Wild Northern Scenes

Sporting Adventures with the Rifle and the Rod

S. H. Hammond

Contents

INTRODUCTORY. 8
CHAPTER I. 11
CHAPTER II. 15
CHAPTER III. 19
CHAPTER IV. 23
CHAPTER V. 28
CHAPTER VI. 36
CHAPTER VII. 40
CHAPTER VIII. 44
CHAPTER IX. 52
CHAPTER X. 56
CHAPTER XI. 62
CHAPTER XII. 70
CHAPTER XIII. 78
CHAPTER XIV. 86
CHAPTER XV. 91
CHAPTER XVI. 98
CHAPTER XVII. 106
CHAPTER XVIII. 115
CHAPTER XIX. 121
CHAPTER XX. 128
CHAPTER XXI. 135
CHAPTER XXII. 142
CHAPTER XXIII. 150
CHAPTER XXIV. 154
CHAPTER XXV. 159
CHAPTER XXVI. 164
CHAPTER XXVII. 170
CHAPTER XXVIII. 174
CHAPTER XXIX. 181
CHAPTER XXX. 185
CHAPTER XXXI. 191

WILD NORTHERN SCENES

SPORTING ADVENTURES WITH THE RIFLE AND THE ROD

BY

S. H. Hammond

WILD NORTHERN SCENES. OR SPORTING ADVENTURES
WITH THE RIFLE AND THE ROD.

BY S. H. HAMMOND.

1857

TO JOHN H. REYNOLDS, ESQ., OF ALBANY.

You have floated over the beautiful lakes and along the pleasant rivers of that broad wilderness lying between the majestic St. Lawrence and Lake Champlain. You have, in seasons of relaxation from the labors of a profession in which you have achieved such enviable distinction, indulged in the sports pertaining to that wild region. You have listened to the glad music of the woods when the morning was young, and to the solemn night voices of the forest when darkness enshrouded the earth. You are, therefore, familiar with the scenery described in the following pages.

Permit me, then, to dedicate this book to you, not because of your eminence as a lawyer, nor yet on account of your distinguished position as a citizen, but as a keen, intelligent sportsman, one who loves nature in her primeval wildness, and who is at home, with a rifle and rod, in the old woods.

With sentiments of great respect,

I remain your friend and servant,

THE AUTHOR.

INTRODUCTORY.

There is a broad sweep of country lying between the St. Lawrence and Lake Champlain, which civilization with its improvements and its rush of progress has not yet invaded. It is mountainous, rocky, and for all agricultural purposes sterile and unproductive. It is covered with dense forests, and inhabited by the same wild things, save the red man alone, that were there thousands of years ago. It abounds in the most beautiful lakes that the sun or the stars ever shone upon. I have stood upon the immense boulder that forms the head or summit of Baldface Mountain, a lofty, isolated peak, looming thousands of feet towards the sky, and counted upwards of twenty of these beautiful lakes--sleeping in quiet beauty in their forest beds, surrounded by primeval woods, overlooked by rugged hills, and their placid waters glowing in the sunlight.

It is a high region, from which numerous rivers take their rise to wander away through gorges and narrow valleys, sometimes rushing down rapids, plunging over precipices, or moving in deep sluggish currents, some to Ontario, some to the St. Lawrence, some to Champlain, and some to seek the ocean, through the valley of the Hudson. The air of this mountain region in the summer is of the purest, loaded always with the freshness and the pleasant odors of the forest. It gives strength to the system, weakened by labor or reduced by the corrupted and debilitating atmosphere of the cities. It gives elasticity and buoyancy to the mind depressed by continued toil, or the cares and anxieties of business, and makes the blood course through the veins with renewed vigor and recuperated vitality.

The invalid, whose health is impaired by excessive labor, but who is yet able to exercise in the open air, will find a visit to these beautiful lakes and pleasant rivers, and a fortnight or a month's stay among them, vastly more efficacious in restoring strength and tone to his system than all the remedial agencies of the most skillful physicians. I can speak understandingly on this subject, and from evidences furnished by my own personal experience and observation.

To the sportsman, whether of the forest or flood, who has a taste for nature as God threw it from his hand, who loves the mountains, the old woods, romantic lakes, and wild forest streams, this region is peculiarly inviting. The lakes, the rivers, and the streams abound in trout, while abundance of deer feed on the lily pads and grasses that grow in the shallow water, or the natural meadows that line the shore. The fish may be taken at any season, and during the months of July and August he will find deer enough feeding along the margins of the lakes and rivers, and easily to be come at, to satisfy any reasonable or honorable sportsman. I have been within fair shooting distance of twenty in a single afternoon while floating along one of those rivers, and have counted upwards of forty in view at the same time, feeding along the margin of one of the beautiful lakes hid away in the deep forest.

The scenery I have attempted to describe--the lakes, rivers, mountains, islands, rocks, valleys and streams, will be found as recorded in this volume. The game will be found as I have asserted, unless perchance an army of sportsmen may have thinned it somewhat on the borders, or driven it deeper into the broad wilderness spoken of. I was over a portion of that wilderness last summer, and found plenty of trout and abundance of deer. I heard the howl of the wolf, the scream of the panther, and the hoarse bellow of the moose, and though I did not succeed in taking or even seeing any of these latter animals, yet I or my companion slew a deer every day after we entered the forest, and might have slaughtered half a dozen had we been so disposed. Though the excursion spoken of in the following pages was taken four years ago, yet I found, the last summer, small diminution of the trout even in the border streams and lakes of the "Saranac and Rackett woods."

I have visited portions of this wilderness at least once every summer for the last ten years, and I have never yet been disappointed with my fortnight's sport, or failed to meet with a degree of success which abundantly satisfied me, at least. I have generally gone into the woods weakened in body and depressed in mind. I have always come out of them with renewed health and strength, a perfect digestion, and a buoyant and cheerful spirit.

For myself, I have come to regard these mountains, these lakes and streams, these old forests, and all this wild region, as my settled summer resort, instead of the discomforts, the jam, the excitement, and the unrest of the watering-places or the sea shore. I visit them for their calm seclusion, their pure air, their natural cheerfulness, their transcendent beauty, their brilliant mornings, their glorious sunsets, their quiet and repose. I visit them too, because when among them, I can take off the armor which one is compelled to wear, and remove the watch which one must set over himself, in the crowded thoroughfares of life; because I can whistle, sing, shout, hurrah and be jolly, without exciting the ridicule or provoking the contempt of the world. In short, because I can go back to the days of old, and think, and act, and feel like "a boy again."

THE RIFLE AND THE ROD.

CHAPTER I.
A GREAT INSTITUTION.

I t is a great institution," I said, or rather thought aloud, one beautiful summer morning, as my wife was dressing the baby. The little thing lay upon its face across her lap, paddling and kicking with its little bare arms and legs, as such little people are very apt to do, while being dressed. It was not our baby. We have dispensed with that luxury. And yet it was a sweet little thing, and nestled as closely in our hearts as if it were our own. It was our first grandchild, the beginning of a third generation, so that there is small danger of our name becoming extinct. A friend of mine, who unfortunately has no voice for song, has a most excellent wife and beautiful baby, and cannot therefore be said to be without music at home. It is his first descendant, and everybody knows that such are just the things of which fathers are very apt to be proud. He was spending an evening with a neighbor, and was asked to sing. He declined, of course, giving as a reason that he never sang. "Why, Mr. H----," said a black-eyed little girl, of seven--"why, Mr. H----, don't you never sing to the baby?" Sure enough! I wonder if there ever was a civilized, a human man, who never sang to the baby. I do not believe that there was ever such a paradox in nature, as a man who had tossed the baby up and down, balanced it on his hand, given it a ride on his foot, and yet never sang to it. I do not care a fig about melody of voice, or science in quavering; I am not talking about sweetness of tone; what I mean to say is, that I do not believe there is a man living, even though he have no more voice than a raven, who is human, and yet never sang to the baby, always assuming that he has one.

"A great institution," I repeated, half in soliloquy and half to my wife.

"What in the world are you talking about?" said Mrs. H----, as she took a pin from her mouth, and fastened the band that encircled the waist of the baby. The nurse was looking quietly on, quite willing that her work should be thus taken off her hands. Will somebody tell me, if there ever was a grandmother, especially one who became such young, who could sit by, and see the nurse dress her first, or even her tenth grandchild, while it was a helpless little thing, say a foot or a foot and a half long? The nurse is so unhandy; she tumbles the baby about so roughly, handles it so awkwardly, she will certainly dress it too loosely, or too tight, or leave a pin that will prick it, or some terrible calamity will happen. So she takes possession of the little thing, and with a hand guided by experience and the instincts of affection, puts its things on in a Christian and comfortable way.

"A great institution!" I repeated again.

"I do believe the man has lost his wits," remarked Mrs. H----, handing the baby to the nurse. "Who ever heard of a baby less than three months old being called an institution?"

"Never heard of such a thing in my life," I replied, "though a much greater mistake might be made."

"What then, in the name of goodness, have you been talking about?" inquired Mrs. H----.

"The COUNTRY of course," I replied.

I had just returned from a business trip to Vermont--who ever thought that Vermont would be traversed by railroads, or that the echoes which dwell among her precipices and mountain fastnesses, would ever wake to the snort of the iron horse? Who ever thought that the locomotive would go screaming and thundering along the base of the Green Mountains, hurling its ponderous train, loaded with human freight, along the narrow valleys above which mountain peaks hide their heads in the clouds? How old Ethan Allen and General Stark, "Old Put," and the other glorious names that enrich the pages of our revolutionary history, would open their eyes in astonishment, if they could come back from "the other side of Jordan," and sit for a little while on their own tombstones in sight of the railroads, and see the trains as they go rushing like a tornado along their native valleys.

I had made up my mind that morning, all at once, to go into the country. It was a sudden resolve, but I acted upon it. Going into the country is a very different thing from what it used to be. There is no packing of trunks, or taking leave of friends. You take your satchel or travelling bag, kiss your wife in a hurry at the door, and jump aboard of the cars; the whistle sounds, the locomotive breathes hoarsely for a moment, and you are off like a shot. In ten minutes the suburbs are behind you; the fields and farms are flying to the rear; you dash through the woods and see the trees dodging and leaping behind and around each other, performing the dance of the witches "in most admired confusion;" in three hours you are among the hills of Massachusetts, the mountains of Vermont, on the borders of the majestic Hudson, in the beautiful valley of the Mohawk, a hundred miles from the good city of Albany, where you can tramp among the wild or tame things of nature to your heart's content.

I had for the moment no particular place in view. What I wanted was, to get outside of the city, among the hills, where I could see the old woods, the streams, the mountains, and get a breath of fresh air, such as I used to breathe. I wanted to be free and comfortable for a month; to lay around loose in a promiscuous way among the hills, where beautiful lakes lay sleeping in their quiet loveliness; where the rivers flow on their everlasting course through primeval forests; where the moose, the deer, the panther and the wolf still range, and where the speckled trout sport in the crystal waters. I had made up my mind to throw off the cares and anxieties of business, and visit that great institution spread out all around us by the Almighty, to make men healthier, wiser, better. I had resolved to go into the country. That was a fixed fact. But where?

There stood my rifle in one corner of the room, and my fishing rods in the other. The sight of these settled the matter. "I will go to the North," I said.

"Go to the North!" said Mrs. H----. "Do tell me if you've got another of your old hunting and fishing fits on you again?"

"Yes," I replied, "I've felt it coming on for a week, and I've got it bad."

"Very well," said my wife, "if the fit is on you, there's no use in remonstrating; your valise will be ready by the morning train." And so the matter was settled.

But I must have a companion, somebody to talk to and with, somebody who could appreciate the beauties of nature; who loved the old woods, the wilderness, and all the wild things pertaining to them; to whom the forests, the lakes, and tall mountains, the rivers and streams, would recall the long past; to whom the forest songs and sounds would bring back the memories of old, and make him "a boy again." So I sallied out to find him. I had scarcely traversed a square, when I met my friend, the doctor, with carpet bag in hand, on his way to the depot.

"Whither away, my friend?" I inquired, as we shook hands.

"Into the country," he replied.

"Very well, but where?"

"Into the country," he repeated, "don't you comprehend? Into the country, by the first train; anywhere, everywhere, all along shore."

"Go with me," said I, "for a month."

"A month! Bless your simple soul, every patient I've got will be well in less than half that time; but let them, I'll be avenged on them another time. But where do *you* go?"

"To my old haunts in the North," I replied.

"To follow the stag to his slip'ry crag,
And to chase the bounding roe."

"But," said he, "I've no rifle."

"I've got four."

"I've no fishing rod."

"I've half a dozen at your service."

"Give me your hand," said he; "I'm with you." And so the doctor was booked.

"Suppose," said the doctor, "we beat up Smith and Spalding, and take them along. Smith has got one of his old fits of the hypo. He sent for me to-day, and. I prescribed a frugal diet and the country. Wild game, and bleeding by the musquitoes, will do him good. Spalding is entitled to a holiday, for he's working himself into dyspepsia in this hot weather."

"Just the thing;" I replied, and we started to find Smith and Spalding. We found them, and it was settled that they should go with us for a month among the mountains. Everybody knows Smith, the good-natured, eccentric Smith; Smith the bachelor, who has an income greatly beyond his moderate expenditures, and enough of capital to spoil, as he says, the orphan children of his sister. By way of saving them from being thrown upon the cold world with a fortune, he declares he will spend every dollar of it *himself*, simply out of regard for *them*. But Smith will do no such thing, and the tenderness with which he is rearing the two beautiful, black-eyed, raven-haired little girls, proves that he will not. But Smith has no professional calling or business, and when his digestion troubles him, he has visions of the almshouse, and the Potters' Field, and of two mendicant little girls, while his endorsement would be regarded as good at the bank for a hundred thousand dollars.

Spalding, as everybody within a hundred leagues of the capitol knows, is a lawyer of eminence, full of good-nature, always cheerful, always instructive; a troublesome opponent at the bar; a man of genial sympathies and a big heart. If I have given him, as well as Smith, a *nom de plume*, it is out of regard for their modesty. We arranged to meet at the cars, the next morning at six, each with a rifle and fishing rod, to be away for a month among the deer and the trout, floating over lakes the most beautiful, and along rivers the pleasantest that the sun ever shone upon.

CHAPTER II.
HURRAH! FOR THE COUNTRY!

Hurrah! Hurrah! We are in the country--the glorious country! Outside of the thronged streets; away from piled up bricks and mortar; outside of the clank of machinery; the rumbling of carriages; the roar of the escape pipe; the scream of the steam whistle; the tramp, tramp of moving thousands on the stone sidewalks; away from the heated atmosphere of the city, loaded with the smoke and dust, and gasses of furnaces, and the ten thousand manufactories of villainous smells. We are beyond even the meadows and green fields. We are here alone with nature, surrounded by old primeval things. Tall forest trees, mountain and valley are on the right hand and on the left. Before us, stretching away for miles, is a beautiful lake, its waters calm and placid, giving back the bright heavens, the old woods, the fleecy clouds that drift across the sky, from away down in its quiet depths. Beyond still, are mountain ranges, whose castellated peaks stand out in sharp and bold relief, on whose tops the beams of the descending sun lie like a mantle of silver and gold. Glad voices are ringing; sounds of merriment make the evening joyous with the music of the wild things around us. Hark! how from away off over the water, the voice of the loon comes clear and musical and shrill, like the sound of a clarion; and note how it is borne about by the echoes from hill to hill. Hark! again, to that clanking sound away up in the air; metallic ringing, like the tones of a bell. It is the call of the cock of the woods as he flies, rising and falling, glancing upward and downward in his billowy flight across the lake. Hark! to that dull sound, like blows upon some soft, hollow, half sonorous substance, slow and measured at first, but increasing in rapidity, until it rolls like the beat of a muffled drum, or the low growl of the far-off thunder. It is the partridge drumming upon his log Hark! still again, to that quavering note, resembling somewhat the voice of the tree-frog when the storm is gathering, but not so clear and shrill. It is the call of the raccoon, as he clambers up some old forest tree, and seats himself among the lowest of its great limbs. Listen to the almost human halloo, the "hoo! hohoo, hoo!" that comes out from the clustering foliage of an ancient hemlock. It is the solemn call of the owl, as he sits among the limbs, looking out from between the branches with his great round grey eyes. Listen again and you will hear the voice of the catbird, the brown thrush, the chervink, the little chickadee, the wood robin, the blue-jay, the wood sparrow, and a hundred other nameless birds that live and build their nests and sing among these old woods.

But go a little nearer the lake, and you will have a concert that will drown all these voices in its tumultuous roar. Compared to these feeble strains, it is the crashing of Julien's hundred brazen instruments to the soft and sweet melody of Ole Bull's violin. Come with me to this rocky promontory; stand with me on this moss-covered boulder, which forms the point. On either hand is a little bay, the head of which is hidden around among the woods. See! over against us, on the limb of that dead fir tree, which leans out over the water, is a bald eagle, straightening with his hooked beak the feathers of his wings, and pausing now and then to look out over the water for some careless duck of which to make prey. See! he has leaped from his perch, has spread his broad pinions, and is soaring upward towards the sky. See! how he circles round and round, mounting higher and higher at every gyration. He is like a speck in the air. But see! he is above the mountains now, and how like an arrow he goes, straight forward, with no visible motion to his wings. He has laid his course for some lake, deeper in the wilderness, beyond that range of hills, and he is there, even while we are talking of his flight. A swift bird, the swiftest of all the birds, is the eagle, when he takes his descending stoop from his place away up in the sky. He cleaves the air like a bullet, and so swift is his career that the eye can scarcely trace his flight. But, hark! all is still now, save the piping notes of the little peeper along the shore. Wait, however, a moment. There, hear that venerable podunker off to the right, with his deep bass, like the sound of a brazen serpent. Listen! another deep voice on the left has fallen in. There, another right over against us! another and another still! a dozen! a hundred! a thousand! ten thousand! a million of them! close by us! far off! on the right hand and on the left! here! there! everywhere! until above, around us, all through the woods, all along the shore, all over the lake is a solid roar, impenetrable to any other sound, surging and swaying, rolling and swelling as if all the voices in the world were concentrated in one stupendous concert.

But, hark! the roar is dying away; voice after voice drops out; here and there is one laggard in the song, still dragging out the chorus. Now all is still again, save the note of the little peeper along the shore. In two minutes that band will strike up again. The roar will go bellowing over the lake through the woods, to be thrown from hill to hill, to die away into silence again; and so it will be through all the long night, and until the sun looks out from among the tree tops in the morning. Touch that solemn looking old croaker on yonder broad leaf of that pond lily, with the end of your fishing rod, while the music is at the highest, he will send forth a quick discordant and cracked cry, like that of a greedy dog choked with a bone, as he plunges for the bottom; and note how suddenly that sound will be repeated, and how quick the roar of the frogs will be hushed into silence. That is a cry of alarm, a note of danger, and every frog within hearing understands its import.

Is it asked *where* we are? I answer, we are on the Lower Saranac Lake, just on the south point, at the entrance of the romantic little bay, at the head of which stands Martin's Lake House, the only human dwelling in sight of this beautiful sheet of water. On the point where we now are, long ago, was the log shanty of a hunter and fisherman, surrounded by an acre or two of cleared land. But its occupant moved deeper into the wilderness, over on the waters of the Rackett, many years since; the log shanty has rotted away, and a vigorous growth of brush and small timber, now covers what once may have been called a field.

But the night shadows are beginning to gather over the forest, throwing a sort of spectral gloom among the old woods, giving a distorted look to the trunks of the trees, the low bushes, the turned up roots, and the boulders scattered over the ground. See what ogre shapes these things assume as the darkness deepens. Look at that cedar bush, with its dense foliage! It is a crouching lion, and as its branches wave in the gentle breeze, he seems preparing for his leap; and yonder boulder is a huge elephant! The root that comes out from the crevice is his trunk, and the moss and lichens which hang down on either side are his pendant ears; and see, he has a great tower on his back, wherein is seated a warrior in his ancient armor, grasping battle-axe and spear. Beyond, through that opening upon the bay, is a castle looming darkly against the sky, with massive towers and arched gateway. Such are the forms which fancy gives to these forest things, in the doubtful twilight of a summer evening. While we have been looking upon these unsubstantial shadows, the sunlight has left the mountain peaks, the stars have come out in the sky, and the moon has started on her course across the heavens.

Let us rest on our oars a moment, here in the bay, to view the scenery around us, as seen by the mellow moonlight. So calm, so still, so motionless are both air and water, that we seem suspended between the sky above, sparkling and glowing with millions of bright stars, and the moon riding gloriously on her course, and a sky beneath, sparkling and glowing with like millions of bright stars, and the same moon, or its counterpart, floating away down in fathomless depths below us. See, how the same hillside, the same line of forest trees, the same ranges and mountain peaks are reflected back from the stirless bosom of the lake. There, above, and just on the upper line of that tall peak, looming darkly and majestically in the distance, hangs a brilliant star, sparkling and twinkling, like the sheen of a diamond; and right beneath, away down just as far below the surface of the water as mountain peak and star are above it, is another mountain peak and bright star, twinned by the mirrored waters. See, away down the lake, that little island with its half dozen spruce trees, clustered together! How like a great war vessel it looks, with sails all set, as seen by the uncertain light of the moon. And that other island, off to the left, with the dead and barkless trees, how like a tall ship with bare masts riding at anchor it seems. That other island, away to the right, with its great boulders and bare rocks rising straight up out of the water, is a fortification, a stronghold surrounded by a wall of solid masonry, and bristling with cannon. We can almost see the sentinel, and hear his measured tramp as he travels his lonely rounds, keeping watch out over the waters. See all along the shore, as you look up the bay towards the Lake House, how the millions of fireflies flash their tiny torches, upward and downward, this way and that, mingling and crossing, and gyrating and whirling--a troubled and billowy sea of millions upon millions of glowing and sparkling gems.

Reader, were you and I gifted with the spirit of poetry, what inspiration would we not gather from the glories which surround us, as we float of a summer evening over these beautiful lakes, sleeping away out here, in all their virgin loveliness, among these old primeval things? But you ask, "what inspiration can there be in a moon and stars, that we see every night, when the sky is cloudless; in a desolate wilderness; the roar of the frogs; the hooting of owls; these useless waters; the phosphorescent flash of lightning bugs; these piled up rocks and barren mountains? Can you grow corn on these hills, or make pastures of these rocky lowlands? Can you harness these rivers to great waterwheels, or make reservoirs of these lakes? Can you convert these old forests into lumber or cordwood? Can you quarry these rocks, lay them up with mortar into houses, mills, churches, public edifices? Can you make what you call these 'old primeval things' utilitarian? Can you make them minister to the progress of civilization, or coin them into dollars?"

Pshaw! You have spoiled, with your worldliness, your greed for progress, your thirst for gain, a pleasant fancy, a glorious dream, as if everything in the heavens, on the earth, or in the waters, were to be measured by the dollar and cent standard, and unless reducible to a representative of moneyed value, to be thrown, as utterly worthless, away. Let us row back to the Lake House.

CHAPTER III.
THE DEPARTURE--THE STAG HOUNDS--THE CHASE--ROUND LAKE.

From Martin's Lake House we were to take our departure in the morning. We had arranged for three boats, and as many stalwart boatmen. Two of these boats were for our own conveyance, and one for our luggage and provisions; the latter to be sent forward with our tents in advance, so as to have a home ready for us always, at our coming, when we chose to linger by the way. These boatmen were all jolly, good-natured and pleasant people, with a vast deal of practical sense, and a valuable experience in woodcraft, albeit they were rough and unpolished. Their hearts were in the right place, and they commanded our respect always for their kindness and attention to our wants, while they maintained at all times that sturdy independence which enters so largely into the character of the border men of our country. Their boats are constructed of spruce or cedar boards of a quarter of an inch in thickness, "clap-boarded," as the expression is, upon "knees" of the natural crook, and weigh from ninety to one hundred and ten pounds each. They are carried around rapids, or from river to river, on the back of the boatman in this wise: A "yoke" is provided, such as every man in the country, especially all who have visited a "sugar bush" at the season of sugar making, has seen. At the end of this yoke is a round iron projection, made to fit into a socket in the upper rave of the boat. The craft is turned bottom upwards, the yoke adjusted to the shoulders, the iron projections fitted into the sockets, and the boatman marches off with his boat, like a turtle with his shell upon his back. He will carry it thus sometimes half a mile before stopping to rest.

With us were to go two staid and sober stag hounds, grave in aspect and trained and experienced, almost, in woodcraft, as their masters; animals that had been reared together, and who possessed the rare instinct of returning always to the shanty from which they started, however far the chase may have led them. It was a glorious sound in the old forests, the music of those two hounds, as their voices rang out bold and free, like a bugle, and went, ringing through the forest, echoing among the mountains and dying away over the lakes. But of that hereafter.

Our little fleet swung out upon the water, while the sun was yet hanging like a great torch among the tops of the trees, on the eastern hills. It was a beautiful morning, so fresh, so genial, so balmy. A pleasant breeze came sweeping lazily over the lake, and went sighing and moaning among the old forest trees. All around us were glad voices. The partridge drummed upon his log; the squirrels chattered as they chased each other up and down the great trunks of the trees; the loon lifted up his clarion voice away out upon the water; the eagle and the osprey screamed as they hovered high above us in the air, while a thousand merry voices came from out the old woods, all mingling in the harmony of nature's gladness. A loud and repeated hurrah! burst from us all as our oars struck the water, and sent our little boats bounding over the rippled surface of the beautiful Saranac.

This is a indeed a beautiful sheet of water. The shores were lined with a dense and unbroken forest, stretching back to the mountains which surround it. The old wood stood then in all its primeval grandeur, just as it grew. The axe had not harmed it, nor had fire marred its beauty. The islands were covered with a lofty growth of living timber clothed in the deepest green. There were not then, as now, upon some of them, great dead trees reaching out their long bare arms in verdureless desolation above a stinted undergrowth, and piled up trunks charred and blackened by the fire that had revelled among them, but all were green, and thrifty, and glorious in their robes of beauty. Thousands of happy songsters carolled gaily among their branches, or hid themselves in the dense foliage of their wide-spreading arms. The islands are a marked feature of these northern lakes, lending a peculiar charm to their quiet beauty, and one day, when the iron horse shall go thundering through these mountain gorges, the tourist will pause to make a record of their loveliness.

Four or five miles down the lake, is a beautiful bay, stretching for near half a mile around a high promontory, almost reaching another bay winding around a like promontory beyond, leaving a peninsula of five hundred acres joined to the main land, by a narrow neck of some forty rods in width. Our first sport among the deer was to be the "driving" of this peninsula. We stationed ourselves on the narrow isthmus within a few rods of each other, while a boatman went round to the opposite side to lay on the dogs. We had been at our posts perhaps half an hour, when we heard the measured bounds of a deer, as he came crashing through the forest. We could see his white flag waving above the undergrowth, as he came bounding towards us. Neither Smith nor Spalding had ever seen a deer in his native woods, and they were, by a previous arrangement, to have the first shot, if circumstances should permit it. The noble animal came dashing proudly on his way, as if in contempt of the danger he was leaving behind him. Of the greater danger into which he was rushing, he was entirely unconscious, until the crack of Smith's rifle broke upon his astonished ear. He was unharmed, however, and quick as thought he wheeled and plunged back in the direction from which he came; Spalding's rifle, as it echoed through the forest, with the whistling of the ball in close proximity to his head, added energy to his flight.

The rifles were scarcely reloaded when the deep baying of the hounds was heard, and two more deer came crashing across the isthmus where we were stationed. The foremost one went down before the doctor's unerring rifle and cool aim, while the other ran the gauntlet of the three other rifles, horribly frightened, but unharmed, away. The hounds were called off, and with our game in one of the boats, we rowed back around the promontory, and passed on towards the Saranac River, which connects by a tortuous course of five miles, the Lower Saranac with Round Lake.

Midway between these two lakes, is a fall, or rather rapids, down which the river descends some ten feet in five or six rods through a narrow rocky channel, around which the boats had to be carried. While this was being done, Smith and Spalding adjusted their rods, eager to make up in catching trout what they failed to achieve in the matter of venison. And they succeeded. In twenty minutes they had fifteen beautiful fish, none weighing less than half a pound, safely deposited on the broad flat rock at the head of the rapids. "One throw more," said Smith, "and I've done;" and he cast his fly across the still water just above the fall. Quick as thought it was taken by a two-pound trout. Landing nets and gaff had been sent forward with the baggage, and without these it was an exciting and delicate thing to land that fish. The game was, to prevent him dashing away down the rapids, or diving beneath the shelving rock above, the sharp edge of which would have severed the line like a knife. Skillfully and beautifully Smith played him for a quarter of an hour, until at last the fish turned his orange belly to the surface, and ceased to struggle. He was drowned.

We had in the morning directed the boatman in charge of the baggage to go on in advance, and erect our tents on an island in Round Lake. When we entered this beautiful sheet of water, about four o'clock, we saw the white tents standing near the shore of the island, with a column of smoke curling gracefully up among the tall trees that overshadowed them. When we arrived, we found everything in order. They were pitched in a pleasant spot, looking out to the west over the water, while within were beds of green boughs from the spruce and fir trees, and bundles of boughs tied up like faggots for pillows. Our first dinner in the wilderness was a pleasant one, albeit the cookery was somewhat primitive. With fresh venison and trout, seasoned with sweet salt pork, we got through with it uncomplainingly.

This little lake is a gem. It is, as its name purports, round, some four miles in diameter, surrounded by an amphitheatre of hills, beneath whose shadows it reposes in placid and quiet beauty. On the northeast, Ballface Mountain rears its tall head far above the intervening ranges, while away off in the east Mount Marcy and Mount Seward stand out dim and shadowy against the sky. Nearer are the Keene Ranges, ragged and lofty, their bare and rocky summits glistening in the sunlight, while nearer still the hills rise, sometimes with steep and ragged acclivity, and sometimes gently from the shore. Here and there a valley winds away among the highlands, along which the mountain streams come bounding down rapids, or moving in deep and sluggish, but pure currents, towards the lake. The rugged and sublime, with the placid and beautiful, in natural scenery, are magnificently mingled in the surroundings of this little sheet of water.

CHAPTER IV.
THE DOCTOR'S STORY--A SLIPPERY FISH--A LAWSUIT AND A COMPROMISE.

There seems to be a law, or rather a habit pertaining to forest life, into which every one falls, while upon excursions such as ours. Stories occupy the place of books, and tales of the marvellous furnish a substitute for the evening papers. Not that there should be any set rule or system, in regard to the ordering of the matter, but a sort of spontaneous movement, an implied understanding, growing out of the necessities of the position of isolation occupied by those who are away from the resources of civilization. The doctor had a genius for story telling, or rather a genius for invention, which required only a moderate development of the organ of credulity on the part of his hearers, to render him unrivalled. There was an appearance of frank earnestness about his manner of relating his adventures, which, however improbable or even impossible as matter of fact they might be, commanded, for the moment, absolute credence.

"They've a curious fish in the St. Lawrence," said the doctor, as he knocked the ashes from his meerschaum, and refilled it, "known among the fishermen of that river as the LAWYER. I have never seen it among any other of the waters of this country, and never there but once. It never bites at a hook, and is taken only by gill-nets, or the seine. Everybody," he continued, "has visited the Thousand Islands, or if everybody has not, he had better go there at once. He will find them, in the heat of summer, not only the coolest and most healthful retreat, and the pleasantest scenery that the eye ever rested upon, always excepting these beautiful lakes, but the best river fishing I know of on this continent. He will not, to be sure, take the speckled trout that we find in this region, but he will be among the black bass, the pickerel, muscalunge, and striped bass, in the greatest abundance, and ready to answer promptly any reasonable demand which he may make upon them. Think of reeling in a twenty-pound pickerel, or a forty-pound muscalunge, on a line three hundred feet in length, playing him for half an hour, and landing him safely in your boat at last! There's excitement for you worth talking about.

"I stopped over night at Cape Vincent, last summer, on my way to 'the Thousand Islands,' on a fishing excursion of a week. I was acquainted with an old fisherman of that place, and agreed to go out with him the next morning, to see what luck he had with the fish. I don't think much of that kind of fishing, though it is well enough for those who make a business of it, for the gill-net works, as the old man said, while the fisherman sleeps, and all he gets in that way is clear gain.

"Well, I rose early the next morning to go out with the old fisherman to his gill-nets. It would have done you good, as it did me, to see how merry every living thing was. The birds, how jolly they were, and how refreshing the breeze was that came stealing over the water, making one feel as if he would like to shout and hurrah in the buoyancy, the brightness, and glory of the morning. But I am not going to be poetical about the sunrise, and the singing birds. We went out upon the river just as the sun came up with his great, round, red face, for there was a light smoky haze floating above the eastern horizon, and threw his light like a stream of crimson flame across the water; and the meadow lark perched upon his fence stake, the blackbird upon his alderbush, the brown thrush on the topmost spray of the wild thorn, and the bob-o'-link, as he leaped from the meadow and poised himself on his fluttering wings in mid air, all sent up a shout of gladness as if hailing the god of the morning.

"We came to the nets and began to draw in. You ought to have seen the fish.

There were pickerel from four to ten pounds in weight, white fish, black bass, rock bass, Oswego bass, and pike by the dozen; and, what was a stranger to me, a queer looking specimen of the piscatory tribes, half bull-head, and half eel, with a cross of the lizard.

"'What on earth is that?' said I, to the fisherman. "'That,' said he, 'is a species of ling; we call it in these parts a LAWYER'

"'A lawyer!' said I; 'why, pray?'

"'I don't know,' he replied, 'unless it's because he ain't of much use, and is the slipriest fish that swims.'

"Mark," continued the doctor, turning to Spalding; "I mean no personality. I am simply giving the old fisherman's words, not my own."

"Proceed with the case," said Spalding, as he sent a column of smoke curling upward from his lips, and with a gravity that was refreshing.

"Well," resumed the doctor, "the LAWYERS were thrown by themselves, and one old fat fellow, weighing, perhaps, five or six pounds, fixed his great, round, glassy eyes upon me, and opened his ugly mouth, and I thought I heard him say, interrogatively, 'Well,' as if demanding that the *case* should proceed at once.

"'Well,' said I, in reply, 'what's out?'

"'What's out!' he answered; '*I'm* out--I'm out of my element--out of water-- out of court--and in this hot, dry atmosphere, almost out of breath. But what have I been summoned here for? I demand a copy of the complaint.'

"'My dear sir,' said I, 'I'm not a member of the court. I don't belong to the bar--I'm not the plaintiff--I'm not in the profession, nor on the bench. I'm neither sheriff, constable nor juror. I'm only a spectator. In the Rackett Woods, among the lakes and streams of that wild region, with a rod and fly, I'm at home with the trout, but;----' "'Oh! ho!' he exclaimed with a chuckle, 'you're the chap I was consulted about down near the mouth of the Rackett the other day, by a country trout, who was on a journey to visit his relatives in the streams of Canada. He showed me a hole in his jaw, made by your hook at the mouth of the Bog river. I've filed a summons and complaint against you for assault and battery, and beg to notify you of the fact.'

"'I plead the general issue,' said I.

"'There's no such thing known to the code,' he replied.

"'I deny the fact, then,' I exclaimed.

"'That won't do,' he rejoined; "'the complaint is put in under oath, and you must answer by affidavit, of the truth of your denial.'

"You see my dilemma. I remembered the circumstance of hooking a noble trout at the place alleged, and as the affair has been settled, I'll tell you how it was. At the head of Tupper's Lake, one of the most beautiful sheets of water that the sun ever shone upon, lying alone among the mountains, surrounded by old primeval forests, walled in by palisadoes of rocks, and studded with islands, the Bog River enters; this river comes down from the hills away back in the wilderness, sometimes rushing with a roar over rocks and through gorges, sometimes plunging down precipices, and sometimes moving with a deep and sluggish current across a broad sweep of table land. For several miles back of the lake, and until a few rods of the shore, it is a calm, deep river. It then rushes down a steep, shelving rock some twenty feet into a great rocky basin; then down again over a shelving rock in a fall of twenty feet into another rocky basin; and then again in another fall of twenty or thirty feet, over a steep, shelving rock, shooting with a swift current far out into the lake. These falls constitute a beautiful cascade, and their roar may be heard of a calm, summer evening, for miles out on the placid water.

"At the foot of these falls, in the summer season, the trout congregate; beautiful large fellows, from one to three pounds in weight; and a fly trailed across the current, or over the eddies, just at its outer edge, is a thing at which they are tolerably sure to rise. Well, last summer, I was out that way among the lakes that lie sleeping in beauty, and along the streams that flow through the old woods, playing the savage and vagabondizing in a promiscuous way. The river was low, and a broad rock, smooth and bare, sloping gently to the water's edge, under which the stream whirled as it entered the lake, and above which tall trees towered, casting over it a pleasant shade, presented a tempting place to throw the fly. I cast over the current, and trailed along towards the edge of the rock, when a three-pounder rose from his place down in the deep water. He didn't come head foremost, nor glancing upward, but rose square up to the surface, and pausing a single instant, darted forward like an arrow and seized the fly. Well, away he plunged with the hook in his jaw, bending my elastic rod like a reed, the reel hissing as the line spun away eighty or a hundred feet across the current, and far out into the lake; but he was fast, and after struggling for a time, he partially surrendered, and I reeled him in. Slowly, and with a sullen struggling, he was drawn towards the shore, sometimes with his head out of water, and sometimes diving towards the bottom. At last, he caught sight of me, and with renewed energy he plunged away again, clear across the current and out into the lake. But the tension of the elastic rod working against him steadily, and always, was too much for his strength, and again I reeled him in, struggling still, though faintly. Slowly, but steadily, I reeled him to my hand. He was just by the edge of the rock, almost within reach of my landing net, when, with a last desperate effort to escape, he plunged towards the bottom, made a dive under the rock, the line came against its edge, slipped gratingly for a moment, snapped, and the fish was gone. He was a beautiful trout, and beautifully he played. He deserved freedom on account of the energy with which he struggled for it.

"You will see, therefore, that, as I said, I was in a dilemma. The action against me was well brought. I could not deny the truth of the facts charged against me in the complaint. In this position of affairs, three alternatives presented themselves; first, a denial of the truth of the complaint, but that involved perjury; secondly, admission of the facts charged, but that involved conviction; and, thirdly, a compromise, and the latter one I adopted.

"'Can't this thing be settled,' said I, to the old lawyer fish of the St. Lawrence, 'without litigation? me and my four companions overboard, place us in *statu quo*, and the action shall be discontinued.'

"'Agreed,' said I, and I reached down to enter upon the performance of my part of the contract.

"'Wait a moment,' said he, curling up his shaky tail, 'the costs--who pays the costs?'

"'The costs!' I replied, 'each pays his own, of course.'

"'Not so fast,' he exclaimed, 'not quite so fast. You must pay the costs, or the suit goes on.'

"There was something human in the tenacity with which that old 'lawyer' clung to the idea of costs. There he was gasping for breath, his life depending upon the result of the negotiation, and still he insisted upon the payment of costs as a condition of compromise."

"Probably out of regard for the interest of his client," said Spalding, gravely;

"but proceed with the case."

"'Fisherman,' said I," resumed the Doctor, "'what is the cost of these five ***lawyers***? How much for the fee simple of the lot?'

"'They ain't worth but ninepence,' he replied.

"'Good,' said I, 'here's a shilling, York currency.'

"'Agreed,' said he, and threw in a sucker, by way of change.

"'Anything more?' I asked of the old cormorant lawyer.

"'No,' he replied; 'all right--so toss us overboard, and be quick, for my breath is getting a little short.' I threw them over, one at a time, the old fellow last, and as he slipped from my hand into the river, he thrust his ugly face out of the water, and said, coolly, 'Good morning! When you come our way again, ***drop in***.'

"'No,' said I, 'I'll ***drop a line.***' I remembered how I 'dropped in,' over on Long Lake, one day, and had no inclination to drop in to the St. Lawrence, especially when there are old lawyer fishes there to summon me for assault and battery on a 'Shatagee trout.'"

"Doctor," said Hank Martin, one of our boatmen, who had been listening to the Doctor's narrative, "I don't want to be considered for'ard or sassy, but I'd like to know how much of these kinds of stories we hired folks are obligated to believe?"

"Well," replied the Doctor, "there are three of you in all, and between you, you must make up a reasonable case, as Spalding would say, of faith in everything you may hear. This you may do by dividing it up among you."

"Very good," said Martin, with imperturbable gravity; "I only wanted a fair understanding of the matter on the start."

CHAPTER V.
A FRIGHTENED ANIMAL--TROLLING FOR TROUT--THE BOATMAN'S STORY.

We sat in front of our tents, enjoying the delightful breeze that swept quietly over the lake, and watching the stars as they stole out from the depths. The whippoorwill piped away in the old forests, and the frogs bellowed like ten thousand buffaloes along the shore. The roar of their hoarse voices went rolling over the lake, through the old woods, and surging up against the mountains to be thrown back by the echoes that dwell among the hills. We had knocked the ashes from our pipes, and were about retiring to our tents for the night, when a long wake in the water across the line of the moon's reflection, attracted our attention. It was evidently made by some animal swimming, and the Doctor and Martin started in pursuit. It proved to be a deer which was apparently making its way to an island, midway across the lake. They had no desire to slaughter it, and they concluded to drive it ashore where we were. They headed it in the proper direction, and followed the terrified animal as it swam for life towards the island on which we were encamped. We understood their purpose, and sat perfectly silent. The deer struck the island directly in front of our tent, and dashed forward in wild affright, right through the midst of us, towards the thicket in our rear, glad to be rid of his pursuers on the water. As he bounded past us, we sprang up and shouted, and if ever a dumb animal was astonished it was that deer. He leaped up a dozen feet into the air, bleated out in the extremity of his terror, and plunged madly forward, as if a whole legion of fiends were at his tail. The stag hounds which were tied to a sapling, by their fierce baying, added vigor to his flight. We heard his snort at every bound across the island, and his plunge into the lake on the other side.

In the morning we sent forward our boatman with the tents and baggage to an island on the Upper Saranac, and coasted this pleasant little lake. On the right, as you approach the head, is a deep bay, skirted by a natural meadow, where the rank wild grass, and the pond lilies that grow along the shore furnish a rich pasture for the deer. We saw several feeding quietly like sheep, on the little plain and upon the lily pads in the edge of the water. We paddled silently to within a dozen rods of them, when, as they discovered us, they dashed snorting and whistling away.

On the right of this meadow, and among the tall forest trees are great boulders which, piled up and partly obscured by the undergrowth, resemble from the lake the massive ruins of some ancient fortification. We landed by a spring, which came bubbling up from beneath one of these great moss-covered rocks, to lunch. It was a pleasant spot, and while we sat there dozens of small birds, of the size and general appearance of the cuckoo, save in their hooked beaks, attracted by the scent of our cold meats, came hopping tamely about on the lower limbs of the forest trees around us. They were called by our boatmen, "meat hawks," and have less fear of man than any wild birds that I have ever seen.

We crossed the carrying place of a quarter of a mile around the rapids, in which distance the river falls some sixty feet, roaring and tumbling down ledges and boiling in mad fury around boulders. We entered the Upper Saranac at the hour appointed, and found our tents pitched and a dinner of venison and trout awaiting us on the island selected for our encampment.

As the sun sank behind the hills, the breeze died away, and the lake lay without a ripple around as, so calm, so smooth, and still, that it seemed to have sunk quietly to sleep in its forest bed. The fish were jumping in every direction, and while the rest of us sat smoking our meerchaums after dinner, or rather supper, Smith rigged his trolling rod, and having caught half a dozen minnows, he with Martin, rowed out upon the water to troll for the lake trout. These are a very different fish from the speckled trout of the streams and rivers. They had none of the golden specks of the latter, are of a darker hue, and much larger. They are dotted with brown spots, like freckles upon the face of a fair-skinned girl. They are shorter too, in proportion to their weight than the speckled trout. They are caught in these lakes, weighing from three to fifteen pounds, and instances have been known of their attaining to the weight of five and twenty. It is an exciting sport to take one of these large fellows on a line of two hundred and fifty or three hundred feet in length. They play beautifully when hooked, and it requires a good deal of coolness and skill to land them safely in your boat. A trolling rod for these large fish should be much stiffer, and stronger than those used for the fly, on the rivers and streams; and the reel should be stronger and higher geared than the common fly reel. Three hundred feet of line are necessary, for the fish, if he is a large one, will sometimes determine upon a long flight, and it will not do to exhaust your line in his career. In that case, he will snap it like a pack-thread. An English bass rod is the best, and with such, and a large triple action reel, the largest fish of these lakes may be secured.

Smith had trolled scarcely a quarter of a mile, when his hook was struck by a trout, and then commenced a struggle that was pleasant to witness. No sooner had the fish discovered that the hook was in his jaw, than away he dashed towards the middle of the lake. The rod was bent into a semicircle, but the game was fast; with the butt firm between his knees and his thumb pressing the reel, the sportsman gave him a hundred and fifty feet of line, when his efforts began to relax, and as Smith began to reel him in, a moment of dead pull, a holding back like an obstinate mule occurred. The trout was slowly towed in the direction of the boat. Then, as if maddened by the force which impelled him, he dashed furiously forward, the reel answering to his movements and the line always taught, he rose to the surface leaping clear from the water, shaking his head furiously as if to throw loose the fastenings from his jaw. Failing in this, down he plunged fifty feet straight towards the bottom, making the reel hiss by his mad efforts to escape. Still the line was taught, pressing always, towing him towards the boat at every relaxation. At last he rose to the surface, panting and exhausted, permitting himself to be towed almost without an effort, to within twenty feet of his captors. When he saw them, all his fright and all his energies too seemed to be restored, and away he dashed, sciving through the water a hundred and fifty feet out into the lake. But the hook was in his jaw, and he could not escape. After half an hour of beautiful and exciting play, he surrendered or was drowned, and Smith lifted him with his landing net, a splendid ten-pound trout, into his boat. By this time the shadows of twilight were gathering over the lake, and he came ashore. A proud man was Smith, as he lifted that fish from the boat and handed it over to the cook to be dressed for breakfast, and though we had seen the whole performance from our tents, yet he gave us in glowing and graphic detail the history of his taking that ten-pound trout.

"Captain," said Hank Wood, who had been quietly whitling out a new set of tent pins, addressing Smith, "you had a good time of it with that trout, but it was nothing to an adventer of mine with an old mossy-back, on this lake, five year ago this summer."

"How was that?" inquired Smith; and we all gathered around to hear Hank Wood's story.

"I don't know how it is," he began, as he seated himself on the log in front of the tents, with one leg hanging down, and the other drawn up with the heel of his boot caught on a projection in the bark, his knee almost even with his nose, and his fingers locked across his shin, "I don't know exactly why, but the catching of that trout makes me think of an adventer I had on this very lake, five year ago this summer. It is curious how things will lay around in a man's memory, every now and then startin' up and presentin' themselves, ready to be talked about--reeled off--as it were, and then how quietly they coil themselves away, to lay there, till some new sight, or sound, or idea, or feelin' stirs 'em into life, and they come up again fresh and plain as ever. Some people talk about forgotten things, but I don't believe that any matter that gets fairly anchored in a man's mind, can ever be forgotten, until age has broken the power of memory. It is there, and will stay there, in spite of the ten thousand other things that get piled in on top of it, and some day it will come popping out like a cork, just as good and distinct as new. But I was talkin' about an adventer I had with a trout, five year ago, here on the Upper Saranac. I was livin' over on the *Au Sable* then, and came over to these parts to spend a week or so, and lay in a store of jerked venison and trout for the winter. I brought along a bag of salt, and two or three kegs that would hold a hundred pound or so apiece, and filled 'em too with as beautiful orange-meated fellows as you'd see in a day's drive. The trout were plentier than they are now. They hadn't been fished by all the sportin' men in creation, and they had a chance to grow to their nateral size. You wouldn't in them days row across any of these lakes in the trollin' season without hitchin' on to an eight, or ten, and now and then to a twenty-pounder.

"Wal, I was on the Upper Saranac, up towards the head of the lake, ten or twelve miles from here, trollin' with an old-fashioned line, about as big as a pipe stem, a hundred and fifty feet long, and a hook to match. Nobody in them days tho't of sich contrivances as trollin'-rods, reels, and minny-gangs. You held your lines in your fingers, and when you hooked a fish, you drew him in, hand over hand, in a human way. It was in the latter part of June, and the way the black flies swarmed along the shore, was a thing to set anybody a scratchin' that happened to be around. It was a clear still mornin', and the sun as he went up into the heavens, blazed away, and as he walked across the sky, if he didn't pour down his heat like a furnace, I wouldn't say so. I had tolerable good luck in the forenoon, and landed on a rocky island to cook dinner. I made such a meal as a hungry man makes when he's out all alone fishin' and huntin' about these waters, and started off across the lake, with my trollin' line to the length of a hundred feet or more, draggin' through the water behind me. The breeze had freshened a little, and my boat drifted about fast enough for trollin', and feelin' a little drowsy, I tied the end of the line to the cleets across the knees of the boat, and lay down in the bottom with my hand out over the side holdin' the line. I hadn't laid there long, when I felt a twitch as if something mighty big was medlin' with the other end of the string. I started up and undertook to pull in, but you might as well undertake to drag an elephant with a thread. I couldn't move him a hair. Pretty soon the boat began to move up the lake in a way I didn't at all like. At first it went may be three miles an hour, then five, ten, twenty, forty, sixty miles the hour, round and round the lake, as if hurled along by a million of locomotives. We went skiving around among the islands, into the bays, along the shore, away out across the lake, crossing and re-crossing in every direction; and if there's a place about this lake we didn't visit, I should like to have somebody tell me where it is. You may think it made my hair stand out some, to find myself flyin' about like a streak of chain lightnin', and to see the trees and rocks flyin' like mad the other way. I tried to untie the line, but it was drawn into a knot so hard, that the old Nick himself couldn't move it. I looked for my knife to cut it, but it had, somehow, got overboard in our flight, besides flyin' about at the rate of sixty mile an hour, kept a fellow pretty busy holdin' on, keepin' his place in the boat.

"After an hour or two we came to a pause, and the old feller that was towin' me about, walked up to the surface, and stickin' his head out of the water, 'Good mornin',' says he, in a very perlite sort of way. 'Good mornin',' says I, back again. 'How goes it?' says he. 'All right,' says I. 'Step this way and I'll take the hook out of your gums.' 'Thank you for nothing,' says he, and he opened his month like the entrance to a railroad tunnel, and blame me, if he hadn't taken a double hitch of the line around his eye tooth, while the hook hung harmless beside his jaw.

"'I've a little business down in the lower lake,' says he, 'and must be movin',' and away he bolted like a steam engine, down the lake. When he straightened up, my hat flew more than sixty yards behind me, and the way I came down into the bottom of the boat was anything but pleasant. Away we tore down towards the outlet, the boat cuttin' and plowin' through the water, pilin' it up in great furrows ten feet high on each side. There is, as you know, sixty feet fall between the Upper Saranac and Round Lake, and the river goes boilin' and roarin', tumblin' and heavin' down the rapids and over the rocks, pitchin' in some places square down a dozen feet among the boulders. No sensible man would think of travellin' that road in a little craft like mine, unless he'd made up his mind to see how it would seem to be drowned, or smashed to pieces agin the rocks. But right down the rapids we went, swifter than an eagle in his stoop, down over the boilin' eddies, down over the foamin' surge, down the perpendicular falls, as if the old Nick himself was kickin' us on end. How we got down I won't undertake to say, but when I got breath and looked out over the side of the boat I saw the old woods and rocks along the shore below the falls, rushin' up stream like a racehorse.

"Wal, we entered Round Lake, crossed it in five minutes, and down the river we rushed over the little falls at a bound, and into the Lower Saranac. I'd got a little used to it by this time, and though it was mighty hard work to catch my breath in such a wind as we made by our flight, yet I managed to sit up and look around me. It was curious to see how the islands on the Lower Saranac danced about, and how the shores ran away behind while I was looking at 'em; and how the forest trees dodged, and whirled, and jumped about one another, as we tore along. After tearin' about the lake a spell, we came to something like a halt, and old Mossyback stuck his head out of water, and openin' his great glassy eyes like the moon in a mist, 'How do you like that?' said he, in a jeerin' sort of way. 'All right,' said I; 'go it while you're young.' I didn't care about appearin' skeered or uneasy, but I'd have given a couple of month's wages just then, to have been on dry land. 'Well,' said he, 'I guess we'll be gittin' towards home.' And away he started for the Upper Saranac, and up the river, across Round Lake, and right up over the rapids we went. Two or three times I made up my mind that I was a goner, as the water piled up around me along over the falls; but somehow our very speed made our boat glance upward at such times, and skim along the surface like a duck. We went boundin' from hillock to hillock, on the mad waters, till we entered the broad lake and went skiving about again among the islands.

"All at once he seemed to take a notion to go down towards the bottom; so shortenin' the line some fifty foot or more, he hoisted his great tail straight up towards the sky, and down he went, the boat standing up on end, and somehow the waters didn't seem to close above us, so rapid was our descent. It was tight work, as you may guess, to hold on under such circumstances, but I managed to keep my place. How deep we went I wont undertake to say, but this much is quite sartin, we went down so far that I couldn't see out at the hole we went in at. There are some mighty big fish away down in them parts, you may bet your life on that; trout that it wouldn't be pleasant to handle.

"By-and-bye we started for daylight again. The fish had to stand out of the way as we rushed like an express train towards the surface; them that didn't we made a smash of. One bull head, I remember, about twice as long as one of our boats wasn't quick enough; the bow of the boat struck him about in the middle and cut him in two like a knife. One old trout seemed to have made up his mind for a fight, and he chased us more than two miles with his jaws open like a great pair of clamps, as if he'd a mind to swallow us boat and all, and from the size of the openin', I'm bold to say he'd a done it too, if he'd have caught us; but as we rounded an island, he run head foremost, jam against a rock. That kind o' stunned him, and he gave in.

"Wal, after we got to the surface, the trout that was towin' me, seemed to let on an extra amount of steam for a mile or so, and let me say the way we went was a caution. I've travelled on the cars in my day, when they made every thing gee again, but that kind o' goin' wasn't a circumstance to the way we tore along. The water rose up on either hand more than twenty feet, and went roarin', and tumblin', and hissin', as if everything was goin' to smash. All at once the line was thrown loose, and the boat went straight ahead bows on, to one of the small islands up towards the head of the lake, and when she struck, I went through the air eend over eend, clear across the island, more than fifteen rods, ca-splash into the lake on the other side.

"Human nater couldn't stand all that, so startin' up I found that while I'd been layin' in the bottom of the boat the wind had ris, and was blowin' a stiff gale. The boat had drifted across the lake and had struck broadside agin the shore, and the waves were makin' a clean breach into her at every surge. I soon got her, head on to the waves, and feelin' something mighty lively at the other eend of the line, hauled in a twelve-pounder."

"Pshaw!" exclaimed one of the audience; "you've only been telling a dream, in this long yarn, we've been listening to."

"Wal," replied the narrator; "some people that I've told it to, have suspicioned that it might be so; but every thing about it seemed so nateral, that I'm almost ready to make my affidavy that it was sober fact. One thing, however, I always had my doubts about: I never fully believed, that *I was actually pitched over that island*. I've hearn it said that when a man has eaten a hearty dinner, and goes to sleep with the hot sun pourin' right down on him, he's apt to see and hear a good many strange things before he wakes up. May be it was so with me."

CHAPTER VI.
THE UPPER SARANAC--SPECTACLE PONDS--THE ACCUSATION AND THE DEFENCE--AN OCTOGE-NARIAN SMOKER.

We spent the next day in rowing about the Upper Saranac, exploring its beautiful bays and islands. We took as many trout in trolling occasionally, as we needed for dinner and supper. It became an established law among us, that we should kill no more game or fish than we needed for supplies, whatever their abundance or our temptation might be. It required some self-denial to observe this law, but we kept it with tolerable strictness. There were times when we had a large supply of both venison and fish, but there were seven men of us in all, and we could despose of a good deal of flesh and fish in the twenty-four hours. We had sent our boat with the luggage across the Indian carrying place, a path of a mile through the forest, to the Spectacle Ponds, three little lakes, from which a stream, known as Stony Brook, rises. This stream is navigable for small boats like ours, five miles to the Rackett River. These lakes contain from a hundred to a hundred and fifty acres each. At the head of the Upper Pond is a beautiful cold spring, near which, upon crossing the carrying place, at evening, we found our tents pitched. We arrived here about sun-down, somewhat wearied with our day's excursion, and with appetites fully equal to a plentiful supper which was soon in readiness for us.

"You are getting me into a bad habit, spoiling my morals in a physical sense," said Smith, addressing us as we sat after supper around our camp-fire; "I find myself taking to the pipe out here, in these old woods, with a relish I never have at home. It seems to agree with me here, and I expect by the time I get back to civilization, I shall be as great a smoker as the Doctor or Spalding. If I do, I shall have to pay for it by indigestion and hypochondria, things that you of the fat kine, know nothing about."

"Well," replied the Doctor, "You will only have to call on me as you did last month, and then send for Spalding to draw your will, as you did the next day, when you were as well as I am, excepting that kink in your head about your going to die."

"Why, the truth is," retorted Smith, "I had made up my mind, after twelve hours consideration, to take the medicine you left, and I appeal to H----here, if it was after that, anything more than a reasonable precaution to be prepared for any contingency that might happen. Your medicines, Doctor, and the testamentary disposition of a man's worldly effects, are very natural associations."

"Very well," said the Doctor; "you'll send for me again in a month after our return, and in that case, it may be, that the money you paid Spalding for drawing your will, will not have been thrown away. But in regard to the use of the pipe; I propose that we call upon Spalding, for a legal opinion, or an argument in its favor. It's his business to defend criminals, and I file an accusation against smoking generally, excepting, however, from the indictments the use of the pipe, as in some sort a necessity, on all such excursions as ours."

"I shall not undertake," said Spalding, "to enter into a labored defence of the use of tobacco in any form. I only move for a mitigation of punishment, and will state the circumstances upon which I base my appeal to the clemency of the court. The exception in the indictment, enables me to avoid the plea of necessity, which I should have interposed, founded upon a huge forest meal, and the abundance as well as impertinence of the musquitoes of these woods."

"I called the other day upon a venerable friend and client, who is travelling the down hill of life quietly, and though with the present summer he will have accomplished his three score years and ten, his voice is as cheerful, and his heart as young, as they were decades ago, when his manhood was in the glory and strength of its prime. I found him sitting in his great arm-chair, smoking his accustomed pipe, reading the evening papers. He seemed to be so calm, and happy, as the smoke went wreathing up from his lips, that I could not for the moment refrain from envying the calmness and repose which were visible all around him. He has smoked his morning and evening pipe, in his quiet way, for nearly half a century. When engaged in the active business of life, struggling with its cares, and fighting its battles, he always took half an hour in the morning, and as long at evening, to smoke his pipe and read the news of the day. He scarcely ever, when at home, under any pressure of circumstances omitted these two half hours of repose, or as his excellent wife used to say, of 'fumigation.' She passed to her rest years ago, leaving behind her the pleasant odor of a good name, a memory cherished by all who knew her.

"Men denounce the use of tobacco, and I do not quarrel with them for doing so. Say that it is a vile and a filthy habit; be it so, I will not now stop to deny it. Say that it is bad for the constitution, ruinous to the health; be it so. I will not gainsay it. Still I never see an old man, seated in his great arm chair, with his grandchildren playing around him, smoking his pipe and enjoying its, to him, pleasant perfume, its soothing influences, without regarding that same pipe as an institution which I would hardly be willing to banish entirely from the world.

"There is a good deal of philosophy, too, in a pipe, if one will but take the trouble to study it; great subjects for moralizing, much food for reflection; and all this outside of the physical enjoyment, the soothing influences of a quiet pipe, when the day is drawing to a close, and its cares require some gentle force to banish them away. It does not weaken the power of thought, nor stultify the brain. It quiets the nerves, makes a man look in charity upon the world, and to judge with a chastened lenity the shortcomings of his neighbors. It reconciles him to his lot, and sends him to his pillow, or about his labors, with a calm deliberate cheerfulness, very desirable to those who come under the law that requires people to earn their bread by the sweat of their brow.

"I said there is a good deal of philosophy in a pipe, and I repeat it. Who can see the smoke go wreathing and curling upward from his lips in all sorts of fantastic shapes, spreading out thinner and thinner, till it fades away and is lost among the invisible things of the air, without saying to himself, 'Such are the visions of youth; such the hopes, the grand schemes of life, looming up in beautiful distinctness before the mind's eye, growing fainter and fainter as life wears away, and then disappearing forever. Such are the things of this life, beautiful as they appear, unsubstantial shadows all.' And then, as the fire consumes the weed, exhausting itself upon the substance which feeds it, burning lower and lower, till it goes out for lack of aliment, who will not be reminded of life itself? the animated form, the body instinct with vitality, changing and changing as time sweeps along, till the spirit that gave it vigor and comeliness, and power and beauty, is called away, and it becomes at last mere dust and ashes. And then again, when the pipe itself falls from the teeth, or the table, or the mantel, or the shelf--as fall it surely will, sooner or later--and is broken, and the fragments are thrown out of the window, or swept out at the door, who can fail to see in this, the type of life's closing scene? the body broken by disease and death, carried away and hidden in the earth, to remain among the useless rubbish of the past, to be seen no more forever? Yes, yes! there is a great deal of philosophy in a pipe, if people will take pains to study it.

"I have a pleasant time of it once or twice a year with an old gentleman, living away in the country; one whom memory calls up from the dim and shadowy twilight of my earliest recollections, as a tall stalwart man, already the head of a family with little children around him. Those who were then little children have grown up to be men and women, and have drifted away upon the currents of life, themselves fathers and mothers, with grey hairs gathering upon their heads. I visit this venerable philosopher in his hearty and green old age, every summer. I see him now, in my mind's eye, sitting under the spreading branches of the trees planted by himself half a century ago, which cast their shadows upon the pleasant lawn in front of his dwelling--discussing politics, morals, history, religion, philosophy--recounting anecdotes of the early settlement of the county of which he was a pioneer; and I see how calmly and deliberately he smokes, while he calls up old memories from the shadowy past, discoursing wisely of the present, or speaking prophetically of the future. I saw him last in July of the past year, and he seemed to have changed in nothing. He had not grown older in outward seeming. His heart was as warm and genial as it was long, long ago; and cheerfulness, calm and chastened, marked as it had for years the conversation of a man who felt that his mission in life was accomplished. 'Why,' said he, addressing me, as a new thought seemed to strike him, 'why, *your* head is growing grey! I never noticed it before. It is almost as white as mine. Well, well!' he continued, as he tapped the thumb nail of his left hand with the inverted bowl of his pipe, knocking the ashes from it as he spoke, 'well, well! it won't be long until we will have smoked our last pipe. Mine, at least, will soon be broken. But what of that? Seventy-eight years is a long time to live in this world. I have had my share of life and of the good pertaining to it, and shall have no right to complain when my pipe is broken and its ashes scattered.' Such was the philosophy of an almost Octogenarian smoker."

"I move for a suspension of sentence," said Smith, "Spalding's defence of the weed, induces me to withdraw the indictment against it, leaving punishment only for the excessive use of it."

The motion was carried unanimously, and by way of confirming the decision, we all refilled our pipes and smoked till the stars looked down in their brightness from the fathomless depths of the sky.

CHAPTER VII.
KINKS!--"DIRTY DOGS"--THE BARKING DOG THAT WAS FOUND DEAD IN THE YARD--THE DOG THAT BARKED HIMSELF TO DEATH.

"The hallucinations of Smith," said Spalding, after we had settled the matter of the pipes, and were enjoying a fresh pull at the weed, "as described by the Doctor, remind me of a slight attack of fever which I had some months ago, and from which I recovered partly through the aid of the Doctor's medicine, and partly through the kindness of a young friend of mine; and of the strange 'kinks,' as you call them, which got into my head between the fever and the Doctor's opiates. Things were strangely mixed up, the real and the unreal grouped and mingled in a manner that gave to all the just proportions and appearance of sober actualities. I remember them as distinctly, and they made as deep and abiding impression upon my mind as if I had seen them all. They are impressed as palpably and indelibly upon my memory now as any actual events of my life."

"Well," said the Doctor, "suppose you give us one of these 'kinks,' while our pipes are being smoked out, as an 'opiate' to send us all to sleep."

"Be it understood, then," Spalding began, "that I like dogs in a general way. They are plain dealing, honest, trusty folk in the aggregate, albeit, there are what Tom Benton calls, 'dirty dogs.' These, however, are mostly human canines, dogs that walk on two legs, and wear clothes. Such curs I *don't* like. But there are such, and they may be seen and heard, barking, and snarling, and snapping in their envy, at honest peoples' heels every day. Let them bark. Mr. Benton was right. They are 'dirty dogs.' But a dog that looks you honestly and frankly in the face, that stands by his master and friend, in all times of trial, in sorrow as in joy, in adversity as in prosperity, in dark days as in bright days, always cheerful, always sincere, earnest, and truthful, and so that his kindness be met, always happy, I like. He is your true nobility of nature below the human. But there **are** 'curs of low degree;' dogs of nei- ther genial instinct nor breeding; senseless animals, that belie the noble nature of their species, are living libels upon their kind. There was one of these over against my rooms, at the time of the sickness I speak of. I say **was** for thanks to the fates, he is among the things that have been; he belongs to history, has been wiped out.

"He was a barking dog. When the moon was in the sky, he barked at the moon. When only the stars shone out, he barked at the stars; when clouds shut in both moon and stars, he barked at the clouds; and when the darkness was so deep and black as to obscure even the clouds, he barked at the darkness. Through all the long night he barked, barked, barked! It was not a bark of defiance, nor of alarm, nor of astonishment, nor of warning. It was not a note of danger, breaking the hush of midnight, saying that thieves were abroad, that murder was on its stealthy mission, or that the wolf was on the walk. It was a senseless, monotonous, idiotic bow, wow! Nothing more, nothing less.

"All Monday night, as I lay tossing upon a bed of pain, when fever was cours- ing through my veins, and every pulse went plunging like a steam engine from the gorged heart to every extremity, and my brain was like molten lead, I heard that terrible bark! It was my evil genius, my destiny. It mingled in every feverish dream, became the embodiment of every vision. I measured the periods of its recurrence by the clock that stands in the corner of our room. I counted the tickings of its silence, and I counted the tickings of its continuance. Every swing of the pendulum became a distinct period of existence. Minutes, hours, were nothing. Forty-four tickings, I said, and that bow, wow! will be heard again! Fifteen tickings, I said, and it will cease; and so I went on until the hours seemed to spread out into a boundless ocean of time. That dog somehow became mixed up with that old family clock that stood in the corner. I heard him scratching and climbing up among the weights, writhing and twisting his way among the machinery, till there, looking out through the face of that old family clock, distinct and palpable as the sun at noonday, or the moon in a cloudless night, I saw the ogre head of that dog; his great glassy, fishy eyes, his half drooping, half erect ears, his slavering jaws, and as he gazed in a stupid meaningless stare upon me, uttered his everlasting bow, wow! Tell me that the room was dark;

that not a ray of light penetrated the closed doors or the curtained windows. What of that? That dog's head, I repeat, was there; I saw it, if I ever saw the sun, the moon or the bright stars. I saw it staring at me through all the gloom, all the thick darkness, and I heard its terrible bow, wow! 'Get out!' I shouted in horror.

"'What's the matter?' cried my wife, springing up in an ecstasy of terror.

"'Drive out that dog,' I replied.

"'What dog?' she inquired.

"'There,' I replied, 'that dog there, in the clock with his great staring, glassy eyes; drive him out!'

"She lighted the gas, and as it flashed up, there stood the old clock, the pendulum swung back and forth, the ticking went on, and its white old-fashioned face, looked out in calm serenity; but the dog was gone. It was all natural as life. The lighting of the gas had frightened the cur back to his yard, and as the forty-fourth tick ceased, his bow wow! was heard again, and it lasted while the pendulum swung back and forth just fifteen times. I took a cooling draft, and counted in feverish agony forty-four, and fifteen, till the daylight came creeping in at the windows, filling with sepulchral greyness the room. The barking ceased, and I slept only to dream of snarling curs and 'dirty dogs' for an hour.

"Through all Tuesday I lay tossing with pain. Fever was in every pulse; my brain was seething, burning lava. I thought and dreamed of nothing but mangy curs and 'dirty dogs.' The night gathered again, and the rumbling of the carriages and the thousand voices that break the stillness of a thronged city, died away into silence. The lights were extinguished, but again that horrible bark! bark! broke the hush of midnight, and worse than all, the quickened senses of fever heard it answered from away over on Arbor Hill; and again away up in State street; and yet again over in Lydius, and still again away down by the river. The East, the North, the West and the South had a voice, and it was all concentrated in a ceaseless, senseless, idiotic bark. I counted again the tickings of the clock, and each swing of the pendulum ended in a bark! As I lay there in the silence and desolation, the restless, tossing anguish of fever, those dogs gathered together in State at the crossing of Eagle, just above my boarding-house, and barked! They came under my windows, and barked! They looked in between the curtains, and barked! They came into my room, and there on the sofa, on the rocking-chair, on the table, on the mantelpiece, on the ottoman, on the stove, and on the top of the old clock, was a dog; and each barked! and barked! I saw them all through the darkness, plain as if it were noonday. They were 'dirty dogs,' filthy brutes, ill-favored mangy curs all, and there they sat and barked at the clock, barked at the mirror, at the stove, barked at one another and at me, with the same monotonous, meaningless, idiotic bow, wow! as of old.

"I had two rifles and a double-barrelled fowling-piece, sitting in the corner of the parlor adjoining our sleeping-room, the gifts of valued friends. My wife, wearied with the day's watching, had sunk into slumber on the bed beside me. I woke her gently.

"'Make no noise,' I said, 'but bring me the guns; do it carefully.'

"'What on earth do you want of the guns?' she inquired in alarm.

"'Don't you see those infernal dogs?' I answered, 'bring me the guns, and I'll make short work with the howling curs.'

"'Why, husband,' said she, 'there are no dogs here,' and as she lighted the gas the curs vanished away. But I saw them in the darkness. It was only when the light flashed through the room, that they fled from it, and I heard them barking in response to each other through all the long night, till the dawn crept over the world again.

"Years ago, I saved a boy from the meshes of the law, in which his evil ways had involved him. I admonished him of the end towards which he was hastening. I showed him that the path he was treading led to destruction, and he left it, as he said, forever. He apprenticed himself to a useful trade, and is now an intelligent mechanic. Out of his time, an industrious, sober youth of two and twenty, supporting by his industry, his mother and sister in comfort and respectability. He heard of my sickness, and on Wednesday morning called to see me, proffering his services as a nurse and watchman, prompted by gratitude for the past. I declined his kindness for the present, as I told him casually of the dog whose midnight barking was killing me. He called again on Thursday morning. The barking had ceased. He inquired if I had been troubled with the yelping of that senseless cur, and I answered truly that I had not, that I had slept soundly, and woke with a softened pulse and a cooled brain.

"'Well,' said he, 'I thought you would rest easier. I looked into the yard as I came along, and saw a dead dog lying there. I thought may be he had barked himself to death.'

"I did not at the time take in the full meaning, the hidden import of his words. I dropped away into slumber, and dreamed of the dog that barked himself to death. I saw him vanish by piecemeal at each successive bark, until nothing but his jaws were left, and as his last bark was uttered, these, too, vanished away, and then all was still.

"I awoke, and thought that a dose of 'dog-buttons,' or a taste of strychnine, administered with a tempting bit of cold steak, or a piece of fresh lamb, or a bone of mutton carefully dropped in his way, might have aided the operation. Be that as it may, whatever of debt may have existed between my young friend and myself for past kind it is all wiped out by the news he brought me, that a 'dead dog lay in the yard over the way.'"

CHAPTER VIII.
STONY BROOK--A GOOD TIME WITH THE TROUT--RACKETT RIVER--TUPPER'S LAKE--A QUESTION ASKED AND ANSWERED.

The next morning we started down Stony Brook, towards the Rackett River, intending to pitch our tents at night on the banks of Tupper's Lake, twenty-three miles distant. Before leaving the Spectacle Ponds, we visited a little island at the north end of the middle pond, containing perhaps half an acre. This island has a few Norway pines upon it, is of a loose sandy soil, and at the highest portion is some twenty feet above the level of the water. It is a great resort for turtle in the season of depositing their eggs. We found thousands of their eggs, some on the surface and some buried in the sand, and if one in a dozen of them brings forth a turtle, there will be no lack of the animal in the neighborhood. Stony Brook is a sluggish, tortuous stream, large enough to float our little boats, and goes meandering most of the way for five miles among natural meadows, overflowed at high water, or thinly timbered prairie, when it enters the Rackett. I discovered on a former visit to this wilderness, when the water was very low, a spring that came boiling up near the centre of the stream, with a volume large enough almost to carry a mill. It was at a point where a high sandy bluff, along which the stream swept, terminated. As we approached this spot, I suggested to Spalding, who was in the bow of the boat, to prepare his rod and fly. We approached carefully along the willows on the opposite shore, until in a position from which he could throw in the direction I indicated. In the then stage of the water, there was no appearance of a spring, or any indication marking it as a spot where the trout would be at all likely to congregate, and Spalding was half inclined to believe that I was practising upon his want of knowledge of the habits of the fish of this region. I had said nothing about the spring, or the habit of the trout in gathering wherever a cold stream enters a river, or a spring comes gushing up in its bed.

"I don't believe there's a trout within half a mile of us," he said, as he adjusted his rod and fly.

"Never mind," I replied, "throw your fly across towards that boulder on the bank, and trail it home, and you'll see."

"Well," said he, "here goes;" and he threw in the direction indicated.

The fly had scarcely touched the water when a trout, weighing a pound or over, struck it with a rush that carried him clear out of the water. After a little play he was landed safely in the boat, and another, and another, followed at almost every throw. Not once did the fly touch the water that it was not risen to by a fish.

"By Jove!" said Spalding, as he handed me the landing-net to take in his third or fourth trout, "this is sport. You use the net, and I'll trail them to you. Let us make hay while the sun shines. The other boat will soon be along, and Smith will be for dipping his spoon into my dish. I want to astonish him when he comes."

We had secured eight beautiful fish when the Doctor and Smith rounded the point above us. We motioned them back, and their boat lay upon its oars. Spalding kept on throwing his fly and trailing the trout to me to secure with the landing-net."

"Hallo!" shouted Smith, "hold on there; fair play, my friends, give me a hand in," and he fell to adjusting his rod and flies.

"Keep back, you lubber," replied Spalding; "what do **you** know about trout-fishing? You'll frighten them all away by your awkwardness."

"No you don't!" shouted Smith, his rod now adjusted. "Drop down, boatman, and we'll see who is the lubber. Wait, Spalding! Don't throw, if you are a true man, until we can take a fair start, and then the one that comes out second best pays the piper."

The boat dropped down to the proper position, and the Doctor, who was seated in the stern, held it in place by pressing his paddle into the sand at the bottom, while the boatman handled the landing net.

"Now!" exclaimed Smith, as the flies dropped upon the water together above the cold spring. There was no lack of trout, for one rose to the fly at every cast.

"I say," said the Doctor, "how many have you in your boat?"

"Sixteen," I replied, after counting them.

"We've got eight, and I bar any more fishing. The law has reached its limit. No wanton waste of the good things of God, you know."

The rods were unjointed and laid away, and such a string of trout as we had, is rarely seen outside of the Saranac woods. We procured fresh grass in which to lay our fish, and green boughs to cover them, and floated on down the stream, entering the Rackett at nine o'clock. The Rackett is a most beautiful river. To me at least it is so, for it flows on its tortuous and winding way for a hundred or more miles through an unbroken forest, with all the old things standing in their primeval grandeur along its banks. The woodman's axe has not marred the loveliness of its surroundings, and no human hand has for all that distance been laid upon its mane, or harnessed it to the great wheel, making it a slave, compelling it to be utilitarian, to grind corn or throw the shuttle and spin. It moves on towards the mighty St. Lawrence as wild, and halterless, and free, as when the Great Spirit sent it forward on its everlasting flow. The same scenery, and the same voices are seen and heard along its banks now as then; and, while man, in his restlessness, has changed almost everything else, the Rackett and the things that pertained to it when the earth was young, remain unchanged. But this will not be so long. Civilization is pushing its way even towards this wild and, for all agricultural purposes, sterile region, and before many years even the Rackett will be within its ever-extending circle. When that time shall have arrived, where shall we go to find the woods, the wild things, the old forests, and hear the sounds which belong to nature in its primeval state? Whither shall we flee from civilization, to take off the harness and be free, for a season, from the restraints, the conventionalities of society, and rest from the hard struggles, the cares and toils, the strifes and competitions of life? Had I my way, I would mark out a circle of a hundred miles in diameter, and throw around it the protecting aegis of the constitution. I would make it a forest forever. It should be a misdemeanor to chop down a tree, and a felony to clear an acre within its boundaries. The old woods should stand here always as God made them, growing on until the earthworm ate away their roots, and the strong winds hurled them to the ground, and new woods should be permitted to supply the place of the old so long as the earth remained. There is room enough for civilization in regions better fitted for it. It has no business among these mountains, these rivers and lakes, these gigantic boulders, these tangled valleys and dark mountain gorges. Let it go where labor will garner a richer harvest, and industry reap a better reward for its toil. It will be of stinted growth at best here.

"I like these old woods," said a gentleman, whom I met on the Rackett last year; "I like them, because one can do here just what he pleases. He can wear a shirt a week, have holes in his pantaloons, and be out at elbows, go with his boots unblacked, drink whisky in the raw, chew plug tobacco, and smoke a black pipe, and not lose his position in society. Now," continued he, "tho' I don't choose to do any of these things, yet I love the freedom, now and then, of doing just all of them if I choose, without human accountability. The truth is, that it is natural as well as necessary for every man to be a vagabond occasionally, to throw off the restraints imposed upon him by the necessities and conventionalities of civilization, and turn savage for a season,--and what place is left for such transformation, save these northern forests?"

The idea was somewhat quaint, but to me it smacked of philosophy, and I yielded it a hearty assent. I would consecrate these old forests, these rivers and lakes, these mountains and valleys to the Vagabond Spirit, and make them a place wherein a man could turn savage and rest, for a fortnight or a month, from the toils and cares of life.

We entered TUPPER'S LAKE towards six o'clock, and saw our white tents pitched upon the left bank, some half a mile above the outlet, where a little stream, cold almost as icewater, comes down from a spring a short way back in the forest. This lake, some ten miles long, and from one to three in width, is one of the most beautiful sheets of water that the eye of man ever looked upon. The scenery about it is less bold than that of some of the other lakes of this region. The hills rise with a gentle acclivity from the shore; behind them and far off rise rugged mountain ranges; and further still, the lofty peaks of the Adirondacks loom up in dim and shadowy outline against the sky. From every point and in every direction, are views of placid and quiet beauty rarely equalled; valleys stretching away among the highlands; gaps in the hills, through which the sunlight pours long after the shadows of the forest have elsewhere thrown themselves across the lake; islands, some bold and rocky, rising in barren desolation, right up from the deep water; some covered with a dense and thrifty growth of evergreen trees, with a soil matchless in fertility; and some partaking of both the sterile and productive; beautiful bays stealing around bold promontories, and hiding away among the old woods. These are the features of this beautiful sheet of water, which none see but to admire, none visit but to praise; and it lies here all alone, surrounded by the old hills and forests, bold bluffs, and rocky shores, all as God made them, with no mark of the hand of man about it, save in a single spot on a secluded bay, where lives a solitary family in a log house, surrounded by an acre or two, from which the forest has been cleared away.

"Will somebody tell me," said Smith, as we sat on the logs in front of our tent after supper, smudging away the musquitoes with our pipes, "will somebody tell me what we came into this wilderness among these musquitoes, and frogs, and owls for? Mind you, I am not discontented; I enjoy it hugely; but what I want to know is *why* I do so? I desire to understand the philosophy of the thing."

"As the question involves, in some sense, a physiological fact," replied the Doctor, "it comes within the range of my professional duties to understand and be able to answer it, for you must know that the enjoyments of this region are primarily physical. Now I've a theory which is this--that every man has a certain amount of vagabondism in his composition that will be pretty certain to break out in spots occasionally. At all events it is so with me, and from my observation of men, I am strong in the faith that it is so with every one who is neither more nor less than human. It is all a mistake to suppose that I come off here, enduring a heap of hardship and toil, simply for the love of fishing and hunting, though I confess to a weakness to a certain extent that way. The charm of this region consists in the fact, that it is the best place to play the vagabond, and in which to do the savage for a season, that I know of. You can go bareheaded or barefooted, without a coat or neckerchief, get as ragged and untidy as you please, without subjecting yourself to remark, or offending the nice sense of propriety pertaining to conventional life. You are not responsible for what you say or do, provided always that you do not offend against the abstract rules of decency, or the requirements of natural decorum. You can lay around loose; the lazier you are the better the boatman in your employ likes it. If you choose to drift leisurely and quietly under the shadow of the hills along the shore, examining the rocks that lie there like a ruined wall, or explore the beautiful and secluded bays that hide around behind the bluffs, or lay off under the shade of the fir trees on the islands, or smoke your cigar or pipe by the beautiful spring that comes bubbling up by the side of some moss-covered boulder, or from beneath the tangled roots of some gnarled birch or maple, you can do any or all of these, and have a man to help you for twelve shillings a day and board, or you can do it just about as well alone.

"You remember LONESOME ROCK, in the Lower Saranac, a great boulder that lifts its head some ten or fifteen feet above the surface, away out near the middle of the lake, around which the water is of unknown depth. This rock, which is always dark and bare, is, as you will remember, of conical shape, sharp pointed at the top, and stands up about the size of a small hay-stack, in the midst of the waters. Do you remember the account that somebody gives in a ragged but terse kind of verse, of the 'gentleman in black,' who, as he walked about,

'Backward and forward he switched his long rail,
As a gentleman switches his cane?'
And of whose dress it was facetiously said:

'His coat was red and his breeches were blue,
With a hole behind for his tail to stick through.'
another author said of him on one of his fishing excursions, that

'His rod, it was a sturdy mountain oak,
His line, a cable which no storm e'er broke,
His hook he baited with a dragon's tail,
And sat upon a rock and bob'd for whale!'

Well, like the ebony gentleman, you can, if you choose, sit upon Lonesome Rock enjoying your meditations, and bobbing, not for whale, for whatever other fish may be found in the Lower Saranac, I believe there are no whale; but you can bob for trout; whether you will catch any or not will depend very much on circumstances. It is a capital place to cast the fly from, or to sink your hook with a bait, and if the trout do not choose to bite, whose fault is that, I should like to know?

"And this reminds me of an anecdote told me by a gentleman I met in June of last year, on the Rackett River among the black flies, of an adventure he met with on Lonesome Rock last season. He had been trolling around the lake in a boat alone, without much success, and concluded he would try deep fishing from this rock, as he had heard that the trout were in the habit of congregating around its base. So he rowed to the rock, and, as he supposed, secured his boat, and climbing up its side seated himself on his boat cushion, on the top. He caught one fine fish at the first throw, and took it for granted that he was going to have a good time of it among the trout. When he mounted the rock, about eleven o'clock, the sky was overcast, and he caught three or four trout of good size in the course of half an hour; but the sun coming out bright and clear, the fish altered their minds, and refused to have anything more to do with his hook. He finally concluded to give up the business, and seek the cooling shadows of the forest trees along the shore. But his boat was gone; and upon looking around he saw it drifting before a light breeze a quarter of a mile distant. Now when you remember that all around the lake was a wilderness, save a single spot at the head of the bay, where Martin's house stands, three or four miles distant, and when you remember also that no boat might be passing during the next twenty-four hours, you will comprehend that his position was none of the pleasantest. There he sat upon the top of his rock, with scarcely room to turn around, with a wide sweep of deep water between him and the nearest land, the fish utterly refusing to bite, and the sun blazing down upon him with heat like a furnace, as it crept with its snail's pace across the sky. At first he was inclined to smile at his ridiculous situation, all alone there on the rock; but as the wind died away, and the sun poured his burning rays right down upon him, and he panted and sweat under its sweltering influences, he began to feel a little more serious. Hours glided away, and the sun crept slowly along down the heavens, but still no boat made its appearance.

"The sun hid itself behind the hills on the West, and still he was alone. The shadows crept up the mountain peaks that stand up like grim giants away off in the East, and twilight began to throw its grey mantle over the lake; still he was alone. The darkness began to gather around him; the forests along the shore to lose their distinctness and to stand in sombre and shadowy outline above the water; still no prospect of relief presented itself. The twilight faded from the West, the stars stole out in the heavens, the milky way stretched its belt of light across the sky, and there he sat alone still on his rock, the night dews falling around him, and the night voices of the forest coming solemnly out over the water. Things had now assumed a serious aspect. He could not stretch his limbs save by standing erect, and it seemed inevitable that he must watch the stars during the night, as he had watched the sun during the day. To sleep there was out of the question. There was no room for a sleeping posture, and the danger of rolling down the rock into the water kept him wide awake. At length the pleasant sound of oars, and voices in jolly converse, fell upon his ear, and he shouted. Two sportsmen were returning from the Upper Lakes, and right welcome was the answer they returned to his call. He was glad enough to be released from his rock, upon which, as he said, 'he had made up his mind that he should be compelled to roost, like a turkey on the ridge of a barn, for the night.'

"To go back from this digression," continued the Doctor, "I repeat that every man has a vein of the vagabond, a streak of the savage in him, which can never be clean wiped out. Educate him, polish him as you may, it will be in him still, and he will love to go off into the old woods at times, to lay around loose for a season, vagabondising among the wild and savage things of the wilderness. It is but indulging the original instincts of our nature. True, he will not relish his savage ways a great while. His old habits will lead him back to civilization, to the luxury of a well-furnished room, the quiet of an easy chair, and the repose of a soft bed. In a word to 'clean up' and shave and dress, so that when he looks into a glass he will see the shadow of a gentleman."

CHAPTER IX.
HUNTING BY TORCH LIGHT--AN INCOMPETENT JUDGE--A NEW SOUND IN THE FOREST--OLD SANGAMO'S DONKEY.

Spalding and Martin went out upon the lake after dark, with one of the boats, to hunt by torch light. This is done by placing a lighted torch, or a lamp upon a standard, placed upright in the bow of the boat, and so high that a man seated or lying upon the bottom of the craft, will have his head below it. He must himself be in someway shaded from the light, which must be cast forward so that both the hunter and the boatman will be in the shadow. A very common method is to make a box, a foot or less square, open, or with a pane of glass on one side; a stick three or four feet long is run through an auger hole in the top and bottom, and wedged fast, which forms a standard; the other end of the stick is run through a hole on the little deck on the forward part of the boat, and placed in a socket formed for the purpose in the bottom, and is wedged at the deck, so as to make it steady. The open or glass front of the box is turned forward, and a common japan lamp placed in a socket prepared for it in the box. This of course throws the light forward, while the occupants of the boat are in the shadow. The hunter sits, or more commonly lies at length on a bed of boughs in the bottom of the boat, with his rifle so far in front that the light will fall upon the forward sight. An experienced boatman will paddle silently up to within twenty feet of a deer that may be feeding along the shore. The stupid animal will stand, gazing in astonishment at the light, until the boat almost touches him.

"That Hank Martin," said Cullen, one of the boatmen, as the hunters disappeared into the darkness, "is a queer boy in his way. You will notice that when he straightens up, and takes the kinks out of him, he stands six feet and over in his stockings, and his arms hang down to his knees. He's the strongest man in these woods, and tolerably active when there's occasion for it. He is a droll, good-natured, easy tempered chap, and don't get angry at trifles. He is fond of a joke himself, and will stand having a good many sticks poked at him without getting riled; but when he does get his back up, it's well enough to stand out of his way, and not step on his shadow. He never struck a man but once in real earnest, and that was over in Keeseville, and on that occasion the people said the town clock had struck *one*. The fellow he struck went eend over eend, and then went down, and when he went down he laid still--he didn't come to tine.

"But what I was going to tell you is, that Hank and I were down at Plattsburgh last fall, and a big fellow who had taken quite as much red eye as was for his good, undertook to pick a quarrel with Hank and give him a beating. Hank, as I said, being a peaceable man, and much more given to fun than to fighting, kept good-natured, and avoided a scrimmage as long as he could. But his patience and his temper at last caved in, and seizing his opponent by the neck with his left hand, and thrusting him down upon the ground, he began very deliberately to cuff him with his right, in a way that seemed anything but pleasant to the individual upon whom his cuffs were bestowed. 'Enough! enough!' cried his assailant. 'Let up! enough! enough!' 'Hold your tongue, you scoundrel!' replied Hank, as he kept on pommeling his enemy, 'hold your tongue, I tell you! You ain't a judge of these things! I'll let you know when you've got enough.' When he'd given him what he thought was about right, he lifted him on to his feet, and, holding him up face to face with himself a moment, 'There,' said he, 'look at me well, so that you'll know me when I come this way again; and when you see my trail, you'd better travel some other road.'"

"Speaking of Plattsburgh," said the Doctor, "reminds me of an incident which occurred to a friend and myself, over in the Chataugay woods, between the Chazy and the Upper Chataugay lakes. I was spending a few days at Plattsburgh, and hearing a good deal of the trout and deer in and about those lakes, my friend and myself concluded to pay them a flying visit. On the banks of the Chazy and near the outlet, a half-breed, that is, half French and half Indian, had built him a log cabin, and cleared about an acre of land around it. His live stock consisted of two homely, lean, and half-starved dogs, and as ragged and ill-looking a donkey as could be found in a week's travel. The half-breed was a sort of half fisherman and half hunter, excelling in nothing, unless it be that he was the laziest man this side of the Rocky Mountains. He succeeded, occasionally, in killing a deer in the forest, and when he did so, he would lead his donkey to the place of slaughter, and bring in the carcase on the long-eared animal's back.

"We were passing from the Chazy to Bradley's Lake, and had sat down on the trunk of a fallen tree to take a short breathing spell. It was a warm afternoon, and the air was calm; not a breath stirred the leaves on the old trees around us; the forest sounds were hushed, save the tap of the woodpecker on his hollow tree, or an occasional drumming of a partridge on his log. It was drawing towards one of those calm, still, autumnal evenings of which poets sing, but which are to be met with in all their glory only among the beautiful lakes that lay sleeping in the wild woods, and surrounded by old primeval things. The path wound round a densely wooded and sombre hollow, the depths of which the eye could not penetrate, but from out of which came the song of a stream that went cascading down the rocks, and rippling among the loose boulders that lay in its course. Beyond us, through an opening in the trees, we could see the lake, sparkling and shining in the evening sunbeams, and we were talking about the beauty of the view, and the calmness and repose that seemed resting upon all things, when, of a sudden, there came up from that shadowy dell a sound, the most unearthly that ever broke upon the astonished ear of mortal man. I have heard the roar of the lion of the desert, the yell of the hyena, the trumpeting of the elephant, the scream of the panther, the howl of the wolf. It was like none of these; but if you could imagine them all combined, and concentrated into a single sound, and ushered together upon the air from a single throat, shaped like the long neck of some gigantic ichthiosaurus of the times of old, you would have some faint idea of the strange sounds that came roaring up from that hollow way. My friend was a man of courage, and, like myself, had been around the world some; had spent a good deal of time, first and last, in the woods, was familiar with most of the legitimate forest sounds, and had heard all the ten thousand voices that belong in the wilderness, but we had never before listened to a noise like that.

"We looked to our rifles and at one another, and it may well be that our hats sat somewhat loosely upon our heads, from an involuntary rising of the hair. 'What, in the name of all that is mysterious,' cried my friend, in amazement, 'is that?' 'It is more than I know,' I replied, as I placed a fresh cap on my rifle. After a few minutes, the sounds were repeated, and the hills seemed to groan with affright as they sent them back in wavy and quavering echoes from their rugged sides.

"'We must understand this,' said my friend, as he led the way with a cautious and stealthy movement towards the depths of the hollow, whence the sounds came, and there, by the stream, on a little sand-bar, stood old Sangamo's donkey, by the side of a deer. Old Sangamo himself was stretched at full length on the bank, fast asleep. How he could have slept on, with such an infernal roaring as that donkey made in those old woods, six or eight miles outside of a fence, is more than I can comprehend. But he did sleep through it all, and was wakened only by a punch in the ribs with the butt of my rifle, instigated by pity for the poor donkey that was being eaten up by the flies. We helped him to load the carcass of the deer on the back of his donkey, and saw him move off lazily towards home. I have heard a good many strange noises in my day, but never, on any other occasion, have I listened to anything to be at all compared with the noise made by the braying of old Sangamo's donkey in the Chataugay woods."

As the Doctor concluded his story, the sharp crack of Spalding's rifle broke the stillness of the night, and went reverberating among the hills, and dying away over the lake. It was but a short distance from our camp, in a little bay hidden away around a wooded promontory below us. In a few minutes, the light was seen, rounding the point that hid the bay from our view, and, as the boat landed in front of our tents, Spalding and Martin lifted from it a fine two year old deer, shot directly between the eyes.

"There," said Spalding, "is the biggest, or what ***was*** the biggest fool of a deer in these woods. Do you believe that he stood perfectly still, gazing in stupid astonishment at our light, until we were within a dozen feet of him, when I dropped him with that ball between the eyes?"

"No," replied Smith, "I really don't believe any such thing."

"It is true, notwithstanding your lack of faith," said Spalding.

"Do you say that as counsel, or as a gentleman?" inquired Smith.

"Look you, Mr. Smith," said Spalding, "you are drawing a distinction not warranted by the authority of the books--as if a lawyer could not tell the truth like a gentleman. I say it as both."

"Very well," remarked Smith, "then I must believe it, of course. But understand, Hank Martin, it will be my turn to-morrow night." And so the matter was settled that the next night hunting was to be done by Smith.

"H----," said the Doctor, as I was stealing quietly out of the tent, in the twilight of the next morning, so as not to awaken my companions, "where now?"

"I'm going to take some trout for breakfast, with our venison," I replied.

"And where do you propose to take them?" he inquired. "Come with me, and I'll show you. I looked the place out last evening, and if you've done sleeping, we'll have some sport."

"Agreed," said he, and we paddled around the point into a little bay, at the head of which a small, but cold stream entered the lake. The Doctor sat in the bow, and, having adjusted his rod, I steered the boat carefully, close along the shore, to within reach of the mouth of the brook, and directed him to cast across it. The moment his fly touched the water, half a dozen fish rose to it together. It was eagerly seized by one weighing less than a quarter of a pound, which was lifted bodily into the boat. He caught as fast as he could cast his fly. They were the genuine brook trout, none of them exceeding a quarter Of a pound in weight. In half an hour, we had secured as many as we needed for breakfast, and paddled back to take a morning nap while the meal was being prepared.

The sweetest fish that swims is the brook trout, weighing from a quarter of a pound down. Rolled in flour, or meal, and fried brown, they have no equal. The lake and river trout, weighing from two to ten pounds, beautiful as they are, have not that delicacy of flavor which belongs to the genuine brook trout. Boiled, when freshly caught, they are by no means to be spoken lightly of. They have few equals, cooked in that way, but as a pan fish, they are not to be compared with the genuine brook trout.

CHAPTER X.
GRINDSTONE BROOK--FOREST SOUNDS--A FUNNY TREE, COVERED WITH SNOW FLAKES.

We crossed over towards a deep bay on the west shore, to where a stream comes cascading down the rocks, and leaping into the lake, as if rejoicing at finding a resting-place in its quiet bosom. The spot where this stream enters, is in the deep shadow of the old forest trees that reach their leafy arms far out from the ledges on which they grow, forming an arch above, and shutting out the sunlight. Here the trout congregate, to enjoy the cool water that comes down from the hills above. We approached it carefully, and Smith, by way of experiment, cast his fly across the current where the stream enters the lake. It was seized by a beautiful fish weighing, perhaps, two pounds. We did not need him, for the place where we proposed to pitch our tents for the night would afford us all the fish required, and after lifting him into the boat with the landing-net and releasing the hook from his jaw, we returned him to the lake again.

Two miles from the head of the lake, on the east side, is a deep bay at the head of which enters a little brook that comes creeping along for a mile among the tangled roots of ancient hemlocks and spruce, singing gaily among the loose stones, sometimes disappearing entirely beneath bridges of moss, and sometimes sparkling in the sunlight, on its way to the lake. This little stream we found swarming with speckled trout of the size of minnows, and at its mouth the large trout congregated. As we rounded one of the points that shut out the view of this bay from the lake, we saw two deer feeding quietly upon the lily pads along the shore, some quarter of a mile from us. We dropped quietly back behind the point, where Smith and one of the boatmen prepared to take a shot at them. Martin took his seat in the stern with his paddle, and Smith lay stretched at length along the bottom of the boat upon boughs prepared for the occasion, with his rifle resting upon the forward end of the boat. It was broad daylight, and to paddle up within shooting distance of a deer under such circumstances, in plain view of an animal the most wary, is a delicate job, but it may be done. I have more than once been thus paddled within thirty yards of a deer while feeding in the water. The wind must be blowing from the deer to the hunter, or the scent will alarm the animal, and he will go snorting and bounding away.

Smith and Martin passed silently out into the bay, and moved slowly towards where the deer were feeding. The boat in which we sat was permitted to float out to a position from which we could see the sportsmen as they approached the game. Slowly but steadily they moved, the paddle remaining in the water, sculling the little craft along as if it were a log drifting in the water. The deer occasionally raised their heads, looking all around, evidently regarding the boat as a harmless thing floating in from the lake. After gazing thus about them they stooped their heads again, and went on feeding, as if no danger were near them. The hunters drifted within seventy or eighty yards of the game, when a column of white smoke shot suddenly up from the bow of the boat, and the report of Smith's rifle rang out sharp and clear over the lake. We saw where the ball struck the water just beyond the deer, passing directly under its belly, possibly high enough to graze its body. At the flash and report of the rifle, the animal leaped high into the air, bounded in affright this way and that for a moment, and then straightened itself for the woods. We heard his snort as he went crashing up the hillside.

Reader, should you ever drift out to this beautiful lake, you will find on the ridge just above where Bog River comes tumbling, and roaring, and foaming over the rocks into the lake, the charred remains of a campfire, built against a great log that was once the trunk of a tall forest tree. If you should visit it within a year or two, you will perhaps notice some forked stakes standing a few feet from the place of the fire, and a bed of withered and dry boughs (now fresh and green). Well, our tents were stretched over those stakes, those boughs were our bed, and those charred chunks are the remains of our campfire, that sent a sepulchral light among the forest trees around.

The sounds that come upon the ear during the night in a far off place like this, are peculiar. The old owl hoots mournfully, the frogs bellow hoarsely along the reedy shore, while the tree toads are quavering from among the branches of the scrubby trees that grow along the rocky banks; the whippoorwill pipes shrilly in the forest depths; the breeze murmurs among the foliage of the tall old pines, while the everlasting roar of the waters, as they go tumbling down the rocks, is always heard. However diversified these sounds may be, they all invite to repose. They fall soothingly upon the ear, and though all are distinctly heard, yet strange as it may seem, there is a strong impression upon the mind of the deep silence pervading the forest. This impression is doubtless occasioned by the utter dissimilarity between the voices one hears in the day, from those which fall upon the ear in the night time. The former are all joyous and happy, full of gladness and merriment, full of life and animation; the latter solemn, deep, profound, lulling to the senses; not sorrowful nor sad, yet still such as form a calm and quiet lullaby, under the influence of which one glides away into slumber, and sleeps quietly until dawn. Then the voice of gladness breaks so tumultuously on the ear, that he must be a sluggard indeed who can resist their wakening influences. How beautifully the sun went down behind the hills, lighting up the western sky, and the fleecy clouds floating in the heavens with a blaze of glory, throwing a mantle of silver over the tall ranges and mountain peaks that loomed up in solemn grandeur away in the east; and how stilly, silently the stars came out from the depths above, and how brightly and truthfully they were given back from away down in depths beneath the placid waters. We had taken half a dozen beautiful trout from the foot of the falls where the current shoots out into the lake. We had eaten them too, and were sitting in front of our tents smoking our evening pipes.

"Spalding," said the Doctor, "How I wish our little boys were out here with us. How they would enjoy themselves among these lakes and rivers. It is a hard lot that the children of our cities have in life. They struggle up to man and womanhood against fearful odds, and the wonder is, that they do not perish in their infancy; that they are not blasted, as the blossoms are, when the cold east wind sweeps over the earth."

"You are right, my friend," replied Spalding. "I should like to have our little boys, and girls too, for that matter, with us for a few days out here on these lakes. It would be a lifetime to them, measuring time by the enjoyment it would afford them. Still their city habits might make them tire of this freedom in a week. You and I enjoy it longer, because it brings back old memories and relieves us from the toils of business and the restraints of conventional life. You are right too in saying that the lot of our city children is a hard one. To live imprisoned between long rows of brick walls, breathing an atmosphere charged with the exhalations of ten thousand cooking stoves, the dust of forges and the smoke of furnaces, machine shops, gas works, filthy streets, and the thousand other manufactories of villainous smells; where the summer air has no freshness, no forest odors, or sweetness gathered from fields of grain, the meadows, or the pastures. To tramp only on stone sidewalks. To know nothing of the pleasant paths beneath the spreading branches of old primeval trees; no soft grass for their little feet to press; never to wander along the streams or the little brooks; to be strangers always to the beautiful things spread out everywhere in the country in the summer time. I always feel sad when I see the pale faces of the little children of the great cities, and marvel how so many of them grow up to be men and women. It is a hard lot to be cooped up in the city, vegitating, as it were, in the shade, where there is no grass for their little feet to press, no fences to climb, or fields to ramble over, or brooks to wade, or running water on which to float chips, and wherein to watch the little chubs and shiners dancing and playing about, or fresh pure air to breathe, or birds to listen to. It is a thousand pities that the cities could not be emptied every summer of their little people into the free and open country, where they could run about, and sport and play, and have free range and plenty of elbow-room. It would make them so much healthier and happier, so much more cheerful; their voices of gladness would ring out so much more joyously in the morning, and their songs be so much more sweet at night."

I remember an anecdote told me of a little child, born in the great metropolis, who had never, until her fifth summer, been outside of the paved streets of New York. Her mother had friends residing in one of the up-river towns, owning a beautiful farm overlooking the Hudson, and in early May she paid them a visit, taking her little daughter with her. Mary, of course, was delighted. Like a bird freed from its cage, she flew about here, there, everywhere, in-doors and out, among the chickens and the pigs, the turkeys and the lambs, enjoying to the full the thousand new things that her eyes rested upon all around her, and her young spirits in wild commotion under the bracing influences of the country air. "Mother! mother!" she exclaimed, as she came dashing into the parlor, her beautiful curls floating wildly over her shoulders, and her bright eyes wide open with wonder; "Mother I mother! come out here, quick! and see this funny tree, all covered over with snow-flakes, and how sweet it smells all around it." It was a plum tree in full blossom. That little child had never seen the beautiful spring blossoms on the fruit trees.

"I have no children of my own," remarked Smith, "and, therefore, may not be regarded as the best authority in regard to the manner of treating, or rearing children; but I have often wondered at the very great mistakes people sometimes make in regard to them. There are parents who mean no wrong, and yet who make no scruple of deceiving them in reply to their simple questionings, forgetting, or regardless of the fact, that a false answer to their innocent inquiries put in good faith, and in the earnest pursuit of truth, may plant an error in their minds, which may take years of experience, and often a painful amount of ridicule to eradicate. I knew a little boy years ago, a thoughtful, philosophic child, who speculated in his simplicity upon what he saw, as great philosophers do, in their wisdom, upon the various phenomena of Nature. His father, had a great barn, above which, as was the fashion long ago, perched upon a staff, a few feet above the ridgepole, was a weather-cock, fashioned out of a piece of board in the shape of a rooster. 'Father,' said the little boy, one day, 'what makes that rooster always point his head one way when the cold wind blows, and the other way when it is warm and pleasant?' 'He always looks towards the place where the wind comes from,' replied the father; 'when he gets too warm, and the sun is too hot for him, he turns his tail to the south, and the north wind is sure to come down, cold and chill, to cool him off.' 'Does he call the cold wind, father, and will it come when he looks, that way?' was the next inquiry. 'Certainly,' replied his father, carelessly. That was a wrong and a foolish answer.

"That little boy, relying in his simple faith upon the wisdom and truthfulness of his father, believed for a long time, that the weathercock on the top of the barn, could bring the cold north, or the warm south wind, by turning upon its perch. He was cured of his error only by being laughed at for his simplicity. Parents should never deceive their children by a careless or a wrong answer to the simple questions put to them by these little searchers after knowledge."

"I remember," said the doctor, "and it is one of the earliest incidents which my recollection has treasured, that I was out one evening in autumn, with a boy older than myself, gathering hazel nuts. The sun had sunk behind the hills, and the shadows of twilight were gathering in the valley. It was a beautiful and calm evening, the solemn stillness of which, was only broken by the 'tza! tza!' of thousands of katydids among the bushes. I asked my companion what it was that made the noise I heard, and he, supposing that I referred to sounds that came up occasionally from the lake, after listening for a moment, answered that it was made by the wild geese. In my simplicity I believed it, and it was not until I caught, the next season, a katydid while it was in the act of singing, that I discovered that the music among the hazel bushes was not made by the wild geese."

"I never respect a man or woman," said Spalding, "whose heart does not warm towards little children, who takes no pleasure nor interest in their society, who has no patience to listen to their simple thoughts expressed in their simple way. 'Mother,' said a little child of four or five years of age, one evening when the summer air was warm, and the skies were bright above, as she sat beside her mother, on a bench beneath the spreading branches of the tall old elms in front of the house; 'mother, what makes the stars come out, only after the dark has come down, and why don't the moon go up into the sky like the sun in the day time?' I listened anxiously for the reply. I knew the kind heart of that mother, how truthful it was, and how earnest and pure in its affection for its gentle and only darling. 'Sit here upon my lap, Mary,' said the mother, 'and I will try and explain it all so that you will understand it.' And she told the little child how God made the sun to rule the day, and the moon and the stars to rule the night; how that the stars were always in the sky, but how the superior brightness of the sun put them out in the day time; how the stars, that twinkled like little rush-lights in the heavens, were great worlds, a thousand times larger than this earth, made and placed away up in the sky, by the same great and good God who made the world we live in. Little Mary was silent and attentive to the simple lecture, until it was finished, and then asked, so simply and confidingly, that I could not help smiling to think that the mind of childhood should be running upon a subject, and seeking a solution of the same question which has puzzled the profoundest philosophers through all time: 'Mother,' said the little one, 'are there people in the moon and in the stars, them great worlds that look to us so like candles in the sky?' 'That question, my child,' said the mother, 'I cannot answer.' 'I believe,' said the child, that there *are* people in the moon, and in all the stars.' 'Why?' asked her mother. 'Because I don't believe God would make such big and beautiful worlds without making people to live in them.' What more has the profoundest philosopher who ever lived said, to prove that those mighty worlds which are seen in the heavens at night, that are scattered all through the universe of God, rolling forever on their everlasting rounds, are peopled by living, moving, sentient beings?"

CHAPTER XI.
A CONVENTION BROKEN UP IN A BOW--THE CHAIRMAN EJECTED.

We sent forward our boatman with the luggage early in the morning, up Bog River towards Mud Lake, the source of the right branch of that river, lying some thirty miles deeper in the wilderness, counting the sinuosities of the stream, and said to be the highest body of water in all this wild region. We were to spend the day on Tupper's Lake, and follow him the next morning. Our boatman built for our accommodation, a brush shanty in the place of our tents. We rowed about this beautiful sheet of water, exploring its secluded bays and romantic islands, trying experiments with the trout wherever a stream came down from the hills, and trolling for lake trout while crossing the lake. Near the shore, on the west bank, perhaps half a mile from the falls, is one of the coldest, purest and most beautiful springs that I ever met with. It comes up into a little basin some six or eight feet in diameter, by two or three in depth. The bottom is of loose white sand which is all in commotion, by the constant boiling up of the clear cold water. From this basin a little stream goes rippling and laughing to the lake. Towards evening we returned to our shanty with abundance of fish for supper and breakfast, taken, as I said, in simply trying experiments as to where they were to be found in the greatest abundance.

If any sportsman who may drift out this way, is fond of taking the speckled trout--little fellows, weighing from a quarter of a pound down, the same he meets with in the streams of Vermont, in Massachusetts, in Northern Pennsylvania, and. Western New York, let him provide himself with angle-worms, and row to the head of the lake. A short distance east of where Bog River enters, say from a quarter to half a mile, he will find a cold mountain stream. Let him rig for brook-fishing and take to that stream. If he does not fill his basket in a little while, he may set it down to the score of bad luck, or some lack of skill on his part in taking them, for the brook trout are there in abundance. Across the lake from Long Island, to the right as you go up the lake, is a bay that goes away in around a woody point. At the head of this bay, "Grindstone Brook" enters. It is a smallish stream, and comes dashing down over shelving rocks some thirty feet, and shoots out into the bay among broken rocks, and loose boulders. The waters of this stream are much colder than those of the lake. Let the sportsman row carefully up towards the mouth of this stream, along towards evening of a hot day, when the shadow of the hill reaches far out over the lake, and cast his fly across the little current, and if he does not take as beautiful a string of river trout as can be found in these parts, let him set it down to the score of accident, for the trout are there in the warm days of August. If he has a curiosity to know what there is above these Little Falls, let him try his angle-worms in the brook just over the ridge, and he will find out. I claim to have discovered these choice fishing places some seasons since, and have kept them for my own private use and amusement. Nobody seemed to know of them. When the trout refused to be taken elsewhere, I have always found them here, abundant, greedy, and ready to be taken by any decently skillful effort. I regard these places as in some sort my private property, and I mention them privately and in confidence to the reader, trusting that my right will be respected.

We finished our evening meal while the sun was yet above the western hills, and sat with our pipes around a smudge, made upon the broad flat rock, which recedes with a gentle acclivity from the shore, where the Bog River enters the lake, looking out over the stirless waters. It was a beautiful view, so calm, so still and placid, and yet so wild. The islands seemed to stand out clear from the water, to be lifted up, as it were, from the lake, so perfectly moveless and polished was its surface. On a grassy point to the right, and a hundred rods distant, two deer were quietly feeding, while in a little bay on the left, a brood of young ducks were sporting and skimming along the water in playful gyrations around their staid and watchful mother. On the outstretched arm of a dead tree on the island before us, sat a bald eagle, pluming himself; and high above the lake the osprey soared, turning his piercing eye downward, watching for his prey.

"I've been thinking," said Smith, as he refilled his pipe, "of what the Doctor was saying the other evening about every body having a streak of the vagabond in him, which makes him relish an occasional tramp in the old woods among the natural things; things that have not been marred by the barbarisms, so to speak, of civilization. I'm inclined to believe his theory to be true, but I see a difficulty in its practical working. Now, suppose, Doctor, that you and I being out here together vagabondizing, as you term it, and your streak of the vagabond being twice as large as mine, you would of course desire to play the savage twice as long as I should. There would, in that case, be a marring of the harmonies. I should be anxious to get back to civilization, while you, being rather in your normal element, would insist upon 'laying around loose,' as you say, for Mercy knows how long."

"Gentlemen," said the Doctor in reply, "only hear this fellow! He's getting homesick already. He has no wife, not a child in the world, no business, nothing to call him home save a superannuated pointer, and an old Tom cat, and yet he would leave these glorious old woods, these beautiful lakes, these rivers, these trout and deer, and all the glad music of the wild things, to-morrow, and go back to the dust, the poisoned atmosphere, the eternal jostling and monotonous noises of the city! Truly a vagabond and a savage is Smith. He's afraid that his family, his mangy old pointer and dropsical cat, will suffer in his absence."

"I scorn to answer such an accusation," retorted Smith, "I shall treat it with dignified contempt, as I do the Doc medicines, which I never take but always pay for, just to keep him from starving, and to make him imagine he cures me. But speaking of cats reminds me of a certain matter which occurred not many years ago. The Doctor here, if his testimony could be relied upon, knows that I used to be troubled with indigestion, and was sometimes a little nervous"----

"A *little* nervous!" interrupted the Doctor, "why he would be as crazy with the hypo as a March hare. He would insist that he was going to die, or to the almshouse. He has made two or three dozen wills, to my certain knowledge, under the firm conviction that he would be in the ground in a week. A *little* nervous, indeed!"

"Well," said Smith, "we won't quarrel about the degree of my nervousness. But in regard to what I was going to say about cats. Some years ago I occupied a suite of rooms in the second story of a house rented by a widow lady, to whom I had been under some obligations in my boyhood, and whom my mother always regarded as her best friend." (Smith supported the excellent old lady in comfort for a decade, under pretence of boarding with her, ministering to the last years of her life with the care and affection of a son.) "The landlord of the premises was the owner of a block of twelve houses--six on Pearl street, and six on Broadway, the lots meeting midway between the two streets. On the rear of these lots are the out-houses, all under a continuous flat roof, some twelve feet high, twenty wide, and say a hundred and fifty feet long. In the rear of the Broadway dwelling-houses, are one story tea-rooms, or third parlors, the roofs of which form a continuous platform, upon which you can step from the second story of the houses."

"Well," said the Doctor, "what of all that?"

"There's a great deal of it," Smith replied. "I don't pretend to know how many cats there were in the city of Albany. Indeed, I never heard that they were included in the census. I do not undertake to say that they *all* congregated nightly on the roofs of those out-houses. But if there was a cat in the sixth ward, that didn't have something to say on that roof every night, I should like to make its acquaintance.

I am against cats. I regard them as treacherous, ungrateful animals, and as having very small moral developments generally. I am against *cat*-terwauling, especially in the night season, when honest people have a right to their natural sleep. I don't like to be woke up, when rounding a pleasant dream, by their growling and screaming, spitting and whining, groaning and crying, and the hundred other nameless noises by which they frighten sleep from our pillows.

"Well, one night, it may have been one o'clock, or two, or three, I was awakened by the awfullest screaming and sputtering, growling and swearing, that ever startled a weary man from his slumbers. I leaped out of bed under the impression that at least twenty little children had fallen into as many tubs of boiling water. I threw open the window and stepped out upon the roof of the tea-room. I don't intend to exaggerate, but I honestly believe that there were less than three hundred cats over against me, on the roofs of the out-houses; each one of which had a tail bigger than a Bologna sausage, his back crooked up like an oxbow, and his great round eyes gleaming fiercely in the moonlight, putting in his very best in the way of catterwauling. Two of the largest, one black as night and the other a dark grey or brindle, appeared to be particularly in earnest, and the way they scolded, and screamed, and swore at each other was a sin to hear. I won't undertake to report all they said; a decent regard for the proprieties of language, compels me to give only a sketch of the debate.

"'You infernal, big-tailed, hump-backed, ugly-mugged thief,' screamed the grey, 'I'd like to know what *you* are out here for this time of night, skulking, and creeping, and nosing about in the dark, poaching upon other people's preserves?'

"'Very well I mighty well!' was the reply, 'for *you*, to talk, you black-skinned, ogre-eyed, growling and sputtering robber, to come upon this roof, sticking up *your* back and taking airs on yourself. I'd like to know what business *you've* got to be prowling about and crowding yourself into honest people's company?'

"'I'm a regular Tom Cat, I'd have you know, and go where I please, and I'll stand none of your big talk and insolent looks.' "'Insolent! Hear the cowardly thief! Insolent! Very well, Mr. Tom Cat! very good, indeed! Now, just take your black skin off of this roof, or you'll get what will make you look cross-eyed foe a month.'

"'Get off this roof, I think you said. Look at this set of ivory, and these claws, old greyback! If you want I should leave this roof, just come and put me off. Try it on, old Beeswax. Yes, yes! try it on once, and we'll see whose eyes will look straight-est in the morning! Come on, old Humpback! Try it on, old Sausage Tail!'

"And then they pitched in, and such scratching and growling, scolding and swearing, and biting, and rolling over and over, I never happened to see or hear before. About that time I dropped a boulder of coal, taken from the scuttle, weigh-ing about half a pound, right among them (accidently of course). Whether it hit any one I can't positively affirm, but I heard a dull heavy sound, a kind of *chug*, as if it had struck against something soft, and the scream of one of the belligerents was brought to a sudden stop, by a sort of hysterical jerk, as though there had been a sudden lack of wind to carry it on. It put an end to the disturbance, and all the rioters, save one, scampered away. That one remained, all doubled up in a heap like, as if it had the sick headache, or been attacked with a sudden inflammation of the bowels. If any body's cat was found the next morning with a swelled head, or a great bunch on its side, and seemed dumpish, it's my private opinion that that's the one that lump of coal fell upon. Still it did'nt do much good in the way of relieving me from the annoyance of these cat conventions. They continued to congregate nightly on that long shed in the rear of my rooms. I wasted more wood upon them than I could well afford to spare. I used up all the brickbats I could lay my hands on. I threw away something less than a ton of coal; and on two occasions came near be-ing taken to the watch-house for smashing a window in the opposite block. All this proved of no avail. Indeed, my tormentors began at last to get used to it, to regard it as part of the performance.

"The matter was getting serious. It became evident that either those cats or myself must leave the premises. I had paid my rent in advance, and was therefore entitled to quiet use and enjoyment, according to the terms of my lease. I made up my mind to try one more experiment. So I bought me a double-barrelled gun, and a quantity of powder and shot, and gave fair warning that I intended to use them.

"Well, the moon came up one night, with her great round face, and went walk-ing up the sky with a queenly tread, throwing her light, like a mantle of brightness, over all the earth. I love the calm of a moonlight night, in the pleasant spring time, and the cats of our part of the town seemed to love it too, for they came from every quarter; from the sheds around the National Garden, from the stables, the streets, the basements, and the kitchens, creeping stealthily along the tops of the fences, and along the sheds, and clambering up the boards that leaned up against the out-buildings, and set themselves down, scores or less of them, in their old trysting place, right opposite my chamber windows. To all this I had in the abstract no objection. If a cat chooses to take a quiet walk by moonlight, if he chooses to go out for his pleasure or his profit, it is no particular business of mine, and I haven't a word to say. Cats have rights, and I have no disposition to interfere with them. If they choose to hold a convention to discuss the affairs of rat-and-mousedom, they can do it for all me. But they must go about it decently and in order. They must talk matters over calmly; there must be no rioting, no fighting. They must refrain from the use of profane language--they must not swear. There's law against all this, and I had warned them long before that I would stand no such nonsense. I told them frankly that I'd let drive among them some night with a double-barrelled gun, loaded with powder and duck-shot--and I meant it. But those cats did'nt believe a word I said. They did'nt believe I had any powder and shot. They did'nt believe I had any gun, or knew how to use it, if I had; and one great Maltese, with eyes like tea-plates, and a tail like a Bologna sausage, grinned and sputtered, and spit, in derision and defiance of my threats. 'Very well!' said I. 'Very well, Mr. TOM CAT! very well, indeed! On your head be it, Mr. TOM CAT! Try it on, Mr. TOM CAT, and we'll see who'll get the worst of it.'

"Well, as I said, the moon came up one night, with her great round face, and all the little stars hid themselves, as if ashamed of their twinkle in the splendor of her superior brightness. I retired when the rumble of the carriages in the streets, and the tramp on the stone sidewalks had ceased, and the scream of the eleven o'clock train had died away into silence, with a quiet conscience, and in the confidence that I should find that repose to which one who has wronged no man during the day, is justly entitled.

"It may have been midnight, or one o'clock, or two, when I was awakened from a pleasant slumber, by a babel of unearthly sounds in the rear of my chamber. I knew what those sounds meant, for they had cost me fuel enough to have lasted a month. I raised the window, and there, as of old, right opposite me, on the north end of that long shed, was an assemblage of all the cats in that part of the town. I won't be precise as to numbers, but it is my honest belief that there was less than three hundred of them; and if one among them all was silent, I did not succeed in discovering which it was. There was that same old Maltese, with his saucer eyes and sausage tail; and over against him sat a monstrous brindle; and off at the right was an old spotted ratter; and on his left was one black as a wolf's mouth, all but his eyes, which glared with a sulphurous and lurid brightness; and dotted all around, over a space some thirty feet square, were dozens more, of all sizes and colors, and *such* growling and spitting, and shrieking, and swearing, never before broke, with hideous discord, the silence of midnight.

"I loaded my double-barrelled gun by candle-light I put plenty of powder and a handful of shot into each barrel. I adjusted the caps carefully, and stepped out of the window, upon the narrow roof upon which it opens. I was then just eighty feet from that cat convention. I addressed myself to the chairman (the old Maltese) in a distinct and audible voice and said, 'SCAT!' He did'nt recognise my right to the floor, but went right on with the business of the meeting. 'SCAT!' cried I, more emphatically than before, but was answered only by an extra shriek from the chairman, and a fiercer scream from the whole assembly. 'SCAT! once,' cried I again, as I brought my gun to a present. 'SCAT! twice,' and I aimed straight at the chairman, covering half a dozen others in the range. 'SCAT! three times,' and I let drive. Bang! went the right-hand barrel; and bang! went the left-hand barrel. Such scampering, such leaping off the shed, such running away over the eaves of the outbuildings, over the tops of the wood-sheds, were never seen before. The echoes of the firing had scarcely died away, when that whole assemblage was broken up and dispersed.

"'Thomas,' said I, the next morning to the boy who did chores for us, 'there seems to be a cat asleep out on that woodshed, go up and scare it away.'

"Thomas clambered upon the shed and went up to where that cat lay, and lifting it up by the tail, halloo'd back to me, 'This cat can't be waked up; it can't be scared away--its dead!' After examining it for a moment--'Somebody's been a shootin' on it, by thunder,' as he tossed it down into the yard.

"You don't say so!" said I. "That cat was the old Maltese--the chairman of that convention. I don't know where he boarded, or who claimed title to him. What I do know is, that it cost me a quarter to have him buried, or thrown into the river; and that I was suffered to sleep in peace from the time I made the discovery that *powder and lead are great quellers of midnight rioting*. They gave *me* quiet at least, and saved me from the wickedness of the nightly use of certain expletives, under the excitement of the occasion, which are not to be found in any of the religious works of the day."

CHAPTER XII.
THE FIRST CHAIN OP PONDS--SHOOTING BY TURNS--SHEEP WASHING--A PLUNGE AND A DIVE--A ROLAND FOR AN OLIVER.

We started early the next morning up Bog River, intending to reach the "first chain of ponds," some twenty miles deeper in the wilderness, as the stream runs, on the banks of which our pioneer had been instructed to pitch our tents. This day's journey, it was understood, would be a hard one, as there were eight carrying places, varying from ten rods to half a mile in length. The Bog River is a deep, sluggish stream for five or six miles above the falls, just at the lake. It goes creeping along, among, and around immense boulders, thrown loose, as it were, in mid channel. At this distance, the stream divides, the right hand channel leading to the two chains of ponds and Mud Lake, where it takes its rise; and the left to Round Pond, and little Tupper's Lake, and a dozen other nameless sheets of water, laying higher up among the mountains. Our course lay up the right hand channel, which, for half a mile above the forks, comes roaring and tumbling through a mountain gorge, plunging over falls, and whirling and surging among the boulders, in a descent of three of four hundred feet in all. Around these, and seven other rapids of greater or less extent, our boats had to be carried.

We reached the lower chain of ponds within an hour of sunset, and found our tents pitched at a pleasant spot which looked out over the easternmost one of these beautiful little lakelets. There are three of them, connected together by narrow passages or straits, the banks of which, as the boat glides along, the oars will touch. They are surrounded by low but pleasant hills, so arranged as to form a varied but delightful scenery. From the western one, the hills rise from the water with a steep acclivity, covered with a gigantic growth of timber, save on the northern side, where a pleasant natural meadow, covered with rank grass and a few spruce and fir trees, stretches away. It contains about two hundred acres, and its waters are deep and pure. The middle one, though smaller, is equally beautiful, skirted on three sides with wood-covered hills, and on the other by a continuation of the same natural meadow. The eastern one, on the western banks of which our tents were located on a beautiful little bay, is the prettiest of them all. It contains perhaps six hundred acres, and the scenery around it is exceedingly cheerful and pleasant. The northern shore is bound by a natural meadow of luxuriant wild grass, between which and the water is a hard sandy beach, at low water some thirty feet wide, and extending between a quarter and half a mile in length.

As we approached these ponds, the river became broad and shallow. Natural meadows, covered with tall grass and weeds, stretching away on either hand. When we came to this portion of the river, the oars were shipped, and our boat-men took their seats in the stern with their paddles. Smith was in the bow of one boat, and Spalding in that of the other, each with rifle in hand, preparatory to the slaughter of a deer, to provide us with venison. It was arranged that the marksman who fired and failed to secure his game, should change places with the one behind him, and that thus the rotation should go on, till we should bring down a deer. We knew that we should see numbers of them feeding along the margin of the stream, and upon the natural meadows that skirted the shore. The stream was winding and tortuous, and at no time could we see more than five-and-twenty rods in advance of us, so crooked is its course.

We were moving up the stream cautiously and silently; the boatman who had charge of the craft in which were Smith and myself, seated in the stern, paddling, and Smith himself seated in the bow, with rifle in hand, ready for anything that might turn up. As the boat rounded a point, a deer started out from among the reeds on the right, and went dashing and snorting across the river directly in front of the boat, and five or six rods ahead, the water being only about two feet in depth. Smith blazed away at him; where the ball went, Mercy knows; but the deer dashed forward with accelerated speed, and a louder whistle, and went crashing up the hill-side. Smith acknowledged to a severe attack of the Buck fever. It was now my turn to take the next shot; and changing places with Smith, we went ahead. In ten minutes a chance to try my skill occurred. But it was a long shot, the game was "on the wing," and I had no better success than did my friend. The deer only increased the length of his bounds, and he too went plunging through the old woods, snorting in astonishment, and huge affright at what he had seen and heard.

Our boat now fell back, and Spalding and the Doctor took the lead. In a short time, a deer was discovered feeding just ahead of us on the lily pads along the shore. The boatman paddled silently up to within eight or ten rods of him. Spalding sighted him long and, as he averred, carefully with his rifle. The deer fed and fed on, and we waited anxiously to hear the crack of the rifle, and see the deer go down; but still the boat glided on unnoticed by the animal that was feeding in unsuspecting security. At length he raised his head, threw forward his long ears, gazed for a second intently at his enemies, and then appreciating his danger, snorted like a warhorse and plunged in a seeming desperation of terror towards the shore. He had ran a few rods when Spalding let drive at him, as he confessed, at random. The ball went wide of the mark, and the game dashed, with more desperate energy, and whistling and snorting like a locomotive, into the brush that lined the banks. It was Spalding's third shot in all his life at a deer, and he insisted, gravely enough, that he did not fire while the game was standing broadside to him, on account of his desire to give the animal a chance for his life. The truth is, that Spalding had a bad, a very bad attack of the aforesaid Buck fever.

The Doctor, by rotation, now became the leading marksman. He was cool and calm, as if going to perform some delicate surgical operation. We soon came in sight of a buck feeding in a shallow pasture, and the boat glided quietly within fifteen rods of it. The Doctor's hand was firm, and his aim steady. There was about him none of that nervous agitation which is so apt to disturb the first efforts at deer slaying. The boat came to a pause a moment, when his rule rang out quick and sharp, waking the echoes of the mountains around and reverberating along the shore. At the crack of the rifle, the buck leaped high into the air, and plunged madly towards the bank, up which he dashed with a prodigious bound, made a single jump among the tall grass, and disappeared from the sight. The Doctor was greatly mortified, supposing he had missed. He declared solemnly that he had taken steady and sure aim just back of the fore-shoulders of the deer, had a perfect sight upon it, and that it did not fall in its tracks, could only be owing to its bearing a charmed life. The boatman, however, knew that the animal, from its actions, was mortally wounded. He said nothing, but paddled quietly to the shore, and there, just over the bank, in the tall grass and weeds, lay the noble buck, stone dead. He had gone down and died without a struggle. A proud man was the Doctor, as he passed his hunting-knife across the throat of the deer, and gazed upon its broad antlers, now in the velvet, pointing to the course of the ball right through its vitals, in on one side and out on the other. We had venison for the next four-and-twenty hours, and we disturbed the deer no more that afternoon.

The deep baying of the stag-hounds, as we entered the little lake, apprised us of the location of our tents, and we were glad to reach them, and stretch our limbs upon the bed of boughs beneath them, for the day had been warm, and our journey a weary one. Our pioneer had made the entire journey the day before, though he had to pass over all the carrying-places three times. We found that he had killed two deer, and had the meat from them, cut into thin slips, undergoing the process of "jerking," in a bark smokehouse erected near the tents. He had also a beautiful string of trout ready for our supper, taken in a way peculiarly his own. He had used neither bait nor fly.

After supper, as we sat looking out over the lake in front of our tents, the Doctor inquired of our pioneer how he had taken his fish, as he had with him neither rod nor flies, and there was no bait to be found in the woods proper for trout.

"Why," said he, "I got lonesome yesterday, all alone up here in the woods, waiting for you, and I thought I'd take a look around the shore of the lake, thinking I might find a gold mine, or a pocketful of diamonds, or something of that sort; so I took my rifle and the two dogs, and started on an explorin' voyage. I didn't find any gold, but I found, just across there by those willows and alders, a cold stream entered the lake, and right in the mouth of it the trout were lyin' as thick as your fingers. They were fine little fellows as I ever happened to see, weighing about a quarter of a pound each. I had a hook or two, and a piece of twine in my pocket, but they were of no sort of use in common fishin', for I had no kind of bait, and couldn't get any. After thinking the matter over, I concluded I'd see if I couldn't bag some of them in a quiet way. So I cut me a long pole, tied the hook and line to the end of it, and reaching out over the water, dropped quietly down among them. I let the line drift gently up against the one I wanted. He didn't seem to mind it, but was rather pleased as the line tickled his sides. After letting it lay there a moment, I jerked suddenly, and up came the trout clean over my head on to the flat rock behind me. However this might have astonished him, it didn't seem to disturb the rest. In that way I caught all I wanted, and could have caught a bushel. It isn't a very science way of fishin', but it answers when a man is hungry, and hasn't got any bait or fly."

"I scarcely know why," said the Doctor, "but Cullen's account of catching his trout, reminds me of a circumstance which occurred when I was a boy, and which for the moment made a deal of sport. I have not probably thought of it in twenty years, but it comes to me now as fresh as though it were the occurrence of yesterday. It must be, as Hank Wood said the other day, that a thing which gets fairly anchored in a man's mind, remains there always, and covered up as it may be by other and later things, it can never be forgotten. It will come drifting back on the current of memory, fresh and palpable as ever.

"Everybody understands, or ought to understand, how sheep are washed. A small yard is built on the bank of a stream adjacent to a deep place. One side of which is open to the water, and into which the flock is crowded. The washers take their places in the water, where it is three or four feet deep, and the sheep are caught by others, and tossed to them, where they undergo ablution (an operation by the way, that they do not seem altogether to enjoy), to wash the dirt and gum from their fleeces. On such occasions, it is regarded as a lawful thing, a standing and ancient practical joke, to pitch any outsider, who may happen to indulge his curiosity by stopping to look on, into the stream. If he is verdant, he will be very likely to be inveigled into the yard, and in an unguarded moment, be made to take an involuntary dive, head foremost into the water.

"A few rods above the place in which my father washed his sheep, was an old dam, the apron of which remained, and beneath which was a basin some five or six feet in depth, and thirty or forty feet in diameter, filled of course with water. On one occasion, a man who was employed to catch the sheep, was one of those shiftless, good-natured, lazy fellows, to be found in almost every neighborhood, who prefer smoking and telling stories in bar-rooms to regular work, and who greatly prefer odd jobs to consecutive labor. Tom G----was one of this genus, full of fun and mischief, but without a particle of real malice in his composition. As he was busy throwing sheep to the washers, a young fellow from the neighboring village happened that way, and becoming somewhat interested in the process, was seduced by Tom G----, inside of the yard, to try his hand at catching and tossing in sheep. About the second or third one he operated upon, his treacherous friend stumbled against him, giving him a tremendous push, and with a sheep in his arms he drove head foremost among the washers. The water was cold, and there was a good deal of puffing and blowing about the time his head came above the surface. He was a sensible chap, and took the joke as a wise man should, especially when the odds are all against him, albeit, it was somewhat rude.

"He came out on the other side of the stream, and after joining in the laugh against himself, and taking off and wringing his garments, he wandered up to the apron of the old dam, and stretching himself along the planks, went to looking anxiously down into the deep water. After a while, he seemed to have discovered something, and called out to his friend below, 'I say Tom, have you got a fishhook in your pocket? Here is a trout that will weigh two pounds, and I want to hook him up.' Now Tom was a fisherman, and a big trout was his weakness; moreover, he was never without half a dozen hooks and lines in his pockets. He left his business at once, and went up to the apron to assist in taking the two-pound trout. A pole was cut, and a couple of feet of line, with a hook attached, was fastened a little way from the top, and the haft of the hook stuck into the end so that by a little force it might be removed, and Tom and his friend got upon the apron, and stooped over to see where the great trout lay.

"'Here he is, Tom, just under the edge of this rock.' Tom stretched himself over to get a view of the fish, when a vigorous shove from the rear sent him like a great frog plump towards the bottom of the pool. This was a consummation that Tom had not bargained for, but there was no alternative but to swim for the shore, dripping like a rat from a flooded sewer. That joke had two points to it, and Tom G----had the worst of them."

"Your anecdote," said Smith, "reminds me of one in which I was an actor, and which was impressed upon my mind by a process which few boys are fond of, but which is very apt to make the impression durable. *I* fished for trout once without line or hook. I got a fine string of them, and myself into a pretty kettle of fish in the bargain. On my father's farm, as it was when I was a boy, was a stream that came down through a gorge in the mountains that bounded the pleasant valley in which that farm lay. In the spring freshets and the summer rains, that stream was a mighty and resistless torrent, that came roaring and plunging down from the plain above, cascading and leaping down ledges and rushing though a gorge, on either side of which precipices of solid rock stood straight up two hundred feet in height. It was a goodly sight to see that stream when its back was up, come rushing and foaming, a mighty flood from the deep and shadowy gulf, rolling in its resistless course great boulders of tons upon tons in weight, and eddying, and twisting, and roaring onward in its furious course towards the lake. In the summer time the drouth lapped up its waters, and it dried away to a little brook, trickling over the falls, and went winding, a small streamlet, around the base of the hill; sometimes it disappeared in the gravel, or among the loose stones, save here and there a pool of narrow limits and shallow depth. It was a fine trout stream at times. Its waters were cold and pure, and the brook trout loved to hide away under the great smooth stones or shelving rocks, and be comfortable in the shade, when the summer sun was hot and fiery in the sky. When the creek was low, they would congregate in the pools and still places, and in times of extreme drouth, might be seen huddled together in such places in great numbers.

"My father, though not a member of any church, was strict in his family discipline in regard to the observance of the Sabbath, the breach of which, on the part of his children, was very apt to be followed by consequences not the most pleasant in the world, for he held that a good switch was an essential article of household furniture, and its occasional use a cardinal principle in the philosophy of family rule. One Sunday, when I was some ten or eleven years old, when the old people were gone to meeting (and they had to go eight miles to find a meeting house), I, with an older brother, tired of lying around the house, concluded to take a stroll along up the brook. It was a time of severe drouth, and the stream was dried up, save here and there a small pool, clear and cold, the bottom of which consisted of smooth and clean-washed stones and pebbles. In one of these was a number of beautiful speckled trout, averaging maybe a quarter of a pound each in weight. Here was a temptation too strong to be resisted. We had no hooks or lines with us, and would not have ventured to use them **on Sunday**, if we had. That would have been fishing. But the taking of those trout with our hands was quite another matter. So, rolling our pants up above our knees (there was no use of talking about shoes and stockings; such luxuries were not within the range of indulgence to boys of our age in those days, save in the frosts and snows of winter, and stubbed toes, stone bruises, and thorns in the feet, come floating along down from the long past, like shadows of darkness on the current of memory. By the way, will some rich man, who was reared in the country in the good old times when boys went barefooted in the summer months, when chapped feet, stone bruises, stubbed toes, and thorns that pierced and festered in their *soles* were the great ills that 'darkened deepest around human destiny,' solve for me a problem of the human mind? Will he tell me whether, in his after life, when he was the owner of broad acres, fine houses, piles of stocks in paying corporations, and huge deposits in solvent banks, he ever felt richer or prouder when counting his gains, and contemplating the aggregate of his wealth, than he did when he pulled on his first pair of boots?) So, as I said, we rolled up our pants, and waded in for the trout. We caught a beautiful string of twenty or more, took them home, dressed them nicely, and sat them carefully away in the cool cellar. We had a notion that the greatness of the prize would wipe away the offence by which it was secured, and that the delicious breakfast they would afford, would be received as a sufficient atonement for the sin of having taken them on a Sunday. But we were never more mistaken in our lives. My father went into the cellar for some purpose in the evening, after his return from meeting, and discovered the trout. An inquiry was instituted, our dereliction was exposed, and we were promised a flogging. Now that was a promise, which, while it was rarely made, was never broken. When my father in his calm, quiet way, made up his mind and so expressed it, that he owed one of his boys a flogging, it became, as it were, a debt of honor, what, in modern parlance, would be termed a confidential debt, and he to whom it was acknowledged to be due, became a prefered creditor, and was sure to be paid.

"Well, the trout were eaten for breakfast, and after the meal was over, my brother and myself were duly paid off, at a hundred cents on the dollar, with full interest. That flogging cured me of 'tickling' trout, especially on Sunday. I am never tempted to take trout with my hands, without feeling a tickling sensation about the back; and though old recollections of the long past, of that pleasant stream and the gorge through which it flowed, with the side hill covered with old forests above it, and the green fields spread out on the other side, of the home of my boyhood, the old log-house, the cattle, the sheep, the old watch-dog, and the thousand other things around which memory loves to linger, come clustering around my heart, yet conspicuous among them all, is the flogging I got for 'tickling' trout on a Sunday."

CHAPTER XIII.

A JOLLY TIME FOR THE DEER--HUNTING ON THE WATER BY DAYLIGHT--
MUD LAKE FUNEREAL SCENERY--A NEW WAY OF TAKING RABBITS--

THE NEGRO AND THE MARINO BUCK--A COLLISION.

As we came down to the lake in the morning to perform our ablations, we saw a fine deer on the opposite shore, feeding upon the pond lilies that grew along in the shallow water. It was nearly half a mile from us, and while we were looking at it, four others came walking carelessly out of the tall grass upon the beach, and commenced playing, as we have seen lambs do, on the sandy shore. They would run here and there, back and forth, at full speed along the sands, leap high into the air, kicking up their heels, and performing all the various antics of which animals so supple and active may be supposed capable. We saw one fellow leap, with a clear bound, over two that were standing looking out over the water, and run some fifty rods up the beach, as if all the hounds in Christendom were at his tail, and then wheel gracefully, and return with equal speed to his companions, when they all commenced jumping and bounding, and running up and down along the shore, as if they were out on a regular spree, and were determined to be jolly. After half an hour of exceedingly active play, they hoisted their white flags, and went bounding over the meadow into the woods.

The deer that was feeding paid no further attention to them than to raise his head and look quietly, and perhaps contemptuously at them occasionally, while he chewed his breakfast, that he was picking up in the shape of lily pads upon the surface of the water. Spalding and a boatman paddled across the lake to make Mm a morning call. It is a curious fact that one skilled in the art will paddle or scull one of these light boats to within a few rods of a deer while feeding, in plain open sight, provided always that the wind blows *from* the direction of the animal, and no noise is made by the boatman. The deer will feed on, and the time for paddling is while his head is down. When he raises it to look about him, in whatever position the boatman is, he must remain immovable. If his paddle is up, it must remain so; not a motion must be made, or the game will be off, with a snort and a rush, for the shore and the woods. The deer may, and probably will look, with a vacant stare, directly at the approaching boat without its curiosity being in the least excited, and then go to feeding again. The marksman must take his aim while the game is feeding; when it raises its head high in the air, throws forward its ears and gazes at him for a moment with a wild and startled look, then is his time to fire. Five seconds at the longest is all that is allowed him when he sees these motions, for within that time, with its fears thoroughly aroused, the game will be plunging for the shelter of the woods.

The boatman paddled Spalding quietly and silently to within twelve or fifteen rods of the deer that was feeding, when a column of white smoke shot suddenly up from the bow of the boat; the sharp crack of the rifle rung out over the water, and the deer went down. Spalding was a proud man as he returned to us with a fine fat spike buck in his boat.

These little lakes are probably sixty-five miles from the settlements, allowing for the winding course of the rivers. Just above, where the river enters, is a dam, built of logs some fifteen feet high, erected by the lumbermen the last winter to hold back the water, so as to float their logs down from this to Tupper's Lake, and so on down the Rackett to the mills away below. Around this dam is the last carrying place between this and Mud Lake, over which our boatmen trudged with their boats, like great turtles with their shells upon their backs. This is still called Bog River, and though above the dam to Mud Lake, where it takes its rise, it is deep and sluggish, yet it is doing it honor overmuch to dignify it by the name of a river. It was large enough, however, to float our little craft. We left our baggage-master here with most of our luggage, to perfect his operations in the way of jerking venison, intending to return the next day. We might have left everything without a guard, so far as human depredations were concerned. No bolts or bars would be necessary for its protection. In the first place, nobody would visit the spot, and if they did, our property would be perfectly protected by the law of the woods. It would be doubtless carefully inspected by any curious banter passing that way, but theft or robbery are unknown here. True, a bottle of good liquor, if handled by a visitor, might lose somewhat of its contents, but it would be drank to the health of the owner, and in a spirit of good fellowship, and not of theft, all which would be regarded by woodsmen as strictly within rule, there being, as Hank Wood said, "no law agin it."

We left the first chain of ponds, and rowed some ten miles up the deep and sluggish but narrow channel of the river, startling every little way a deer from its propriety by our presence as it was feeding along the shore. Few sportsmen ever visit this remote region, and it is above the range of the lumbermen. We came to some rapids near the outlet of the second chain of ponds, around which we walked, and up which the boatmen pushed their little craft. These rapids are a quarter of a mile in length, with no great amount of fall, but still enough to prevent the passage up them of a loaded boat. Directly at the head of these rapids is the "second chain of ponds," three pleasant little lakelets, of from two to four hundred acres each, surrounded by dense forests, and shores in the main walled in by huge boulders and broken rocks. We passed through these, in which were several loons, or great northern divers, quietly floating, and as they watched us, sending forth their clear and clarion voices over the water. We took each a passing shot at them, but with no other effect than to make them dive quicker and deeper, and stay under longer than usual; at the flash of our rifles they would go down, and in a few minutes would be again on the surface sixty rods from us, laughing aloud, as it were, with their clear and quavering voices, at our impotent attempts to shoot them.

We left the "second chain of ponds" by the narrow and sluggish inlets, still the Bog River, here so small that the boatman's oars spanned the narrow channel, and as crooked a stream as it is possible for one to be. It flows for miles through a low and marshy region, with dense alderbushes clustering along the shore, and scattering fir-trees, dead at the top, standing between these and the forests in the background. The bottom, much of the way, is of clean yellow sand, in which are imbedded millions of clams, resembling, in every respect, those of the ocean beach. Some of these we opened, and found the living bivalves in appearance precisely like their kindred of the salt water. I have seen occasionally muscle shells in other streams, and along the shores of the lakes, but I never before saw any such as these save near the ocean, where the salt water ebbs and flows, and not even there in such quantities. One might gather barrels and barrels of them, large and apparently fat, and yet there would be hundreds or thousands of barrels left. The mink, the muskrat, and other animals that hunt along the water, and have a taste for fish, have a good time of it among them, for we saw bushels of shells in places where the fish had been extracted and devoured.

We arrived at Mud Lake towards evening, and pitched our tent on a little rise of ground on the north side, a few rods back from the lake, among a cluster of spruce and balsam, and surrounded by a dense growth of laurel and high whortleberry bushes. We saw a deer occasionally on our route, and the banks of the stream in many places were trodden up by them like the entrance to a sheep-fold. Why this sheet of water should be called Mud Lake is a mystery, for though gloomy enough in every other respect, its bed is of sand, and it is surrounded by a sandy beach from fifteen to forty feet wide. It is perhaps four miles in circumference, its waters generally shallow, and so covered with pond lilies, and skirted with wild grass, as to form the most luxuriant pasture for the deer and moose to be found in all this region. Of all the lakes I have visited in these northern wilds, this is the most gloomy. Indeed it is the only one that does not wear a cheerful and pleasant aspect. It seems to be the highest water in this portion of the wilderness, lying, as one of our boatmen expressed it, "up on the top of the house." In only one direction could any higher land be seen, and that was a low hill on the western shore, not exceeding fifty feet in height. There are no tall mountain peaks reaching their heads towards the clouds, overlooking the waters; no ranges stretching away into the distance; no gorges or spreading valleys; no sloping hillsides, giving back the sunlight, or along which gigantic shadows of the drifting clouds float. All around it are fir, and tamarac, and spruce of a stinted and slender growth, dead at the top, and with lichens and moss hanging down in sad and draggled festoons from their desolate branches. It is, in truth, a gloomy place, typical of desolation, which it is well to see once, but which no one will desire to visit a second time. We noticed on the sandy beach tracks of the wolf, the panther, the moose, and in one place the huge track of a bear. He must have been of monstrous growth, judging by the impression of his great feet and claws in the sand. But we saw none of these animals, and so gloomy is the place, so sepulchral, such an air of desolation all around, that it brings over the mind a strong feeling of sadness and gloom, and we resolved not to tarry beyond the nest morning, even for the chance of taking a moose, a panther, or a bear.

We pitched our tent, as I said, a little way back from the lake, near a cold spring, that came boiling up through the white sand in a little basin, eight feet wide, the bottom of which, like that on the bank of Tupper's Lake, was all in commotion, boiling and bubbling, as the water forced its way up through it. I was in the forward boat as we approached the lake, and was surprised to see the number of deer feeding upon the lily pads in the shallow water, and the wild grass that grew along the shore. Some stood midside in the water, some with only the line of their backs and heads above it. Some were close along the shore, feeding upon the grass that grew there. Others still were nibbling at the leaves of the moosewood upon the bank, and one large buck stood by the side of a fir tree, rubbing his neck up and down against it, as if scratching himself against its rough bark. We had not been discovered, and waited for the other boats to arrive. Great was the astonishment of my companions, when they saw the number of deer that were feeding in this little lake. Neither of them had ever seen the like, nor had I, save on one occasion, and that was in a small lake, the name of which I have forgotten, lying a few miles beyond the head of the Upper Saranac.

"You see that clump of low balsam trees on that point yonder," said my boatman, as we lay upon our oars, pointing in the direction indicated. "Well, from that spot, three years ago, I shot a moose out upon the bar there, as it was feeding upon the lily pads and flag grass.

"I had heard from an old Indian hunter, about this lake, and the abundance of game to be found here, and I made up my mind to see it. So another hunter and myself agreed to come up here in July, and take a look at matters, and find out whether the old copperhead told the truth or not. We started about the middle of July, with our rifles and provisions for a fortnight, and came up. We saw any quantity of deer on the way. On the second chain of ponds, we saw, as we were rowing along, a large panther walk out on to the top of a great boulder, and look around, lashing his sides with his long tail, and then sit down on his haunches with his tail curled around his feet, just as you've seen a cat do. He was too far off for us to shoot him, and he saw us before we got within proper distance, and stole away into the woods, and we passed on. As we rounded the point just below the lake there, and looked out upon the broad water, I saw the moose I spoke of, feeding. We sat perfectly still, and permitted the boat to drift back down the stream until we were out of sight. We then landed, and I crept carefully and silently to that clump of fir trees. I had my own and my companion's rifle both properly loaded. Having got a right position, I sighted for a vital part, and fired. The animal rushed furiously forward two or three rods, with its head lowered as if making a lunge at an enemy, then stopped, and looked all around, standing with its back humped up, and its short stump of a tail working and writhing at a furious rate. I sighted it again with the other rifle, and pulled. The animal plunged furiously for again for a few rods, stopped a moment, and then settled slowly down, and fell over on its side, dead. It was a cow-moose and would weigh as killed five or six hundred pounds. I was a pretty proud man then, as that was my first moose, and about as big feeling a chap as was Squire Smith the other day, when he brought down that buck. I have shot two others here since, one at each visit I have made."

The season for moose hunting along the water pastures, was nearly over. They go back upon the hills in August, the food there being by that time abundant. The tracks we saw were old ones, the animals having passed there several days previously. I would not have it supposed that the moose are abundant in any portion of this wilderness. They have come to be few and far between, and exceedingly wary at that. I could hear of none having been killed the present season; but that there are some left, as well as bears, and wolves, and panthers, the tracks we saw gave unmistakable evidence.

We saw no appearance of trout in this lake, or in the outlet of it above the upper chain of ponds. The stream swarmed with chub and dace, a rare circumstance with the streams of this region. Towards evening, we saw numbers of little grey wood rabbits, hopping around among the dense undergrowth on the ridge where our tents were situated, squatting themselves down and cocking up their long ears, as they paused occasionally to examine the strange visitors who had come among them. They were very tame, not seeming to regard our presence as a thing of much danger to them.

"Seeing those rabbits," remarked Smith, "reminds me of an anecdote of my boyhood, which at the time occasioned me an amount of mortification equalled only by the amusement it affords me, when I think of it in after years. On my father's farm was a bush field, a place that had been chopped and burned over, and then left to grow up with bushes, making an excellent cover for wild wood rabbits. I had seen them hopping about, when I went to turn away the cows in the morning, or after them at night. I had a longing to 'make game' of them. I had a brother a good deal older than myself, who was as fond of a joke as I was of the rabbits, and who was quite as ready to make game of me, as I was of them; so he told me, one day to put an apple on a stick over their paths, high enough to be just above their reach, and a handful of Scotch snuff on a dry leaf on the ground under it, and the rabbits, while smelling for the apple, would inhale the snuff, and sneeze themselves to death in no tune. Well, I was a child then and simple enough to be gammoned by this rigmarole. I set the apple and the snuff, but I got no rabbit, while I did get laughed at hugely for my credulity. This satisfied me that people should never impose upon the simplicity of childhood. I remember my mortification on the occasion. It was so long ago that it stands out by itself, a mere fragment of memory, with *all* beyond it a blank, and a wide gap out this side. It is an isolated fact, fixed in my recollection by the pain it occasioned me."

"Your anecdote of the rabbits," said the Doctor, "reminds me of a story told of a Dutchman, who discovered an owl on a limb above him, and noticed that its face, and great round eyes, followed him always as he walked around the tree, without its body moving at all. Seeing this he concluded in his wisdom, that he would travel round the tree, till the owl twisted its head off in watching him. So round and round he went for an hour, and stopped only by having the conviction forced upon his mind that the owl had a swivel in its neck."

"Strange," remarked Spalding, "how the hearing of one story reminds us of another. I always admired the 'Arabian Nights,' because the stories contained in that work hang together so like a string of onions, or a braid of seed corn. The first is a sort of introduction to the second, and the second an usher to the third, and so on through the whole. But why the story of the Dutchman and the owl should remind me of another, in which an old negro and a bellicose ram were the actors, is a matter I do not pretend to understand, unless it be the extreme absurdity of both. A gentleman of my acquaintance long ago (he was a middle-aged man when I was a small boy. He was an upright and a good man. He has gone to his rest, and sleeps in an honored grave, having upon the simple stone above him no lying epitaph), had an old negro who rejoiced in the name of Pompey, and a Merino buck, the latter a valiant animal, that was ready to fight with anybody, or anything, that crossed his path. Between him and the 'colored person,' was an 'eternal distinction,' an active and irreconcilable antagonism, that developed itself on every possible occasion. The old Guinea man was winnowing wheat one day, with an old-fashioned fan (did any of you ever see one of these primitive machines for separating wheat from the chaff, used by our fathers before the fanning mill was invented? It was an ingenious contrivance, by which a man with a strong back and of a strong constitution, could clean some twenty bushels in a single day). While stooping over to fill his fan with unwinnowed grain, the buck, taking advantage of his position, came like a catapult against him, and sent him like a ball from a Paixhan gun, head foremost into the chaff. Great was the astonishment, but greater the wrath of Pompey, and dire the vengeance that he denounced against his assailant. Gathering himself up, and rubbing the part battered by the attack of his enemy, he retreated around the corner of the barn, and procuring a rock weighing some twenty pounds, returned to the presence of his foe, who was quietly eating the wheat that the negro had been cleaning, evidently regarding it as the legitimate spoils of victory. Getting down on all fours, and managing to hold the stone against his head, Pompey challenged his enemy to combat. The buck, nothing loth, drew back to a proper distance, and shutting both eyes, came like a battering *ram* against the stone on the other side of which was the negro's head. As might have been expected, the challenger went one way, and the challenged the other by the recoil, both knocked into insensibility by the concussion. Pompey was taken up for dead, but his wool and the thickness of his scull saved him. He gave the buck a wide berth after that. He regarded him always with a sort of superstitious awe, never being able to comprehend how he butted him through that big stone. Explain the matter to him ever so scientifically, demonstrate it on the clearest principles of mechanical philosophy, still Pompey would shake his head, and as he walked away, would mutter to himself, 'de debbil helps dat ram, *sure*. Dere's no use in dis nigger's tryin' to come round *him*. He's a witch, dat ram is, and ain't nuffin else.'"

CHAPTER XIV.

A DEER TRAPPED--THE RESULT OF A COMBAT--A QUESTION OF MENTAL PHI-

LOSOPHY DISCUSSED.

We returned the next day to our camping ground. On the "Lower Chain of Ponds," we found our pioneer and his goods all safe, no visitors having passed that way in our absence. Smith knocked over a deer on our passage down. I have said that just above our camp was a dam. It was made in this wise: first, great logs were laid up, across the stream, in the same fashion as the side of a log house, to the height of about twelve feet, properly secured, and upon these, other and smaller logs were laid, side by side, transversely, and sloping up the stream at an angle of forty-five degrees, like one side of the roof of a house. These long, slender logs, reached out over and beyond those that were laid up across the stream, the lower part covered with brush, and then with earth, so as to make a tight dam, the upper ends, even when the dam was full, extending several feet above the top water line. These logs, or perhaps they had better be called large and long poles, for, when compared with the foundation timbers, they were nothing more, have, of course, above where they are covered with brush and earth, interstices, or crevices, between them.

On our return, and as we came in sight of the dam, I, being in the forward boat, saw a small deer, laying stretched out upon these poles, dead, hanging, as it were, by one foot. My impression was, that it had been shot, and dragged up there, and left by our pioneer for the present. We found, however, upon examination, that the deer had walked up on the dam, probably to take a look at what was below, and on the other side, when his foot slipped down between the poles, and he was caught as in a trap. His leg was badly broken, and nearly severed by his efforts to get loose, and the bark of the poles was worn away within reach of his struggles. He had died where he thus got hung; and there he was, stone dead, but not yet cold, when we found him. He was a fine, fat, young deer, and died by one of the thousand accidents to which the wild animals of the forest, as well as man, are exposed.

Upon relating this incident to an old hunter, I was told by him that he once, while out in the woods, came upon the skeletons of two large bucks, that, in fighting, had got their horns so interlocked and wedged together, that they could not separate them, and thus, locked in the death grapple, they had starved and died. There lay their bones, the flesh eaten from them by the beasts and carrion birds, and, bleached by the sun and the storms, the two skulls with the horns still interlocked; and the narrator told me he had them yet at home, fast together, as he found them, as one of the curiosities to be met with in the Rackett woods.

"I've been thinking," said Spalding, in his quiet way, as we sat towards evening, looking out over the pleasant little lake, watching the shadow chasing the retiring sunlight up the sides of the opposite hills, "I've been thinking how differently we act, and feel, and talk--aye, and think, too--out here in these old woods, from what we do when at home and surrounded by civilization. However we four may deny being old, we cannot certainly claim to be young. We have all reached the meridian of life, and though feeling few, if any, of the infirmities of age, still, our next move will be in the downhill direction. Yet, notwithstanding all this, we talk and act, and think, and feel, too, like boys. I do not speak this reproachfully, but as a fact which develops a curious attribute of the human mind."

"Well," replied the Doctor, "while it may be curious, it is exceedingly natural. We have thrown off the restraints which society imposes upon us; we have thrown off the cares which the business of life heaps upon us. We have gone back for a season to the freedom, the sports, the sights, the exercises which delighted our boyhood. And can it be called strange that the feelings, the thoughts, and emotions of our youth should come welling up from the long past, or that with the return of boyish emotions, the language and actions of boyhood should be indulged in again?"

"You will find," said Smith, "your old feelings of sobriety, of thoughtfulness, your cautiousness, coming back just in proportion as you tire of this wilderness life, and that by the time you are ready to return to civilization, you will have become as staid, sober, and reflective men of the world, as when you started, with as strict a guard upon your expression of sentiment, or opinion, as ever."

"It is that 'guard' of which you speak," remarked Spalding, "over the emotions, the sentiments of the heart, stifling their expression, and chaining down under a placid exterior their manifestations, that constitutes one of the broad distinctions between youth and manhood. It is when that guard is set, that the process of fossilization, so to speak, begins; and if no relaxing agency intervenes, the heart becomes cold and hard, even before white hairs gather upon the head. I often imagine that if men who really *think*, who have the power of analyzation, of weighing causes and measuring results, would dismiss that rigid espionage over themselves, would stand in less awe of the world, in less dread of its accusation of change, and with the fearless frankness of youth, declare the truth, and stand boldly up for the right as they, *at the time*, understand it to be, without reference to consistency of present views and opinions with those of the past, the world would be much better off; progress would have vastly fewer obstacles to contend against. But it is not every man, even of those who *think*, who in politics, in religion, in science, in anything involving a possible charge of inconsistency, of the desertion of a party, a sect, or a principle, dare avow a change of conviction or opinion, however such change may exist. This should not be so. It belittles manhood, and makes slaves and cowards of men. It is a proud prerogative, this ability and power of thinking. It is a priceless privilege, this freedom of thought and opinion, and he is a craven who moves on with the heedless and thoughtless crowd, conscious of error, himself a hypocrite and a living lie, through fear of the charge of 'inconsistency,' the accusation of change. 'Speak your opinions of to-day,' says Carlyle, 'in words hard as rocks, and your opinions of to-morrow in words just as hard, even though your opinions of to-morrow may contradict your opinions of to-day.' There is a fund of true wisdom in this beautiful maxim, if men would appreciate it. It would correct a vast deal of error in politics, in religion, in philosophy, in the social relations of life. Times change, and struggle against it as they may, men's convictions will change with the times. The man who says that his opinions never alter, is to me either a knave or a fool. For a thinking man to remain stationary, when everything else is on the move, is a simple impossibility. Time was when the stage coach was the model method of travelling. It carried us six, sometimes eight miles the hour, in comfort and safety. But who thinks of the lumbering stage coach now, with its snail's pace of eight miles the hour, when the locomotive with its long train of cars, lighted up like the street of a city in motion, rushes over the smooth rails literally with the speed of the wind. The scream of the steam-whistle has succeeded the old stage-horn, and the iron horse taken the place of those of flesh and blood. Change is written in great glowing letters upon everything. It stands out in blazing capitals everywhere.

All things are on the move! Forward! and forward! is the word. And who would, who CAN, stand still amidst the universal rush? Only a century ago, from the valley through which the majestic Hudson rolls its everlasting flood, westward to the mighty Mississippi, westward still to the Rocky Mountains, and yet westward to the Pacific, was one vast wilderness; interminable forests, standing in all their primeval grandeur and gloom; boundless prairies, covered with profitless verdure, over which the silence of the everlasting past brooded; and above all these, mountain peaks, covered with perpetual snows, upon which the eye of a white man had never looked, stood piercing the sky. From the Atlantic coast to the Mississippi, that old forest has been swept away. The broad prairies have been, or are being, subjected to the culture of human industry; even the Rocky Mountains have been overleaped, and beyond them is a great State already admitted into the family of the Union, and a territory teeming with an adventurous and hardy population, knocking at its door for admission. The march of civilization has crossed a continent of more than three thousand miles, sweeping away forests, spreading out green fields, planting cities and towns, making the old wilderness to blossom as the rose, scattering life, activity, progress, all along the road it has travelled. The great rivers that rolled in silence through unbroken forests, have become the highways of trade, upon whose bosoms the white sails of commerce are spread, and through whose waters countless steamboats plough their way. These stupendous changes are the results of human energy, and they reach, in their moral prestige, their progressive influence, through every vein and artery of governmental and social compacts, affecting political institutions, shaping national policy, and forcing, by their resistless demonstrations, change and mutations of opinions upon all men.

"As it has been in the past century, so it is now, and so it will be through all the long future. Forward, and forward, is the word, and forward will be the word for centuries to come. And why? Because all men here, in this free Republic, are free to think, free to speak, free to will, free to act. No traditions of the past bind them; no hereditary policy controls their action; no customs, covered with the dust of ages, fetter them; no physical or intellectual gyves, corroded by the rust of centuries, are eating into their flesh. Because thinking American men everywhere live in the present, ignoring and defying the dead past, and building up the mighty future. Because they 'speak their opinions of TO-DAY in words hard as rocks, and their opinions of TO-MORROW in words just as hard, although their opinions of to-morrow may contradict their opinions of to-day.' They are fearless of personal consequences. As free men, they will think, as free men they will speak, and as such they will act, regardless of the jibe and sneer of those who accuse them of change, of inconsistency, of being mutable and unstable of purpose. The point to the march of improvement, the advance in the actualities of life, and ask, 'When every thing else is on the move, shall we stand still? Shall the opinions of a quarter of a century, a decade, a year, a month ago, remain unchanged, immutable, fixed as a star always, amidst the new demonstrations looming up like mountains everywhere around us?'

"Man's life is short at best; a little point of time, scarcely discernible on the map of ages; his aspirations, his hopes, his ambition, more transient than the lightning's flash; but his opinions may tell for good upon that little point occupied by his generation, and he should 'speak them in words hard as rocks.' They may aid in illuminating the darkness of the present, and he should therefore 'speak them in words hard as rocks.' They may have some influence in building up and ennobling human destiny in the future, and he should therefore 'speak them in words hard as rocks,' regardless of the contumely heaped upon him by little minds for having thus spoken them. What if the ridicule, the denunciations of the unthinking, the sensual, the profligate, the unreflecting fools of the world be poured upon him? What of that? To-day, may be one of darkness and storm. The cloud and the storm will pass away, and the brightness and glory of the sunlight will be all over the earth to-morrow. Let him 'speak his opinions then of to-day in words hard as rocks, and his opinions of to-morrow in words just as hard.' Let him speak his opinions thus on all subjects within the range of human investigation, upon science, philosophy, politics, religion, morals; and leave to little minds to settle the question of consistency or change. Let his be the eagle's flight towards the sun, and theirs to skim in darkness along the ground, like the course of the mousing owl."

After it became dark, Smith and Martin went out around the lake night hunting, and the rest retired to our tents. We heard the report of Smith's rifle from time to time, and concluded that we should have to court-martial him for a wanton destruction of deer, contrary to the law we had established for our government on that subject. But on his return, we ascertained that, though having had several shots, he had succeeded in killing or, according to Martin's account, even wounding but one, and that a yearling, and the poorest and leanest we had seen since we entered the woods. Though it was thus diminutive in size, Smith declared that he had seen, and shot at, some of the largest deer that ever roamed the forest. He insisted that he had seen some, by the side of which the largest we had looked upon by daylight, were mere fawns, and thereupon he undertook to establish a theory that the large deer fed by night and the smaller ones by day. This would have been all well enough, were it not for the fact, understood by every experienced night-hunter, that by the spectral and uncertain light of the lamp, or torch, a deer, when seen standing in the water, or on the reedy banks, is in appearance magnified to twice its actual dimensions. To this Smith at last assented, since to deny the proposition, involved the conclusion that he had killed the wrong deer; for the one he shot at, as it stood in the edge of the water, though much smaller than some he had seen, appeared greatly larger than the one he killed.

CHAPTER XV.
HOOKING UP TROUT--THE LEFT BRANCH--THE RAPIDS--A FIGHT WITH A BUCK.

We started down stream in the morning, towards the forks, intending to ascend the left branch to Little Tupper's Lake. We reached the forks at three o'clock. Directly opposite to where the right branch enters, a small cold stream comes in among a cluster of alder bushes on the eastern shore. At the mouth of this little stream, which one can step across, the trout congregate. We could see them laying in shoals along the bottom; but the sun shone down bright and warm into the clear water, and not a trout would rise to the fly, or touch a bait. We wanted some of those trout, and as they refused to be taken in a scientific way and according to art, it was a necessity, for which we were not responsible, which impelled us to a method of capture which, under ordinary circumstances, we should have rejected. I took off the fly from my line, and fastened upon it half a dozen snells with bare hooks, attached a small sinker, and dropped quietly among them. A large fellow worked his way lazily above where the hooks lay on the bottom, eying me, as if laughing at my folly in attempting to deceive him, with fly or bait. I jerked suddenly, and two of the hooks fastened into him near the tail. That trout was astonished, as were half a dozen or more of his fellows, when they came out of the water tail foremost, struggling with all their might against so vulgar and undignified a manner of leaving their native element. We got as beautiful a string in this way as one would wish to see, albeit they laughed at our best skill with fly and bait; and the cream of the matter was, that we had our pick of the shoal.

We pitched our tents at the foot of the second rapids, on a high, moss-covered bank. The roar of the water sounded deep and solemn among the old woods, as it went roaring and tumbling, and struggling through the gorge. The night winds moaned and sighed among the trees above us, while the night bird's notes came soothingly from the wilderness around as.

"What a strange diversity of tastes exists among the people of this world of ours," said the Doctor, addressing himself to me, as we sat in front of our tents, listening to the roar of the waters. "You and I, I take it, enjoy a fortnight or so, among these lakes, and old forests, with a keener relish than Spalding or Smith here. I judge so, because we indulge in these trips every year, while this is their first adventure of the kind. But even you and I, however much we may love the woods, however we may enjoy these occasional tramps among their shady solitudes, would not enjoy them as a residence; and yet I have sometimes thought I should love to spend the summers in a forest home, alone with nature, with my pen and books, a fishing-rod and rifle to supply my wants, and a friend to talk with occasionally.

"Many years ago, I was out on the Western prairies, some sixty days beyond the region of bread; we had encamped on the banks of a stream, along which a narrow belt of timber grew. More than a quarter of a century has passed since I took that trip to look upon the Rocky Mountains. There was no gold region laying beyond them then, or rather, the enterprise of the Anglo-Saxon had not discovered its existence, and the greed of the white man had not made the trail over the mountains, or through their dismal passes, a familiar way. Along in the afternoon we were visited by a trapper, who had, in his wanderings, discovered the smoke of our camp fires. He was a weather-beaten, iron man, of the solitudes of nature, who had wandered away from his home in New England, and from civilization, into that limitless wilderness. He was glad to see us, inquired the news from the outer world, talked about

York State, Vermont, the Bay State, and then, after an hour's converse, as if his social instincts and sympathies had been satisfied, he shouldered his rifle and started
off across the plain, towards a belt of timber lying dim and shadowy, like a low
cloud, upon the distant horizon. I watched him for an hour or more, as he trudged
away over the rolling prairie, growing less and less to the view, until he became
like a speck in the distance, and then vanished from my sight. There was a solemn
sort of feeling stole over me, as this lonely hunter wended his way into the deep
solitudes of the prairies, to be alone with nature, communing only with himself and
the things scattered around him by the great Creator. He seemed to be contented
and happy. How different were his tastes from yours or mine, my friends; and yet
I felt as though it would have been easy for me to have been like him, an isolated
and solitary man, had circumstances in early life thrown me into a position to have
followed the original bent of my nature."

"And yet," said Spalding, "if you will look into the philosophy of the matter,
you will see that this diversity of tastes, as you call it, is not so great after all; that is,
that the origin of the impulse which sends some men away from society among the
solitudes of the wilderness, and of that which holds others in constant communion
with the busy scenes of life, is very nearly the same. It is the love of adventure, of
excitement, a restlessness for something new, a desire for change. This impulse
is controlled, shaped by circumstances of early life, by education and association;
but the foundation of it at last is the thirst for excitement, the love of adventure.
One man wanders away into the wilderness in pursuit of it. Another plunges into
society in pursuit of the same thing. These hardy men who are here with us, who
were reared on the borders of civilization, enjoy the solitudes of their wilderness
quite as much, and upon the same general theory, as we do the society to which we
have been accustomed; and they plunge alone into the one with quite as much zest
as we do into the other, in the pursuit of excitement. Here is Cullen, now, who has
spent more time alone in the wilderness than almost any other man outside of the
trappers and hunters of the prairies of the West, I appeal to him if it is not rather
a love of adventure than of nature which sends him on his solitary rambles in the
forests?"

"May be the Judge is right," replied Cullen, as he rubbed the shavings of plug
tobacco in the palm of his left hand with the ball of his right, while he held his short

black pipe between his teeth, preparatory to filling it, "may be the Judge is right, I rather think he is, and let me tell you I've met with some queer adventures, as you call them, in these woods too; some that I wouldn't have gone out arter if I'd known what they were to've been afore I started. I've been movin' back from what you call civilization for five and twenty year, because I didn't like to live where people were too thick, and where there was nothing but tame life around me. I've a kind of liking for the deer and moose, and haven't any ill will towards, now and then, a wolf or a painter. I like a rifle better than I do the handles of a plow, and I'd rayther bring down a ten-pronger than to raise an acre of corn, and I don't care who knows it. There's a place in the world for just such a man as I am yet, and will be till these old woods are gone. Do you see that?" said he, rolling up his pantaloons to his knees, revealing a deep scar on both sides of the calf of his leg, as if it had been pierced by a bullet. "And do you see that?" as he exhibited another deep scar above his knee. "And that?" as he showed another on his arm, above the elbow. "Wal, I reckon I had a time of it with the old buck that made them things on my under-pinin', and on my corn-stealer, as they say out West. Fifteen years ago I was over on Tupper's Lake, shantyin' on the high bank above the rocks, just at the outlet, fishin' and huntin', and layin' around loose, in a promiscuous way, all alone by myself, havin' nobody along but the old black dog that you," appealing to Hank Wood, who nodded assent, remember. "That dog," continued Cullen, "was human in his day, and if anybody has another like him, and wants a couple of months lumberin' in the place of him, I'm ready for a trade; he may call at my shanty. Wal, Crop and I had Seen about all there was to be looked at about Tupper's Lake, and havin' hearn some pretty tall stories about the deer and moose up about the head of Bog River from an Ingen who'd hunted that section, I mentioned to Crop one mornin' that we'd take a trip into them parts. 'Agreed,' said he, or leastwise he didn't say a word agin it, and, by the wag of his tail, I understood him to be agreeable.

"Mud Lake, as you've discovered, aint very near now, and it was a good deal farther off then. The settlements hadn't been pushed so far into the woods then as now. But we put out, Crop and I, for Mud Lake; we passed the eight carryin' places afore night, and reached the first chain of ponds while the sun was hangin' like a great torch in the tree-tops. I've seen a good many deer in my day, but the way they stood around in those ponds, and in the shallow water of the river below, among the grass and pond lilies, was a thing to make a man open his eyes *some.* I saw dozens of 'em at a time, and if it didn't seem like a sheep paster I would'nt say it. I had my pick out of the lot, and knocked over a two-year-old for provision for me and Crop. I aint at all poetical, but if there was ever a matter to make a man feel like stringin' rhymes, that evenin' that Crop and I spent on the lower chain of ponds, or little lakes on Bog River, was a thing of that sort. The sun threw his bright red light on the tops of the mountains away off to the East, spreading it all over the lofty peaks, like a golden shawl, while the gorges and deep valleys around their base rested in deep and solemn shadow. The loon spoke out clear, like a bugle on the lakes, and his voice went echoin' around among the hills; the frogs were out and out jolly, while the old woods were full of happy voices and merry songs as if all nater was runnin' over with gladness and joy; even the night breeze, as it sighed and moaned among the tree-tops, seemed to be whisperin' to itself of the joy and brightness and glory of such an evenin'. As the night gathered, the moon, in her largest growth, came up over the hills and walked like a queen up into the sky, and the bright stars gathered around her, twinklin' and flashin' and dancin', as if merry-makin' in the brightness of her presence. Away down below the bottom of the lake were other mountains and lakes, another moon with bright stars shinin' and twinklin' around her, other broad heavens just as distinct and glorious as those which arched above us. Don't laugh, Judge, for me and Crop saw and heard all that I've been describin' to you, and we felt it too, may be quite as deeply as if we'd been bred in colleges and stuffed with the larnin' of the books.

"I heard the cry of the painter, the howl of the wolf, and the hoarse bellow of the moose that night, and Crop crept close alongside of me, in our bush-shanty, and answered these forest sounds by a low growl, as if sayin' to himself, that while he'd rayther keep oat of a fight, yet, if necessary, in defence of his master, he was ready to go in. Wal, we started on up stream next mornin', passed the second chain of lakes, and went along up the crooked and windin' course of the stream, till towards night we came in sight of Mud Lake. That lake is anything but handsome to my thinkin'; you saw it was gloomy and solemn enough, situated as it is away up on the top of the mountain, higher than any other waters I know of in these parts. All about it are fir, and tamarack, and spruce, the lichens hanging like long grey hair away down from their stinted branches, while all around low bushes grow, and moss, sometimes a foot thick, covers the ground. That, Judge, is the place for black flies and mosquitoes in June. The black flies are all gone before this time in the summer, but if you'd a taken this trip the latter part of June, you'd have admitted that I'm tellin' no lie. If there's any place in the round world where mosquitoes have longer bills, or the black flies swarm in mightier hosts, I don't know where it is, and shan't go there if I happen to find out its location. I've a tolerably thick hide, but if they didn't bite me *some*, I wouldn't say so. But you ought to have seen the deer feedin' on the pond-lilies and grass in that lake I They were like sheep in a pasture; and out some fifty rods from the shore was a great moose, helpin' himself to the eatables that grew there. I laid my jacket down for Crop to watch, and waded quietly in towards where the moose was feedin'. I got within twelve or fifteen rods of him, and spoke to him with my rifle. He heard it, you may guess. Without knowin' who or what hurt him, he plunged right towards me for the shore; but he never got there alive. You ought to have seen the scampering of the deer at the sound of my rifle! Maybe there wasn't much splashin' of the water, and whistlin', and snortin', and puttin' out for the shore among 'em.

"The next mornin', I got up just as the sun was risin', and a little way down on the shore of the lake I saw a buck. Wal, he was one of 'em--that buck was. The horns on his head were like an old-fashioned round-posted chair, and if they hadn't a dozen prongs on 'em, you may skin me! He wasn't as big as an ox, but a two-year-old that could match him, could brag of a pretty rapid growth. I crept up behind a little clump of bushes to about fifteen rods of where he stood on the sandy beach, and sighting carefully at his head, let drive. My gun hung fire a little, owin' to the night-dews, but that buck went down, and after kickin' a moment, laid still, and I took it for granted he was dead. So I laid down my rifle, and went up to where he was, and with my huntin' knife in my hand, took hold of his horn to raise his head so as to cut his throat. If that deer was dead, he came to life mighty quick; for I had no sooner touched him, than he sprang to his feet, and with every hair standin' straight towards his head, came like a mad bull at me. In strugglin' up he overshot me; and as he made his drive one prong went through the calf of my leg. I plunged my knife into his body, and the blood spirted all over me. But it wasn't no use. He smashed down upon me again, and made that hole in my leg above the knee. I handled my knife in a hurry, and made more than one hole in his skin, while he stuck a prong through my arm. I hollered for Crop, who was watching the shanty as his duty was. The old buck and I had it rough and tumble; sometimes one a-top, and sometimes the other, and both growin' weak from loss of blood. May be we didn't kick and tussle about, and tear up the sand on the beach of the lake *some!* The buck was game to the backbone, and had no notion of givin' in, and I had to fight for it, or die; so up and down, over and over, and all around, we went for a long time, until Crop made up his mind that my callin' so earnestly meant something, and round the point he came. When he saw what was goin' on, you ought to've seen how *he* went in! He didn't stop to ask any questions, but as if possessed by all the furies of creation he lit upon that buck, and the fight was up. He with his teeth, and I with my knife, settled the matter in less than a minute. But, Judge, let me tell you, that buck was dangerous; and if Crop hadn't been around, may be ther'd have been the bones of man and beast bleachin' on the sandy beach of Mud Lake! I bound up my wounds as well as I could--but it was tough work backin' my bark canoe over the carryin' places on Bog River, and across the Ingen carryin' place, and from the Upper Saranac to Bound Lake, with them holes in my leg and arm, and the other bruises I received. When I got out to the settlements I was mighty glad to lay still for six weeks, and when I got around again I was a good deal leaner than I am now.

"My gun hangin' fire made my bullet go wide of the spot I aimed at. It had grazed his skull and stunned him for a little time, and crazed him into the bargain. I learned more fully a fact that I'd an idea of before, by my fight with that deer, and it is this--that it's best to keep out of the way of a furious buck with tall, sharp horns on his head. He's a dangerous animal to handle.

"That's one of the adventures that I went out into the wilderness arter, and found without lookin' for it; and I've found a good many others that put me and Crop in a tight place more than once. I backed him over all the carryin' places between Little Tupper's and the Saranacs once, when he was too lame and weak to walk, and nussed him for a month afterwards. But that's an adventer I'll tell another time. There's a deal of excitement, as the Judge calls it, outside of the fences, if people will take the pains to look for it there."

CHAPTER XVI.
ROUND POND--THE PILE DRIVER--A THEORY FOR SPIRITUALISTS.

We put up our tents the next evening, on a bold bluff near the outlet of Round Pond, a picturesque and pleasant sheet of water, some eight or ten miles in circumference. It lay there still and waveless, in that calm summer evening, as glassy and smooth as if no breeze had ever stirred its surface. All around it were old forests, old hills and rocks, and away off in the distance were the tall peaks of the Adirondacks, standing up grim, solemn, and shadowy in the distance. These peaks are seen from almost every direction. They tower so far above the surrounding highlands, that they seem always to be peering over the intervening ranges, as if holding an everlasting watch over the broad wilderness beneath them. This lake is probably more than a thousand feet above the Rackett, and the river falls that distance principally at the two rapids around which our boats were carried. The rest of the way it is a deep, sluggish stream, so that the descent may be reckoned within less than three miles. A ledge of rocks forms the lower boundary of the lake, through which the water, at some remote period, broke its way, and it goes roaring down rapids for three-quarters of a mile, then moves in a sluggish current across a plain of several miles in extent; then plunges down a steep descent for over a mile and a half to subside again into quiet, and move on with a sluggish current to plunge down the ledges again into Tupper's Lake. There are no perpendicular falls of more than twenty feet, but the water goes plunging, and boiling, and foaming down shelving rocks, and eddying, and whirling around immense boulders, rushing and roaring through the gorges with a voice like thunder. These falls are all useless here, and probably will be for centuries to come; but were they out in the "living world," in the midst of civilization, with a fertile and populous region about them, they would soon be harnessed to great wheels, and made utilitarian; the clank of machinery would soon be heard above the roar of their waters. They would do an immensity of labor on their returnless journey to the ocean. But here, they are utterly valueless, wasting their mighty power upon desolate rocks, rushing in mad and impotent fury forever through a region of barrenness and sterility, so far as the uses of civilization are concerned, a region where the manufacturer or the agriculturist will never tarry, until the world shall be so full of people that necessity will drive them to the mountains, to build up the waste places of the earth. Opposite, and across the bay from where our tents were pitched, I noticed that a small stream entered the lake, and Smith and myself crossed over to experiment among the trout I knew would be gathered there. We were entirely successful, for we took one at almost every throw. I have more than once stated, that the trout of these lakes and rivers, in the warm season, congregate where the cold streams enter; and if the sportsman will search out the little brooks, no matter how small, and cast his fly across where their waters enter the lake or river, he will be sure to find trout in any of the hot summer months.

We returned to camp before the sun went behind the hills, with our fish ready for the pan, and our boatmen provided us with a meal of jerked venison, pork, and trout, which an epicure might envy, and to which a hard day's journey and an appetite sharpened by the bracing influence of the pure mountain air, gave a peculiar relish. It was a pleasant thing to see the moon come up from among the trees that formed a dark outline to the lake away off to the east, and travel up into the sky; to see how faithfully it was given back from down in the stirless waters, and how the stars twinkled and glowed around it in the depths below, as they did in the depths above. There was the moon, and there the stars, all bright and glorious in the heavens above; and there another moon, and other stars, as bright and glorious, down in the vault below; the lake floating, as it were, an almost viewless mist, a shadowy and transparent veil between. As we sat, in the greyness of twilight, in front of our tents, a curious sound came over the lake from the opposite shore, so like civilization that it startled us for a moment. Here we were, fifty miles from a house, away in the forest beyond the sound of anything savoring of human agency, and yet we heard distinctly what was for all the world like the blows of an axe or hammer upon a stake, driving it into the earth. It had the peculiar ring, which any one will recognise who has driven a stake into ground covered with water, by blows given by the side instead of the head of an axe. These blows were given at intervals so regular, that we all suspended smoking, certain that there were other sportsmen beside ourselves in the neighborhood of this lake.

"Who in the world is that?" asked Smith, of Martin, who seemed to enjoy our astonishment.

"That," replied Martin, "is a gentleman known in these parts as the 'Pile-driver.' He visits all these lakes in the summer season, and though, as a general thing, he travels alone, yet he sometimes has half a dozen friends with him. If you'll listen a moment, may be you'll find that he has a friend in the neighborhood now who will drive a pile in another place."

Sure enough, in a moment the same ringing blows came from a reedy spot in a different part of the bay.

"The bird that makes that noise," said Martin, "is about the homeliest creature in these woods. It is a small grey heron, that lights down among the grass and weeds to hunt for small frogs and such little fish as swim along the shore. When he drives his pile, he stands with his neck and long bill pointed straight up, and pumping the air into his throat, sends it oat with the strange sound you have heard. It is the resemblance of the sound to that made by driving a stake into ground covered with water, that gives him his name. He's an awkward, filthy bird, but he helps to make up the noises one hears in these wild regions."

"My first thought was," said Smith, "that we had got among the spirits of the woods, and that they were 'rapping' their indignation at our presence, there was something so human about it."

"By the way," remarked the Doctor, "and you remind me of the subject, what a strange delusion is this Spiritualism, to the 'manifestations' of which you refer, and how singular it is that men of strong natural sense and cultivated minds, should be drawn into it. We all know such. Their delusion, too, is stronger than mere speculative belief. It is a faith which to them appears to amount to absolute knowledge. They have no doubt or hesitancy on the subject. Their convictions are perfect; such, that were they as strong in their faith as Christians, as they are in the reality of Spiritualism, they would be able to move mountains."

"I have noticed this intensity of their faith," said Smith; "and while I utterly reject the whole theory of Spiritualism, I could never join in the ridicule of its earnest devotees. There is something that commands my respect in this strong faith, when honestly entertained, however stupendous the error may be to which it clings. There is something, to my mind, too solemn for derision in the idea of communing with the spirits of the departed, or that the time is approaching when living men and the souls of the physically dead, are to meet, as it were, face to face, and know each other as they are. It is one which I can, and do reject, but cannot ridicule. The world, however, regards it differently. And yet with all the contempt and derision that has been poured upon this singular delusion, its devotees have multiplied beyond all precedent in the history of the world. They number, it is said, in this country alone, millions, and have some forty or more newspapers in the exclusive advocacy of their theory."

"The wise people of this world," said Spalding, "that is, those who are wise in their day and generation, laugh at the believers in this modern theory of Spiritualism. They pity them, too, as the unhappy devotees of a faith which sober reason and all the experience of the past prove to be as unsubstantial as the moonbeams that dance upon the waters at midnight. Still these same devotees point to the demonstrations of what they regard as living facts, phenomena palpable to the senses, things that appeal to the eye, the ear, and the touch, and say that these are higher proofs than all the dogmas of philosophy, all the observation and experience of former times, all the logic of the past. And here is the issue between Spiritualism and the mass of mankind who deride and condemn it.

"Now, be it known to you, that I am no Spiritualist. I reject not all the evidences of the phenomena upon which it is based, but I utterly deny that such phenomena are the works of disembodied spirits. I myself have seen what utterly confounded me, and while I reject all idea of supernatural agencies, all interposition of departed spirits, yet I have become thoroughly satisfied that there are more things in heaven and earth than are dreamed of in our philosophy. These phenomena of which the Spiritualists speak, I will not undertake to pronounce all lies. Some of them are doubtless impostures--the work of knaves, who speculate upon the credulity and superstitions which are attributes of the human mind; but they are not all such. But while I admit their reality, I insist that such as are so, are the results of natural laws, which will one day be discovered, and which will turn out to be as simple as the spirit which presides over the telegraph, or that which constitutes the life of a steam engine. There may be, and probably is, a great undiscovered principle which underlays these spiritual manifestations, as they are called, and MIND is after it, looking for it carefully; and what MIND has once started in pursuit of earnestly, it seldom fails to overtake.

"I have sometimes amused myself by endeavoring to furnish a theory for the Spiritualists to stand upon, based upon the demonstrations of the past, the evidences brought to light by the researches of science, which at all events should have about it truth enough to give color and respectability even to an error as stupendous as that of Spiritualism. This theory I have predicated upon the progress of the material world, aside from animal life, showing that what may have been impossible thousands of years ago, may be possible, or about becoming possible now; that we are about entering upon a new era in the advancement of all things towards perfectability, and that the advent of that era may be marked by an established communication between the living and the spirits of the departed.

"Science demonstrates that the material world presents in its history an illustration of the great principle and theory of progress. It is quite certain that our planet was once a very different thing from what it is now; it differed in form, in substance, in compactness, in everything from its present condition. We do not *know* that it was once wholly aeriform, mere gasses in combination, too crude to admit of solidarity; but reasoning back from established facts, the conclusion is almost irresistible, that this earth, now so rock-ribbed and solid, so ponderous, so ragged with mountain ranges, and cloud piercing peaks, was once but vapor, floating without form through limitless space, drifting as mere nebulous matter among the older creations of God. However this may be, it is regarded as quite certain, that time was when ft was entirely void of solidity, void of dry land, with no continent, island, or solid ground, with no living thing within its circumference. It was thus passing through one of the remote eras of its existence. It was then young, just emerging, as it were, from nothingness, growing into form, assuming shape, and gathering attributes of fitness for exterior vitality, preparing the way for higher existences than mere inorganic matter. How long this era existed, science has failed to demonstrate, but it passed away, and solid land marked the next era of the earth's progress. It was surrounded by an atmosphere absolutely fatal to animal life; an atmosphere which, while it stimulated vegetable growth, no living thing could breathe and continue to live. Hence it was, that vegetation, gigantic almost beyond conception, covered its surface. Fern, which is now a pigmy plant, nowhere higher than a few feet, grew tall and overshadowing like great oaks, while oaks, it is fair to presume, towered thousands of feet towards the sky. These stupendous forests stood alone upon the surface of the earth; no animals wandered through their fastnesses; no birds sported amidst their mighty branches; noxious exhalations came steaming up from their tangled recesses, and their gloomy shadows lay a mantle of darkness over dreary and lifeless solitudes. The storms raged, and the winds howled; the sun travelled its daily rounds, with its light dimmed and clouded by the pestilential vapors it exhaled, and silence, so far as the sounds of animal life were concerned, reigned supreme--the stillness of the grave, the quiet of utter desolation, save the voice of the wind or the storm, was unbroken all over the face of the earth. Onward, and onward, rolled this mighty orb on its pathway through the heavens, bearing with it no animal existences, freighted with no human hopes--carrying with it nothing of human destiny. Man, with all his lofty aspirations, his mighty schemes, his glory, and his pride, was a thing of the future. He had not yet emerged from the eternity of the past, to grapple with the present, or encounter the retributions of the eternity which is to come. This was the era of gigantic vegetable growth, and it had its uses; for it was preparing the way for higher and more complicated existences. As the gases that surrounded the earth became consolidated into vegetation, as this stupendous growth decomposed the noxious atmosphere, drawing from it its grosser particles and working them up into solid matter, extracting from it what was fatal to animal life, this earth entered upon another era of its progress.

"Animal life made its appearance. It was weak and feeble at first, but a step removed from vegetable matter. The molusca, the polypi, and the rudest forms of fishes, were, beyond question, the first of living things. Science demonstrates that the water brought forth the first creations endowed with animal vitality. How long this era continued no man can tell. Then came the amphibise, gigantic animals of the lizard kind; the sauruses, that could reach with their long necks and ponderous jaws across a street and pick up a man, if street and man there had been. Then came land animals, monstrous in growth, by the side of which the elephant dwindles to the diminutive stature of the dormouse. In all these advances, was a succession of steps, mounting higher and higher, in complication of structure, each more perfect in organism than its predecessor. Vegetation itself became more complicated, and as it approached perfection lost its gigantic growth. Solidarity, compactness in all things, became the order of nature; the atmosphere surrounding the earth, became more and more fitted for the higher and more complicated animal organizations. At last when time was ripe for his advent, when the earth was fitted for his residence, and the air for his breathing, MAN, the last and most perfect in his structure, the most delicate and finished in his organization of all living things, made his appearance. He stepped from the hand of God, the only thinking, reflecting, the only intellectual, responsible being, in all the world. He stood at the head of created matter, with all things on the earth subject to his will, and corresponding to his, condition, his attributes, his necessities, and his instincts.

"Thus this great earth itself, has been but one continued illustration of the great theory and principle of progress. From a beginning, lost in the thick darkness of a past eternity, it has been marching forward in a career as pause-less as the sun in his journeyings through the sky, as clearly demonstrable as the growth of the germ that starts from the buried acorn, and moves on to its full development in the great oak. Science records with unerring certainty the progress of the earth, and of animal life, from the lowest existences in the mollusca and polypi, up to the superlatively complicated, and delicate structure of man, tracing it step by step, until it is finished in the noblest work of God, a human body coupled with an immortal soul!

"And here arises a question which science has not solved, and to which the philosophy, the wisdom, the logic of the past can give no answer. The earth, and the things of the earth, have been moving forward, marching on towards perfectability always. Is this forward movement finished? We have, in looking at the subject in the light of science, a time when there was not on the earth, in the air, or in the water, any living thing. We have an era when animal life was but a span removed from vegetable vitality; we have an era of gigantic vegetable growth; an era of gigantic but rude animal growth, and so on step by step down to the advent of man. The previous combinations of animal life and vegetable life passed away with the era in which they flourished; one class succeeding another, each emerging from, and stepping over the annihilation of its predecessor, till we come down to the present--is there no future progress for this earth as a planet? Is there to be no other era, where man himself, like the sauruses, like the mastodon, shall have passed away, to be succeeded by some nobler animal structure, some loftier intelligence, some more cunning invention of the infinite mind?

"Man, great in intellect, powerful in mind, gifted with reason, and having within him a spirit that is immortal, proud, glorious, aspiring as he is, falls very far short of perfection in every attribute of his nature. To say, therefore, that the prescience, the creative power of the Almighty, reached the limit of its achievements in the creation of man, is to impeach the omnipotence of God himself. Will any man insist that the ingenuity of the Almighty is exhausted? May it not be, then that the time will come when some sentient beings, as far superior to man, as man is to the animals of the era of the lizards and the amphibia, shall, like the geologists of the present day, be delving among the rocks and rubbish of vanished ages, for evidences of the existences of our own proud species at, to them, some remote period of the world's progress?

"If these questions cannot be answered by the learned and the wise, if science makes no response, and philosophy furnishes no solution of them, who dare say that the world is not, even now, entering upon a new era of progress, taking another step in the forward movement? May it not be, that the time is coming when the barrier between the living, and the disembodied spirit is to be broken down? When that viewless essence, that mystery of mysteries, the spirit of life, the immortal soul, shall be permitted to come back from the unknown country, to impart to the people of this world, the wisdom, the mysteries, and the glory of the next? May not this be the new era that is about opening in the progress of all things? It may be asked, is it not possible that a new principle is about being evolved, that will admit of communication between the living and the physically dead? May it not be that the world and its surroundings, have become so changed, that what was impossible thousands, or even hundreds, of years ago, may have become, or be about to become possible now? That the same process which carried this earth forward from the beginning, that so changed the atmosphere of old, rendered it fit to sustain animal life in its rudest structure, that so changed it again, as to make it capable of sustaining a higher order of animal organism, that kept on changing, and improving the whole face of the earth, that so arranged organic matter, as to make this world, at last, a fit residence for man, may be going on still; approaching all things nearer, and nearer to perfection, until we have arrived upon the threshold of an era, when living men may commune with the spirits of the physically dead? An era as yet but in its dawn, when the stupendous future can be seen only as through a glass darkly?

"Remember, I do not assert my faith in a theory which is indicated by an affirmative answer to these inquiries, for I have none. I give the record of the earth's progress in the past, as it is written upon the rocks, standing out upon precipices, brought to light by the researches, and translated by the energy of science from forgotten and buried ages. The deductions to be drawn from it, I leave to those who have a taste for the speculative, neither believing in, nor quarrelling with the theory which they may predicate upon it."

CHAPTER XVII.
LITTLE TOPPER'S LAKE--A SPIKE BUCK--A THUN-DER STORM IN THE FOREST--THE HOWL OF THE WOLF.

We spent the next day in coasting Round Pond, looking into its secluded bays, and resting, when the sun was hot, beneath the shadows of the brave old trees that line the banks. In floating along the shore of this beautiful sheet of water, one can hardly help imagining that in the broken rocks and rough stones piled up along the margin of the lake, he sees the rains of an ancient wall, the mortar of which has become disintegrated by time, and the masonry fallen down. He will see at intervals what, from a little distance, seems like a solid wall of stone, laid with care, and upon which the lapse of centuries has wrought no change, so regular are the strata of which it is composed, while an occasional boulder, large as a house, and covered with moss, reminds him of the ruined tower of some stronghold. He will see, as he rounds some rocky point, half a dozen of these gigantic boulders piled together, leaning against each other with great cavernous openings between, through which he can walk erect, and he involuntarily looks around him for the armor of the ancient giants who piled up these stupendous rocks and walled in the lake with these massive boulders.

As we swept around a point near the south shore of the lake, we saw a deer at a quarter of a mile from us, feeding upon the lily pads that grew along the shore. Spalding and myself were in advance of our little fleet, and our boatman paddled us carefully and silently towards the animal, using the paddle only when its head was down. He would feed for a minute or two and then look carefully all around him. Of us he took no particular notice, although we were within a hundred and fifty yards of him; and even when we were within sixty yards he seemed to regard us only as a log floating upon the water, or something else which might be regarded as perfectly harmless. Spalding was in the bow of the boat, and when within some eight rods of the game, we lay perfectly quiet for a moment, when his rifle spoke out and its voice rung and re-echoed among the surrounding hills as if a whole platoon of musketry were blazing all around us. The deer made three or four desperate leaps in a zigzag direction, and then went down. When we got to him, he was dead. He was a fine two year old buck, with spike horns, and in excellent condition. We took his saddle and skin and passed on.

From Bound Pond we rowed up the inlet, a broad and sluggish stream, full of grass and lily pads, to Little Tapper's Lake. We saw several deer feeding along the shore that, discovering us as we rowed carelessly along, went whistling and snorting away into the forest. As we approached the lake, dark clouds gathered in the West; great ugly looking thunderheads came rolling up from behind the hills higher and higher; perfect stillness was all around us; the leaves were moveless on the trees, and the voices of the birds were hushed.

"Squire," said Martin to me "I'm thinkin' we'd better go ashore and put up our tents; there's a mighty big storm over the hill, and he'll be down this way before many minutes."

And we rowed to a high point at a small distance, covered with spruce and fir trees, and put up our tents on the lee side of it, so as to be sheltered from the wind as well as the rain. This was the work of only ten minutes; but before we had finished, the deep voice of the thunder came rolling over the forest, and we could see the storm rising over the hills, in a long black line, all across the Western sky. The lightning darted down towards the earth, or across from cloud to cloud, and the thunder boomed and rolled along the heavens, its deep rumble shaking the ground like an earthquake. Presently, the hills were hidden from our view, we heard the rush of the storm in the forest on the other side of the river, then the splash of the big drops on the water, and then the wind and the rain were upon us. For a few minutes, I thought our tents would have been lifted bodily from the ground, but the skill of our pioneer had provided against the blast, and they remained standing safely over us. In a short time the wind passed on, leaving the heavy rain to pour down in torrents, and the deep voiced thunder to come crashing down to the earth, or go rolling solemnly and heavily along the sky. It rained for an hour as it can do only among these mountain regions. The clouds and the rain at length swept on, and the bow of promise spanned the rear of the retiring storm; a new joy seemed to take possession of the wild things, and gladness and merriment sounded from every direction in the old woods; a thin and shadowy mist hung like a veil over the water, and a refreshing coolness, as well as brightness and glory, were all around us. These storms of a hot summer day in this high region, if one is prepared for them, are full of pleasant interest; they rise so majestically, sweep along with such power, and pass away so triumphantly, leaving behind them such a calm sweetness in the air, that a journey to this wilderness would be imperfect in interest without witnessing them.

We entered Little Tripper's Lake towards evening, at the north end, and look-ing down south, one of the most beautiful views imaginable opened upon our vi-sion. Surrounded by low and undulating hills, dotted with islands, with long points running far out into the lake, and pleasant little bays hiding around behind wooded promontories, it presented a wild yet pleasing landscape, on which a painter's eye could not rest but with delight, and which, transferred to canvas, would make a picture of which any artist might be proud.

By the way, I wonder that our artists do not summer among these mountains and lakes, sketching and painting the transcendently beautiful views they every-where present. There is nothing like them on all this continent. We talk about the scenery of Lake George. It is all tame and spiritless compared with what may be seen here; it possesses not a tithe of the variety, the bold and grand, the placid and beautiful, all mingled, and changing always, as you pass from point to point along these lakes. Why do not the artists whose business it is to make the "canvas speak," drift out this way, and deal with nature in all her ancient loveliness, clothed in her primeval robes, and smiling in her freshness and beauty, as when thrown from the hand of Deity? It would repay them for their labor, and yield them a rich harvest of gain.

We had heard of the shanty in which we were to encamp, and we rowed straight through the whole length of the lake towards it. We reached it as the sun was going down, and stowed away our luggage before the darkness had gathered over the forest. We took possession by the right of squatter sovereignty, the owner being unknown, or at all events, absent from the woods. This lake is one of the few in all this region that I had never visited before, and is next in beauty to its namesake, two days' journey nearer to civilization. It is about twelve miles in length, and from one to two miles in width, with many beautiful bays stealing around behind bold rocky promontories, and sleeping in quiet beauty under the shadows of the tall forest trees that tower above their shores. It is dotted, too, with beautiful islands, some rising with a gentle slope from the water, covered with scattering Norway pines, and a dense undergrowth of low bushes; others are covered with tall spruce, fir, and hemlocks, standing up in stately and solemn grandeur, their arms lovingly intertwined, through the everlasting verdure of which the sun never shines; and others still are gigantic rocks, rising up out of the deep water, all treeless and shrubless, remaining always in brown and barren desolation, on which the eagle and osprey devour their prey, and the flocks of gulls that frequent the lake 'light to rest from their almost ceaseless flight. Civilization has not as yet marred in anything this beautiful sheet of water; even the lumberman has not forced his way to the majestic old pines that tower in stately grandeur above the forest trees of a lesser growth; not a foot of laud has been cleared within thirty miles of it. The old woods stand around it just as God placed them, in all their pristine solemnity, stately and motionless; the wild things that roamed among them in the day of old, are there still, and the same species of birds that sported in their branches thousands of years ago, are there still. We heard the howl of the wolf at night; we heard the scream of the panther; we saw the tracks of the moose, and where he had fed on the pastures along the shore; we saw the footprints of a huge bear in the sand on the beach, and the deer-paths were like those that lead to a sheep-fold. It was a pleasant thing to row along the shore, into the bays, around the islands, and into the creeks that came in from other little lakes deeper in the wilderness. The banks are mostly bold and bluff, the rocks standing up four or eight feet from the water, or broken and fallen like an ancient wall. Here and there is a long stretch of beautiful sandy beach, on which the tiny waves break with a rippling song, and from which bars go out with a gentle slope into the water.

We intended to remain here quietly for a few days, taking things easy, rowing, and fishing, and hunting enough for exercise only. There is plenty of deer, and trout, and duck, and partridge here, to be taken with small labor; there are bears, and wolves, and panthers, in the woods around. But these are fewer and harder to be come at than the other game; there is an occasional moose too. We saw the tracks of all these animals hereabouts, and we hoped to get a shot at some or all of them before leaving the woods.

Reader, did you ever hear the wolves howl in the old woods of a Still night! No? Then you have not heard *all* the music of the forest. Some deep-mouthed old forester will open his jaws, and send forth a volume of sound so deep, so loud, so changeful, so undulating and variable in its character, that, as it rolls along the forest, and comes back in quavering echoes from the mountains, you will almost swear that his single voice is an agglomerate of a thousand, all mixed, and mingled, and rolled up into one. May be, away in the distance, possibly on the other side of the lake, or across a broad valley, another will open his mouth and answer, with a howl as deep, and wild, and variable, as the first; and possibly a third and fourth, one on the right, and another on the left, will join in the chorus, until the whole forest seems to be fall of howling and noise; and yet not one of these animals may be within a mile of you. To a timid man, there is something terrific in the howl of the wolves; but in truth, they are harmless as the deer, quite as wild and shy, and full as cowardly in the presence of a man. They will fly as frightened from his approach, unless, possibly, in the intense cold and desolation of winter, when driven together and rendered desperate by hunger, they might be emboldened by starvation to attack a man, but even this is among the apocryphal legends of the wilderness.

"Hearing them wolves howlin'," said Hank Martin, as we sat in the evening around our camp fire, "reminds me of a story Mark Shuff tells of his experience with the critters; but mind, I don't pretend to swear to its truth, for I don't claim to know anything about the facts myself. I'll tell it as Mark told it to me, and if it turns out to be too tough a yarn to take down whole, don't lay it to me. You know Mark Shuff," said he, appealing to me, "and you may believe such parts of it as you may be able to swallow, and the rest may be divided up, as the Doctor said the other day, among the company."

"Go ahead," said the Doctor, "I'll take a quarter as my share of the story, and you may cut it off of either end, or carve it out of the middle. I'll take a quarter, tough or tender."

"You may set down a quarter to my account," said Smith, "and Spalding shall take another." "Very well, then," said Martin, "I'll believe a quarter of it myself, and so the case is made up, as the judge would say."

"Well," repeated Martin, "you know MARE Shuff?" "Of course I know Mark Shuff; and who, that has visited these lakes and woods don't know him? He is a stalwart man, six feet in his stockings, strong, healthy, and enduring as iron, I have had him as a boatman and guide about Tupper's Lake, and the regions beyond it, more than once. He works at lumbering in the winter, and if there is one among the hundreds, I had almost said thousands, who make war, in the snowy season of the year, upon the old pines of the Rackett woods, who can swing an axe more effectually than Mark Shuff, his light is under a bushel--his fame obscured. Mark works hard for four or five months, and lays around loose the balance of the year. In the summer, he holds a cost as a thing of ornament rather than use, and boots or shoes as luxuries, not to be reckoned as among the necessaries of life. His hat, as a general thing, is of straw, and minus a little more than half the brim. He would be out of place, and out of uniform, as well as out of temper with himself, if he was for any considerable length of time without the stub of a marvelously black pipe in his mouth, filled with plug tobacco, shaved and rubbed in his hand into a proper condition for smoking. Mark, though by no means an intemperate man, is fond of a drop now and then, and when he has just a thimbleful too much, the way he will swear is emphatically a sin. And yet he is anything but quarrelsome or contrary, even when a shade over the line of strict sobriety. He is a great, strong, square-shouldered, big-breasted, good-natured specimen of the genus homo, a giant in physical strength, and were I a wolf, I would prefer letting him alone to any man in these parts. When he gets just the least grain "shiny" (and he never gets beyond that), and his oar goes a little wrong, or a twig brushes him ungently, or his seat gets a little hard, he will express his sense of its improper deportment by incontinently damning its eyes, and so forth, as if it were a sentient thing, and understood all his profane denunciations; but with all this, Mark never forgets to be respectful, and, in his way, courteous to his employers. He has, moreover, a sharp, clear eye in his head, and can see a deer, or any other game, as quick, and shoot it as far as the best, and has as good a knowledge of where they are to be found, as any man in these woods."

"Well," continued Martin, as he lighted his pipe by dipping it into the embers and scooping up a small coal; "Well, Mark Shuff and a friend of his by the name of Westcott, had a shanty one winter over on Tupper's Lake; they were trappin' martin, and mink, and muskrat, and wolves, when they could get one. They shantied on the outlet, just at the foot of the lake, below the high rocky bluff round which the little bay there sweeps. There wasn't any house then nearer than Harriets Town, down by the Lower Saranac; but there was a company of lumbermen having a shanty up towards the head of the lake, near where the Bog River enters. Mark, one cold winter's morning, started on an errand to the lumber shanty I speak of, calculatin' to return the same evening. The lake was frozen over, and he took to the ice, as being the nearest and best travelin'. The winter had set in airly, and the snow had lain deep for months, and the game of the woods had got pretty well starved out. Mark did'nt take his rifle with him, thinkin' of course that he would see no game on the ice worth shootin', and a gun would only be an incumbrance to him. Well, he did his errand at the shanties, and started for home. I don't know whether he took a drop or not, but they generally keep a barrel of old rye in the lumber shanties, and my opinion is that Mark was invited to take a horn, in which case, I'm bold to say, the horn was taken.

"However that may be, Mark started for home along in the afternoon, and took to the ice, as he did when he went up in the morning. Everything went right until he got within may be a mile of home, when he heard, from a point of land, a little to the left of him, a sharp, fierce bark, and turning that way, he saw a great shaggy, fierce-looking wolf trot out from behind a boulder and squat himself down on his haunches, and eye him as if calculating the probabilities of his making a good supper. While Mark was looking at him, feelin' a little oneasy, he heard another sharp bark, and from a point just ahead of him another great wolf trotted out on to the ice, and sat himself down, eyeing him with suspicious intensity. In a moment, another came out right opposite to him, and then another, and another, until Mark swears to this day that there were more than a dozen of these fierce and hungry savages squatted on their haunches within fifty yards of him.

"Mark, as I said, had no rifle, his only weapons being a hunting knife and a heavy walking stick, which he carried in his hand. To say that he was not frightened, would be stating what I don't believe to be true, and I've heard him tell how his huntin' cap seemed to be lifted right up on his head, as if every hair pointed straight towards the sky. He looked at the wolves a moment, and then walked on; but the animals trotted along with him, still, however, keepin' at a respectful distance. Those in advance seemed inclined to cross his path, as if to turn him towards the centre of the lake, while those behind went further and further from the shore, as if to surround him; and thus they travelled for near half a mile, Mark making for the open water, which in the coldest weather is always to be found near the outlet of the lake, determined, if they came to close quarters, to take to that and swim for it. He had heard and knew that almost every animal is afraid of the voice of a man; so he shouted at the top of his voice, and as he said, ripped out some select and choice oaths, which for a moment alarmed the wolves, and they fell back a few rods, still, however, keepin' in a kind of half circle around him. But it was'nt long before they began to gather in on him again, and though his shoutin' and swearin' kept them at a good distance, yet they seemed to be gettin' used to it, and it didn't alarm them as it did at first. Mark had now got within reach of the water, and he felt comparatively safe. He was not more than a quarter of a mile from home, and cold as it was, he felt sure that he could swim that distance.

"Before being compelled to take to the water, it occurred to him to halloo for Westcott, which he did with all his might. The wolves did'nt appear to care much about his hallooing, but kept trottin' along between him and the shore, and before and behind him, drawin' the circle closer and closer every ten rods; and Mark expected every moment when they'd make a rush on him, in which case he'd made up his mind to make a dive into the water, along which he was now travelin'. Presently he saw Westcott, with his double-barrelled rifle, stealin' along the shore, hid from the kritters by a high rocky point, within some twenty rods of him. He felt all right then, for he knew that when Westcott pinted that rifle at anything, something had to come. It was a dangerous piece, that rifle was, 'specially when loaded and Westcott was at one end of it.

"Mark was not more than fifteen rods from the shore, but that ground was occupied by the wolves; on the right was the water, into which he might at any moment be compelled to plunge; while both before and behind him his advance and retreat was alike cut off. He had noticed that whenever he stopped, the wolves stopped, as if the time for the rush had not yet come, and it puzzled him to understand why they delayed the onset. Seeing Westcott with his rifle, Mark determined to treat his assailants to a choice lot of profane epithets, and the way he opened on the cowardly rascals, he said, astonished even himself. But while he was thus swearing at his enemies, he discovered, as he thought, the reason why they had not attacked him sooner. A troop of a dozen or more wolves broke cover some distance up the lake, and came runnin' down towards where he stood, for whose presence, no doubt, those around him were waiting. Just then he saw WESTCOTT'S huntin' cap above the rocks on the point, and saw his double-barrel poked out in the direction of the leader of the pack, and he knew that that old grey-back's time had come. Mark let off a fresh volley of profanity, and as the wolves seemed preparing for a rush, WESTCOTT'S rifle broke the frozen stillness of the woods, and old grey-back turned a summerset and went down. The astonished wolves clustered together for a moment in confusion, and the other barrel spoke out. Another of the pack bounded into the air, and as he came down kicked and thrashed about in a most oncommon way, and then laid still--while the way the rest put out for the point, some distance up the lake, was a thing to be astonished at. Mark threw up his hat, and hollered, and shouted, and swore, till the last wolf disappeared into the forest, and then shoulderin' one of the dead kritters, and WESTCOTT the other, started on home. The hides, and the bounty on the scalps, made a good day's work of it; but Mark swears to this day, that if the last dozen of wolves had been a little earlier, or Westcott a little later, he'd a-been driven like a buck to the water, cold as it was; and if they'd been a little earlier still, he'd have been a goner. He never goes far from home since, without a rifle; although with that he has no fear of wolves, yet he concludes that a hunting-knife and a stick are no match for a whole pack of the kritters, when made savage by the starvation of winter."

[Illustration: Westcott's rifle broke the frozen stillness of the woods, and old greyback turned a summerset and went down. The astonished wolves clustered together for a moment in confusion, and the other barrel spoke out.]

While we were listening to the story of Mark Shuff and the wolves, the old fellow over the water made the forest ring again with his howling. He was answered from miles away down the lake by another. Their voices kept the forest echoes busy, until we laid ourselves away in our blankets, where we slept till wakened by the glad voices of the birds in the early morning.

CHAPTER XVIII.

AN EXPLORING VOYAGE IN AN ALDER SWAMP--A BEAVER DAM--A FAIR SHOT
AND A MISS--DROWNING A BEAR--AN UNPLEASANT PASSENGER.

We started the next morning on an exploring voyage round the lake, to look into the bays and inlets, try the fish and deer, and see what we could see generally. We struck across to an island opposite our landing-place, containing five or six acres, covered with a dense growth of spruce, hemlock, and fir, with an occasional pine standing with its tall head proudly above the other forest trees, while along the ground the low whortleberry bushes, loaded with fruit, now just ripening, grew. This island is near the south shore, and separated from it by a narrow channel some twenty rods in width. We landed, and were regaling ourselves upon the berries, leaving our boats and guns on the lake side of the island. We had wandered near the centre of the island, when three deer started up within two rods of us, and rushed whistling and snorting in huge astonishment across the island in the direction of the mainland, and dashing wildly into the water, swam to the shore and disappeared into the forest. We, in truth, were little less astonished than they, for we certainly expected no such game to be hiding there, and when they leaped up so suddenly and plunged away, crashing and snorting through the brush, it startled us somewhat; but our boats and guns were on the other side of the island, and we could only look on as they swam boldly to the shore without the power to harm them.

At the east end of the lake a large stream, deep, sluggish, and tortuous enters, which we voted came from a lake or pond, back at the base of the hills, seen some three or four miles distant in that direction, and while the other boats passed in another direction, Spalding and myself started upstream to explore it. As we advanced, the alders and willows encroached more and more upon the channel, until it became too narrow for rowing. Our boatman took his paddle, and seated in the stern of our little craft, propelled it up stream for an hour or more. The alders gradually contracted, the channel becoming narrower until we were passing under a low archway of branches, covered with dense foliage, through which the sunlight could not penetrate. The arch grew lower and lower, and the channel narrower, until we at last absolutely stuck fast among the branches of the alders which, here grew almost horizontally over the stream. We could not turn round, and to go further was absolutely impossible; there was but one mode of extrication, and that was to back straight out the way we had entered. Our boatman changed his position to the bow of the boat, and after much labor and exertion, we started down stream. After two hours of hard work, pushing with the oars and pulling by the branches, we emerged into daylight, came out into the open stream, not a little fatigued by our efforts to find the imaginary pond at the base of the mountains.

This stream, with the broad alder marsh that stretches away on either side, was doubtless once a beaver dam; and we thought we could discover where these singular and sagacious animals had erected the structure that made for them an artificial lake. Our theory on this subject may have been true or false, but this much is a fact, that in all this region of lakes and rivers, I have seen no alder or other marsh of any considerable extent, save this. In the times of old, when the Indian and his brother the beaver, lived quietly together, before the greed of the white man had built up a war of extermination between them, this must have been a glorious country for the beaver. The lakes are so numerous and the ponds and rivers so fitted for them, that they must have had a good time of it here for centuries. The Indians never disturbed them, never made war upon them; their flesh was not needed or fitted for food, and the value of their fur was unknown. Tradition, speaking from the dim and shadowy past, tells us of the vast numbers of these sagacious and harmless animals which congregated in these regions, living in undisturbed quiet and happiness all the year, building their dams, their canals, and cities on all the ponds, rivers, and lakes hereabouts. But they are all gone now. I inquired if any had been seen of late years, and could hear of but a single family, which some ten years ago were said to dwell somewhere in the vicinity of Mud Lake, the highest and wildest of all these mountain lakes. The last of these was taken four or five years ago, since which no sign of the beaver has been discovered. They are doubtless all gone, and as this was their last abiding-place, they may be regarded as extinct on this side of the Alleghany ranges, and probably on this side of the eastern slopes of the Rocky Mountains. Like the beaver, the Indian who turned against him, will soon be gone too. Annihilation is written as the doom of both. The wild man must pass away with the woods and the forests, before the onward rush of civilization, and history will soon be all that will remain of the Indian and his ancient brother the beaver.

Well, be it so, and who will regret it? It is a sad thing to see a whole race perish, wiped out from the aggregate of human existence. But in this instance, its place will be filled by a higher and nobler race, and the hunting-ground of the savage and the pagan, be converted into cultivated fields; where stood the wigwam, will stand the farm-house; where the council-fires blazed, will stand the halls of enlightened and Christian legislation; churches and school-houses, and all the accompaniments of Christianity and civilization will take the place of ancient forests; and educated, intellectual, cultivated minds take the place of the rude, untaught, and unteachable men and women of the woods.

As we re-entered the lake, we saw a noble buck feeding along the shore, a short distance from us. We dropped behind a point of willows, from the outer edge of which we would be in shooting distance. We paddled silently round the point, and there, within fifteen rods of us, he stood, broad side to us, presenting as beautiful a mark as a man could wish. I counted him certainly ours, when I drew upon him with my rifle. Well I blazed away, and as I did so, he raised his head suddenly, gazed in astonishment at us for a moment, with his ears thrown forward, and in an attitude of wildness, and then dashed madly away into the forest, snorting like a war-horse at every bound. I had not touched him, and I knew it the moment I fired. Our little boat was light and rollish, and just as I pressed the trigger, it rolled slightly on the water and my ball passed over, but mighty close to the back of that deer. I was mortified enough at this mishap, for I prided myself on my coolness and marksmanship, and here was a failure apparently more inexcusable than any that had occurred. But there was no help for it. The deer was gone, and Spalding and the boatman indulged in a hearty laugh at my expense.

Some half a mile up the lake, we saw a great turtle sunning himself on a rock which was partly out of water. He was twice as large as any of the fresh-water kind I had ever seen. His shell was all of two feet in diameter, and his scaly arms, as they hung loosely over the side of the rock, were as large as the wrists of a man. He was some six or eight rods from us, and Spalding gave him a shot with his rifle. The ball glanced harmlessly from his massive shell against the ledge behind him, and starting from his sleep, he clambered lazily and clumsily into the water.

We threw out a trolling line as we passed up the lake; but we caught no trout. Along the shore, however, we caught small ones in plenty with the fly. These shore trout, as I call them, seem to be a distinct species, differing in many respects from the other trout of the lakes or streams. They are uniform in size, rarely exceeding a quarter of a pound in weight. They are of a whitish color, longer in proportion than the lake, river, or brook trout, have fewer specks upon them, and those not of a golden hue, but rather like freckles. They are found among the broken rocks where the shores are bold and bluff, or near the mouths of the cold brooks that come down from the hills. I caught them at every trial, and whenever we wanted them for food. Their flesh is white and excellent--better, to my taste, than that of any other fish of these waters.

We rejoined our companions in a little bay that lay quietly around a rocky promontory, where we found them enjoying a dinner of venison and trout, under the shade of some huge firtrees, by the side of a beautiful spring that came bubbling up, in its icy coldness, from beneath the tangled roots of a stinted and gnarled birch. Happily, there was enough for us all, and we accepted at once the invitation extended to us to dine. Towards evening, we rowed back to our shanty. The breeze had entirely ceased, and the lake lay still and smooth; not a wave agitated its surface, not a ripple passed across its stirless bosom; the woods along the shore, and the mountains in the back ground, the glowing sunlight upon the hill-tops were mirrored back from its quiet depths as if there were other forests, and other mountains and hills glowing in the evening sunshine away down below, twins to those above and around us. We saw on our return along the beach, the track of a bear in the sand, that had been made during the day, and we had some talk of trying the scent of our dogs upon it. But it was too near night, to allow of a hope of securing him, even if the dogs could follow, and we gave up the idea, promising to attend to bruin's case another day.

As we sat with our meerschaums, in the evening, speculating upon the chances of securing a bear, or a moose, before leaving the woods, a wolf lifted up his voice on the hill opposite as, and made the old forest ring again with his howling. He was answered as in the night previous, from away down the lake, and by another from the hill back of us, and another still from the narrow gorge above the head of the lake. However discordant the music appeared to us, they seemed to enjoy it, for they kept it up at intervals during all the early part of the night.

"Seeing that bear's track, and hearing the howl of those wolves," said the Doctor, "reminds me of a story I heard told by an old Ohio pilot, whom I found in drifting down that noble river in a pirogue, some five and twenty years ago. We tied up one night by the side of another similar craft, that had gone down ahead of us, the people on board of which had landed and built a camp-fire, and erected their tent. They were strangers to us, but in those days everybody you met in the wilderness which skirted the Upper Ohio was your friend, if you chose to regard him so. I was a mere boy then, and was in company with my father and three other gentlemen, who owned a township of land not far from Cincinnati; that is not far now, considering the difference in the mode of travelling between then and now, and we were on our way to explore that township. I did not regard it as of much value then, though it has since brought a heap of money to its owners. We found the company belonging to the other boat busily employed in cooking a supper of venison and bear-meat, they having in the course of the day killed two deer and a bear that they found swimming the river. We were invited to help ourselves; an invitation which, being cordially given, we as cordially accepted. We had been passing during most of the day through unbroken forests, standing up in stately majesty on both sides of the river, and stretching back the Lord knows how far. After the darkness gathered, the wolves made the wilderness vocal with their howling. It was the first time I had ever heard them, and for that matter the last, until since we have been in these woods: but when that old fellow over the lake lifted up his voice last night, I recognized it at once. I can't say I admired it as a musical performance then, and I don't appreciate its harmony now. If there are those who like it, why, *de gustibus non*, and so forth.

"But I set out to tell the story that the old Ohio pilot told that night, while the travellers sat smoking around their camp-fires, and the wolves were howling in the wilderness about us. I do not, of course, vouch for its truth; I simply tell it as he told it to us. He seemed to believe it himself, for he told it with a gravity of face, and a seriousness of manner, which would ill comport with its falsity. His hearers did not seem to regard it as passing belief, but they laughed at the idea of drowning a bear.

"'Twenty odd years ago,' said the old pilot, as he lighted his pipe and seated himself on the head of a whisky-keg, 'there warn't a great many people along the

Ohio, except Ingins and bears, and we didn't like to cultivate a very close acquaintance with either of them, for the Ingins were cheatin', deceivin', and scalpin' critters, and the bears had an onpleasant way with 'em, that people of delicate narves
didn't like. I came out for some people over on the east side of the mountains,
lookin' land, in company with four men who had hunted over the country. Ohio
warn't any great shakes then, but let me tell you, stranger, it had a mighty big pile
of the tallest kind of land layin' around waitin' to be opened up to the sunlight. It's
goin' ahead now, and people are rushin' matters in the way of settlin' of it, but you
could stick down a stake most anywhere in it then, and travel in any direction a
hundred miles climbin' a fence.

"'Wal, we came down the Alleghany in two canoes, and shantied on the Ohio,
just below where the Alleghany empties itself into it. We hid our canoes, and struck
across the country, and travelled about explorin' for six weeks, and when we got
back to our shantyin' ground, we were tuckered out you may believe. We rested
here a couple of days, layin' around loose, and takin' our comfort in a way of our
own. Early one morning, when my companions were asleep, I got up and paddled
across the river after a deer, for we wanted venison for breakfast. I got a buck, and
was returnin', when what should I see but a bear swimmin' the Ohio, and I put
out in chase right off. I soon overhauled the critter, and picked up my rifle to give
him a settler, when I found that in paddlin' I had spattered water into the canoe,
wettin' the primin' and makin' the gun of no more use than a stick. I didn't understand much about the natur of the beast then, and thought I'd run him down, and
drown him, or knock him on the head. So I put the canoe right end on towards
him, thinkin' to run him under, but when the bow touched him, what did he do,
but reach his great paws up over the side of the canoe, and begin to climb in. I
hadn't bargained for that; I felt mighty onpleasant, you may swear, at the prospect
of havin' sich a passenger. I hadn't time to get at him with the rifle, till he came
tumblin' into the dugout, and as he seated himself on his stern, showed as pretty a
set of ivory as a body would wish to see. There we sat, he in one end of the dugout
and I in the other, eyein' one another in a mighty suspicious sort of way. He didn't
seem inclined to come near my end of the dugout, and I was principled agin goin'
towards his. I made ready to take to the water on short notice, but at the same time
concluded I'd paddle him to the shore, if he'd allow me to do it quietly.

"'Wal, I paddled away, the bear every now and then grinnin' at me, skinnin' his face till every tooth in his head stood right out, and grumblin' to himself in a way that seemed to say, 'I wonder if that chap's good to eat?' I didn't offer any opinion on the subject; I didn't say a word to him, treatin' him all the time like a gentleman, but kept pullin' for the shore. When the canoe touched the ground, he clambered over the side, and climbed up the bank, and givin' me an extra grin, started off into the woods. I pushed the dugout back suddenly, and gave him, as I felt safe again, a double war-whoop that seemed to astonish him, for he quickened his pace mightily, as if quite as glad to part company as I was. I larned one thing, stranger, that mornin', and it's this, never to try drownin' a bear by runnin' him under with a dugout. It won't pay.'"

CHAPTER XIX.
SPALDING'S BEAR STORY--CLIMBING TO AVOID A COLLISION--AN UNEXPECTED MEETING--A RACE.

"That story," said Spalding, "reminds *me* of a bear story. I shall do as the Doctor did, tell it as it was told to me. I did not see the bear, but I know the man who was the hero of it, and his brother told the story in his presence one day, and he made no denial. He at least is estopped from disputing it, and we lawyers call that *prima facie* evidence of its truth. It occurred a long time ago, when there were fewer green fields in Oswego county and especially in the town of Mexico, than there are now. The old woods stood there in all their primeval grandeur. The waves of Ontario laved a wilderness shore, and their dull sound, as they came rolling in upon the rocky beach, died away in the solitudes of a gloomy and almost boundless forest. Here and there a 'clearing' let in the sunlight, and the woodman's axe broke the forest stillness as he battled against the brave old trees. The smoke of burning fallows was occasionally seen, wreathing in dense columns towards the sky. Civilization, enterprise, energy and new life were just starting on that career of progress which has moved onward till the wilderness, under the influence of their mighty power, has been made to blossom as the rose. Those were pleasant times, as we look upon them now, just fading into the dim and shadowy past, but they were times of toil and privation. The arms of the men of those times were nerved by the hope of the future, and the spirit that sustained them was that of faith in the fact that the promise of reward for their labor was sure.

"Do the men of the present day ever think what a gigantic labor that was of clearing away those old forests? Contemplate a wilderness, reaching from the Atlantic to the Mississippi, from the great lakes and the majestic St. Lawrence to the Gulf of Mexico, every acre of which was covered with tall trees which had to be cut away one by one, not with some great machine which mowed them down in broad swaths like the grass of a meadow, but by a single arm and a single axe. Talk about the Pyramids, the Chinese Wall, the great canals of the earth! They sink into utter insignificance when compared with the prodigious labor of clearing away the American forests, and spreading out green fields where our fathers found only a limitless wilderness of woods. The sons of these men who performed that labor, in my judgment, have a better patent to preferment and honors than those who come from other lands to claim their inheritance after it has been thus perfected by such toil and hardships, and dangers as the history of the world cannot parallel."

"I think, if I remember rightly," said the Dr., "you set out to tell a bear story. You are now indulging in a sermon on progress. Allow me to call your attention to the bear."

"I appeal to the court," said Spalding, addressing Smith and myself, "against this interruption."

"The counsel will proceed," said Smith, with all the gravity of a judge; "we hope the interruption will not be repeated."

"Well," said Spalding, resuming his narrative, "some fifty years ago, two enterprising men (brothers) marched into the woods in the town of Mexico, now in Oswego county, with their axes on their shoulders, and stout hearts beating in their bosoms. They located a mile or more apart, and began a warfare, such as civilization wages, against the old forest trees. Men talk about courage on the battle-field, the facing of danger amid the conflict of armed hosts, and the crash of battle. All that is well, but what is such courage, stimulated by excitement and braced by the ignominy which follows the laggard in such a strife, to that calm, enduring, moral courage of him who encounters the toil and hardships incident to the settlement of a new country, and battles with the dangers, the long years of privation, which lie before the pioneer who goes into the forest to carve out a home for himself and his children? How much more noble is such courage, how infinitely superior is such a warfare, one which mows down forest trees instead of men, which creates green pastures, broad meadows, and fields of waving grain, instead of smouldering cities, and desolated homes! How much more pleasant is the sound of the woodman's axe, than that of the booming cannon! How much more cheerful the smoke that goes up from the burning fallow, than that which hangs in darkness over the desolation of the battle field, beneath which lie the dead in their stillness, and the wounded in their agony! But I am losing sight of the bear."

"Exactly so," said the Doctor; "and we have not as yet had the pleasure of making his acquaintance. Suppose you give us an introduction to the gentleman."

"These interruptions are entirely out of order," gravely remarked Smith; "they must not be repeated. The counsel will proceed."

"Well," resumed Spalding, bowing deferentially to the court, "one of these settlers started one day across the woods to visit his brother. There were few roads in those times, and these were laid out without much reference to distance; they went winding and crooking every way to avoid this hill, or that creek, or water course, or any other impediment which nature may have thrown in the way, and a blind footpath, or a line of marked trees, was more commonly travelled from one forest house to another. The forester was tramping cheerfully along, thinking doubtless of the good time coming, when his farm would be shorn of all its old woods, when flocks and herds would be grazing in luxurious pastures, tall grain waving in fields, the summer grass clothing in richness meadows reclaimed by his labor from the wilderness, and he should be at ease among his children. First settlers of a new country think of these things, and it is because they think of them, that their hearts are strong and buoyant with hope. They live in the future, enduring the darkness and privation of the present, in their faith in the brightness of the years to come. Thus they wait in patience for, while they command success, and the end of their toil is an old age of competence, and in the closing years of life, quiet and repose. Well, he was enjoying these pleasant visions when he saw, some thirty rods ahead of him, a huge bear, with her cubs, 'travelling his way,' as the saying is, in other words coming directly towards him. He was no hunter, and had with him no weapon. He had heard strange stories of the ferocity of the bear when her cubs were by her side, and to say that he was not horribly frightened would be a departure from the strict requirements of truth. He had heard, too, that a bear could not climb a small, straight tree, and *he* could. The question then was between climbing and running. He was not much in a race, and he decided to climb; so selecting a smooth-barked, perpendicular ash sapling, he started with might and main towards the top. He went up, as he supposed, till he was out of the reach of the bear, and held on, all the time keeping his eye on the animal, and making as little noise as possible. The bear, doubtless seeing that he was beyond her reach, passed on out of sight, and after he remained till the danger was over, he concluded to come down. He was astonished to find that his efforts to descend were powerless. He seemed to have frozen to the tree. Upon looking around, to his utter amazement, he found himself sitting on the ground, *with both legs and arms locked fast around the, tree! He had not climbed an inch, and the bear had not been aware of his presence in the woods!*

"That ash sapling was safe from that day. It stood then in the old forest. The woodman's axe spared it. It stands now in the open field, a majestic tree; its great trunk, eight feet in circumference, its long arms covered with foliage, casting a broad shadow over the pasture beneath, in which cattle and sheep seek for coolness and ruminate in the heat of the summer days. It is pointed out as the tree which the man who was frightened by a bear *didn't* climb, and is referred to as evidence of the truth of my story, as the Dutchman proved the authenticity of his Bible, 'by the pictures.'"

"And that," said I, "puts *me* in mind of a bear story, which has this merit over both of yours--it is true. I can speak of it as a thing of personal knowledge, occurring within my own personal experience. I began the study of law in Angelica, the county seat of Alleghany county, and as it was a good many years ago, it is fair to assume that I was a good many years younger than I am now, and that the country in that region was younger too. Everybody knows that Alleghany county is, or used to be, a great place for whirlwinds and tornadoes. If they do not, they may understand and be assured of the fact now. A few years (less than twelve) ago, a black cloud came looming up in the northwest, and started on its career towards the southeast. As it swept along, it sent its fierce winds crashing, and howling, and roaring, through the old forests, uprooting, hurling to the ground, and scattering everything that encountered its fury. Houses, barns, haystacks, fences, trees, everything were prostrated, and to this day its track is visible in the swath it mowed through the old woods, from sixty to a hundred rods wide, plain and distinct still, for miles and miles. It was not of that tornado, however, that I propose to speak. Others had preceded it, and in the country all about Angelica were what were called 'windfalls.' These windfalls were neither more nor less than the old tracks of these whirlwinds and tornadoes, that had swept down the forest trees. Fire had finished what the whirlwind begun. In time, blackberry-bushes had grown up among the charred trunks of the old pines, and other trees, bearing an immensity of fruit; and it was a pleasant resort for young people, one of those windfalls, when the blackberries were ripe and luscious. These windfalls were great places, too, for rabbits, partridges, and 'such small deer,' and it was no great thing to boast of, to kill a dozen or two of the birds of an afternoon.

"I went out with a friend one day to one of these windfalls, partly after blackberries, and partly for partridges. We were both boys, younger than fifteen, then, and each possessing, probably, quite as much discretion as valor. We had separated a short distance from each other, he to gather berries, and I, with a small fowling-piece, in pursuit of game. Presently I saw my friend crashing through the brush towards me, and also towards the fields, without his basket, and bare headed, his hair standing straight up, putting in his very best jumps, as if a thousand tigers were at his heels. Without heeding for a moment my anxious inquiries as to what was the matter, he kept right on, leaping the logs like a deer, looking neither to the right hand nor the left, but with his coat tail sticking out on a dead level behind, making a straight wake for home. Fear is said to be contagious, and I believe in the doctrine that it is so. I caught it bad; and without knowing what I was afraid of, I started, and if any fourteen year old boy can make better time than I did on that occasion, I should like to see him run. I kept possession of my fowling-piece, and came out neck and neck with my friend. We scrambled over the outer fence, and ran some dozen rods or more in the open field, without either of us looking back. Then, however, we made the astounding discovery, that there was nothing after us, and we both paused to take breath, and, so far as I was concerned, to ascertain, if possible, what had occasioned the race. I learned that my friend, after I left him, had gone into the windfall, and was standing upon the long trunk of a fallen tree, picking berries, when he saw, a few rods from him towards the other end of the log on which he was standing, a great black hand reach up and bend down a tall blackberry-bush that was loaded with berries. This alarmed him somewhat, for whoever the great black hand belonged to was concealed by the thick bushes and their foliage from his view. Presently, two great black hands were placed upon the log, and a huge black bear clambered lazily up, and, for a second, stood in utter amazement, face to face, and within fifty feet of my friend. Both broke at the same instant, in affright; my friend in one direction, and the bear in the other--my friend for the fields, and the bear for the deep woods--and each as anxious as fear could make him to put a 'broad belt of country' between them. My friend dropped his basket, as he leaped from the log; it was no time to stop for a basket; a limb caught his hat and pulled it off; he had not time to stop for his hat. The truth is, he was in a hurry, and something more than a hat or a basket was required to stay his progress towards home."

"The Squire's story," said Cullen, as he knocked the ashes from his pipe, and commenced shaving a fresh supply of tobacco with his jack-knife, and depositing it in the palm of his left hand, "the Squire's story reminds me of an adventer Crop and I met with, over towards St. Regis Lake, a good many year ago; and I'll state the circumstances of the case, as the Judge would say. It was an adventer that don't happen often--leastwise, not in the same way. It made me understand some things that I hadn't much idea of before. Let me tell you, Judge, if you don't want a fight with an animal that's got long claws and sharp teeth, don't come close upon him onawares, or may be there'll be trouble. Give him time to think, and ten to one he'll take to his heels. Most animals have more confidence in their legs than they have in their teeth and claws, and they'll be very likely to use 'em, if you'll give 'em time to consider. But if you find a painter, or a bear, takin' a nap in your path, and don't want to have a clinch with him, wake him up before you get right onto him, or he'll be very likely to think he's cornered, and them animals have onpleasant ways with 'em when they're in that fix.

"Wal, as I was sayin', Crop and I was over on St. Regis Lake, layin' in a store of jerked venison, and trappin' martin, and mink, and muskrat, and huntin' wolves, and sich other wild animals as came in our way. The scalp of a wolf was good for fifteen dollars in them days, and a backload of furs was worth a heap of money. We had a line of martin traps leadin' back to the hills, and over into a valley beyond, where the animal was plentier than they were on our side. In passin' along this line, we had to round the end of a hill that terminated in a sharp point of rocks. In a deep gully at its foot, a stream went surgin' over rapids; the bank on the side towards the hill was, may be, twenty feet high, and a right up and down ledge. Above this ledge, and between it and the rocky point, was a narrow path, only three or four feet wide, that turned short around the end of the hill. On the left hand was the ledge, and at the bottom of it were broken rocks, and on the right was a bluff point of rocks, that made up the end of the hill, standin' straight up, may be, fifty feet. Around this point, the path turned sharp almost as your elbow.

"I was passin' quietly round this pint, lookin' down into the gully, with Crop at my heels, when, on turnin' the short elbow, there I stood, face to face, and within ten feet of a mighty big bear, that was travellin' my way, as the Judge said. I had no idee that he was around, and I'm quite sartain he didn't expect to meet a human in such a place. Of course, we were naterally astonished at seein' one another just then, and the meetin' didn't seem to be altogether agreeable to either party. I ain't easily scared when I've time to prepare for a scrimmage, yet, I'm free to say, I'd have given a couple of wolf-scalps to've been on the other side of the gully, just at that time. The bear seemed to expect me to begin the fight, for, after gruntin' out in a very oncivil way his surprise at makin' my acquaintance, he reared himself up on eend, and, with a fierce growl, showed a set of ivory that wasn't pleasant to look at. I should have been willin' myself, to've backed down, and apologized for my rudeness in crossin' his path, for I was carryin' my rifle carelessly in my left hand, and our meetin' was so sudden that I scarcely had time to bring it to bear upon the kritter. I rather think I should have dodged back, any how, but Crop seemed to think his master was in danger, and that he was obligated, live or die, to go in. So, quick as a flash, he rushed by me, and threw himself into the very face of the desperate brute. Crop made a great mistake when he calculated he was a match for that bear, for, with one cuff, the animal sent him eend over eend down the bank, upon the broken rocks below. But the little time that was so occupied saved me a deal of trouble and danger, for it lasted just long enough for me to bring my rifle into position, which I did about the quickest, you may bet your life on that. I run my eye along the barrel, sighted him between the eyes, and pulled. The bear keeled over onto his back with a jerk, gave a spiteful kick with both hind feet, and he, too, went over the ledge onto the sharp rocks below. I looked over, and saw Crop staggerin' to his feet, and lookin' about in a bewildered way, as if not quite understandin' how he came there. I went round a little way, and got down into the gully where the animals were. I found the bear stone dead, and Crop with two ribs broken and his shoulder out of joint, whinin', and moanin' piteously with pain. I set his shoulder as well as I could, and, after takin' the skin off the bear, I backed him two miles to my shanty. It was a fortnight before he 'left the house,' but he learned a little piece of wisdom by that cuff that sent him down the bank, and got a little insight into the nater of an angry bear."

CHAPTER XX.

THE CHASE ON THE ISLAND--THE CHASE IN THE LAKE--THE BEAR--GAMBLING FOR GLORY--ANECDOTE OF NOAH AND THE GENTLEMAN WHO

OFFERED TO OFFICIATE AS PILOT ON BOARD THE ARK.

We had as yet had no use for our dogs since we left the Saranac. They had travelled quietly with us as we moved from place to place, or stayed inactive at the tents while we remained stationary. The game was so abundant, that the real difficulty was to restrain ourselves from destroying more than was needful for our use. We had indeed, failed to live strictly up to the law we had imposed upon ourselves, for we had at all times trout and venison beyond our present wants, excusing ourselves on the ground that an excess of supply was always preferable to a scant commissariat. More than one deer was slaughtered, if the truth must be told, for no better reason than that given by an Irishman for smashing a bald head he chanced to see at a window: it presented a mark too tempting to be resisted the lake from our camping ground. We stationed two of our boats between the island and the shore nearest the main land, and the other on the opposite side, and sent Cullen upon the island to beat for game. It was scarcely five minutes, before the voices of the dogs broke upon the stillness of the morning, in a simultaneous and fierce cry, as if they had started the game suddenly, and fresh from his lair. Away they went in full cry across the island, the deer sweeping around the upper end, and returning on the opposite side, as if loth to take to the water; but true to their instincts, the hounds followed, making the hills and the old woods ring again with the music of their voices. Presently, a noble buck broke cover, directly opposite to where the Doctor and Smith's boat lay. As our object was rather to enjoy the music of the chase, than to capture the deer, they shouted and hallooed as he entered the water, and he wheeled back, and went tearing in huge affright through the woods, up the island again. Still the howling was upon his trail, and as he approached the upper end, he again took to the water, to be frightened back by Martin and myself, and with renewed energy he bounded across to a point stretching out into the lake on the opposite side. Here Spalding and Wood were stationed, and they, by their shouting, drove him back again to the thickets. By this time, the poor animal began to appreciate the full peril of his position, for turn where he would he found an enemy in front, while the cry of his pursuers followed him like his destiny. Thus far every effort to escape by taking to the water had failed, and he seemed to think, as Martin expressed it, that "day was breaking." He essayed it again on the land side, and was driven back by us, and thus he coursed three times round the island, until, in desperation, he plunged into the broad lake and struck boldly out for the opposite shore, three quarters of a mile distant. Spalding shouted to us, and when we rounded the headland, we saw that he and Wood had headed, and were driving him towards a small island, of less than half an acre, covered only with low bushes, half a mile down the lake. We did not propose to harm him, but we intended to drive him upon that little island, and by surrounding it, keep him there for a while by way of experimenting upon his fears, or rather as Martin said, "to see what he would do." As he approached the shore, he bounded upon the island, and tossing his head from side to side, as if looking for a place of concealment or escape. Finding none, he dashed across to the opposite side and plunged into the lake. He was met by the Doctor and Smith, and turned back. He rushed in another direction, across the island, to be headed by the boat in which I was seated, and again in another direction to be headed by Spalding. Thus met and driven back at every turn, he at last stationed himself on a high knoll, near the centre of the island, apparently expecting that the last struggle for life was to be made there. We rested upon our oars, making no noise, and watching his movements. The bushes were low, coming only up midside to the animal. He watched us latently for half an hour, tossing his head up and down, looking first at one, then at another, as if calculating from which the attack upon his life was to come. At last, as if overcome by weariness, or concluding that after all there was no real danger, he laid quietly down. In answer to his confidence in the harmlessness of our intentions, we rowed away back to the island where we started him. We had not reached it, however, when we saw him enter the water, and swim to the main land, and glad enough he seemed to be when he had regained the protection of his native forests.

We took our dogs from the island, and rowed to the broad channel of the inlet which enters the lake on the left hand side, as you look to the south. There are two of these inlets, which enter within a quarter of a mile of each other, each of which comes down from little lakes, or ponds, deeper in the wilderness. The one we entered flows in a tortuous course through a natural meadow, stretching away on either hand forty or fifty rods, to a dense forest of spruce, maple, and beech, above which gigantic pines stand stately and tall in their pride. Three miles from the lake, the hills approach each other, and the little river comes plunging down through a gorge, over shelving rocks, and around great boulders, as if mad with the obstructions piled up in its way.

As we approached these falls, Smith, who sat in the bow of the boat, motioned to the boatman to lay upon his oars, and pointed to an object partly concealed by some low bushes, forty or fifty rods in advance of us. Remaining perfectly still a moment, we saw a bear step out upon a boulder, look up and down the stream, and stretch his long nose out over the water, as if looking for a good place to cross the rapids. After scratching his ear with one of his hind feet, and his side with the other, he turned and walked deliberately from our sight into the forest. By this time, the boat with the dogs came in sight, and we beckoned its occupants to come to us. One of the hounds only had ever seen game of this kind. But Cullen declared that there was no game that they would not follow when once fairly laid on. We wanted that bear. It was the only one we had seen; indeed it was the only one I had ever seen wild in the forest. We went to the spot where we last saw him, and there in the sand, by the side of the boulder, was his great track, almost like a human foot. Cullen called the attention of the dogs to it, and hallooed them on. They took the scent cheerfully, and with a united and fierce cry they dashed away in pursuit. They had ran but a short distance, when they seemed to become stationary, and deep, quick baying succeeded the lengthened and ringing sound of their voices.

"Treed, by Moses!" cried Cullen, as he dashed forward, the rest of us following as fast as we could.

"Not too fast," said Martin, "not too fast. There's no hurry; he won't come down unless our noise frightens him. Let us go quietly; there's plenty of time. Belcher has got his eye on him, and will stay by him till we come." We travelled quietly, and as silently as we could for near half a mile, and as we rounded a low but steep point of a hill, there sat bruin, some twelve rods from us, in the forks of a great birch tree, forty feet from the ground, looking down in calm dignity upon the dogs that were baying and leaping up against the tree beneath him. Did anybody ever notice what a meek, innocent look a bear has when in repose? How hypocritically he leers upon everything about him, as if butter would not melt in his mouth? Well, such was the look of that bear, as he peered out first on one side, then on the other of the great limbs between which he was sitting, secure, as he supposed, from danger. But he was never more mistaken in his life. In watching the dogs he had failed to discover us. We agreed that three should fire upon him at once, reserving the fourth charge for whatever contingency might happen. Smith, the Doctor, and Spalding sighted him carefully, each with his rifle resting against the side of a tree, and blazed away, their guns sounding almost together. It was pitiful the scream of agony that bear sent up. It was almost human in its anguish. It went ringing through the woods, dying away at last almost in a human groan. After struggling and clasping his arms for a moment around the great branch of the tree, his hold relaxed, he reeled from side to side, and then fell heavily to the ground, with three balls within an inch of each other, right through his vitals. He was larger than a medium sized animal of his species, and in excellent case.

The next thing in order was to transport him to our boats. This was done by tying his feet together, then running a long pole, cut for the purpose, between them, and lifting each end upon the shoulder of a boatman, he was "strung up," as Allen expressed it, clear from the ground. They stumbled along as best they could, over the rough ground, and through the tangle brush, towards the river. It was a heavy load considering the unevenness of the path, and the men were compelled to halt every few rods to breathe. We got him safely to the landing at last, and tumbling him into the bottom of one of the boats, started down stream towards our shanty. A proud trio were Spalding, Smith, and the Doctor that afternoon, returning with their game across the lake; and they certainly had some occasion to congratulate themselves, for this was the first wild, uncaged bear either of us had ever seen, and him they had succeeded in capturing.

We dined that afternoon on a roasted sirloin of bear, stewed jerked venison, fried trout, and pork. I cannot say that I altogether relished the roast, though some of our company took to it hugely. The truth is, that with some of them venison and trout were beginning to be somewhat stale dishes, they did not relish fat pork, and a change therefore to roasted bear meat was peculiarly acceptable.

"Gentlemen," said Smith to the Doctor and Spalding, as we sat after our meal, enjoying our pipes, "what say you to selling out your interest in that bear? If you're open for a bargain, I'll make you a proposition."

"Why," the Doctor replied, "there'll be nothing left but the skin, and that will be of no special value except as a trophy."

"Not exactly," resumed Smith. "I'll deal frankly with you, gentlemen. There'll be a good many stories to be told about the killing of that bear, and my object is to appropriate the glory of the achievement. Now it wont be a matter to boast of, to say that we three fired into one bear, and that none of the largest."

"Oh! as to that," said the Doctor, "I intend to enlarge upon the subject, exaggerating the size of the bear, describing the terrible conflict I had with him, how I happened to save myself by remembering my double-barrelled pistol; how I made the three ball holes in him, while you and Spalding were running away, and how he bit me in the arm, and almost hugged me to death, while I was trying to get at the pistol. I shall shine in that bear story! Yes! yes! I shall shine!"

"Hear the cormorant!" exclaimed Smith. "Hear him! And he'll do precisely as he says he will, only a great deal worse. We must buy him out, Spalding. We must purchase his silence for our own credit."

"Well, gentlemen," replied Spalding, "settle it between you--you are welcome to my share of the achievement. The scream of mortal agony which that bear sent up when our three balls went crashing through its body rings in my ears yet. I don't feel quite so proud of the shot as I otherwise should have done. You are welcome to my share of the glory."

"Spoken like a liberal and free-hearted gentleman," said Smith. "Well, Doctor, name the amount and nature of the blackmail you intend to levy upon me. But have a conscience, man! have a conscience!"

"It will be making a great sacrifice on my part," the Doctor replied, "but out of friendship for you, I'll make you a proposition. We'll toss op a dollar, and the one that wins shall have the honour of having killed the bear, and of telling the story in his own way, and the others shall indorse it."

"Agreed," said Smith, "but if you win, I shall have to borrow a conscience of Spalding, or some other lawyer, for there'll be need of a pretty elastic one."

"Yours will answer, I think," drily remarked Spalding.

"It appears to me, gentlemen," said I "that I've something to say about the killing of that bear."

"You," exclaimed the Doctor, "what had you to do with it, pray? There stands your rifle, with the same ball in it that you placed there this morning. You haven't discharged your rifle to-day."

"Notwithstanding that," I replied, "I am entitled to a portion of the glory, as I am chargeable with my share of the responsibility, of killing the bear. I was one of the first who discovered him; I was among the foremost in the pursuit; I was present, aiding and advising in the manner of the killing; I had my weapon in my hand, and was restrained from using it, only because you might fail to accomplish what my reserved bullet would have made secure. Now, if this bear had been human, and we were accused of killing him, I would be regarded in the eye of the law as equally guilty with you. I appeal to Spalding if this is not so?"

"H----is right," replied Spalding, as he sent a column of smoke wreathing upward from his lips. "Such is the law."

"We must buy this fellow off, Smith," said the Doctor, "we must buy him off. He's an old hunter, known as such, and he'll take to himself all the glory; and what is worse, the world will believe him. He'll spread himself beyond all bounds. He'll shine beyond endurance upon the strength of this bear. We must buy him off. It is against all conscience, but there is no help for it. We must buy him off. There's an impudence in this claim which reminds me of an anecdote related by Noah."

"By Noah?" asked Smith, interrupting him, "Noah who?"

"What ignorance there is in this world, even in these days of educational enlightenment!" remarked the Doctor to Spalding and myself. "Now, here is a decently informed gentleman, claiming to be a Christian man, to have studied the Bible, and don't know who Noah was. Such an instance of human ignorance in these times, is shocking."

"Oh! I understand now," said Smith, "he was the gentleman who built the ark. Well, go on with your anecdote."

"Well, as I was saying," the Doctor resumed, "this claim of H----'s to a share of the glory of slaying the bear, reminds me of an anecdote related by Noah soon after the subsidence of the flood, and it shows that impudence is, at least, not postdeluvian in its origin. It seems that there were in the world before, as well as after the flood, some very meddling impudent fellows, who were always interfering with other people's business, claiming a share of other people's credit, trying to make the world believe that they were great things, and persuading everybody that whatever remarkable achievement was accomplished, occurred through their counsel and advice, and as a consequence, claiming a large share of all the honors going.

"Well, after the rain had continued falling for a number of days, and the valleys were all full of water, and the angry surges went roaring, with the voice of ten thousand thunders, high up along the sides of the hills, one of these pestilent fellows--deriding the miraculous exhibition going on all around him--undertook, in his self-conceit, to lead the people to a place of safety. So he selected a lofty peak that shot up from a range of mountains, and commenced travelling up its steep acclivities. But the flood followed him, roaring, and boiling, and heaving, in its onward rush. Day by day, night by night, it crept up, and up, higher and higher, until the self-confident leader, who scoffed at the supernatural warning, had but a mighty small place above the surge, whereon to shelter himself from the destruction that surrounded him. About that time the Ark, with Noah and his people, all safe and snug, came drifting that way.

"'Halloo!' says the occupant of the rock, 'send us a boat, and take us aboard. The freshet is getting pretty bad, and it is getting a little damp, up here.'

"'I can't do it,' says Noah, 'my craft is full of better people.'

"'But,' says the applicant for admission into the Ark, 'let me in, and I'll superintend the navigation. I'll man the wheel, and see that the sails are all right, and we can pick up a deal of floating plunder as we go along.'

"'Can't do it,' says Noah, 'we've got a good steersman and safe navigators on board already.'

"'Well,' says the applicant, 'I'll work my passage as a deck hand, asking only a small portion of such spoils as we may pick up. Come, bring us aboard.'

"'Can't do it,' says Noah, 'can't think of such a thing."

"'Then,' said the persevering applicant for a passage in the Ark, 'I'll go along for nothing--giving the benefit of my counsel and assistance free gratis; more than all that, I'll stand the liquor all round.'

"'No use in talking,' says Noah, 'you can't come on board of my craft, on any terms. You'd corrupt my people, and set them by the ears in a week. You can't have a berth on any conditions. Good-bye!'

"'Then go to thunder with your old Ark,' indignantly responded the occupant of the rock, 'I don't believe there's going to be much of a shower, after all.'

"In a day or two, Noah drifted that way again. The mountain peak had disappeared beneath the waters, and the occupants were all gone." "I give up my claim," said I, "Doctor, in consideration of your anecdote. Take the glory of killing the bear. I see you're not disposed to give me a place in your Ark. So toss up the dollar."

The dollar was tossed up, and Smith won the glory.

CHAPTER XXI.
THE DOCTOR AND HIS WIFE ON A FISHING EXCURSION--THE LAW OF THE CASE--STRONG-MINDED WOMEN.

The right to the glory of having killed the bear being settled, the Doctor, addressing himself to Spalding, remarked--"There was something in H----'s appeal to you about the law of his case, that reminded me of a little scene between my wife and myself, many years ago, when we were both younger than we are now, and certainly had never anticipated the dark years of trial, through which we were unexpectedly called upon to pass. You know that I started in life, like Smith here, a gentleman of fortune, calculating, like him, to live at my ease, without troubling myself with the cares of any particular business, as I passed along. Still I thought, or rather my father thought, that it would be well enough, even for a gentleman, to have at least a nominal title to some profession. So I studied the law, and was admitted as an attorney and counsellor of the courts. Never intending to practise, I did not become very profoundly learned in the profession; still I became, to some extent, indoctrinated with its mysteries. I did not like it; and when the necessity for some active employment came looming up in the distance, I chose a different calling, and at six-and-twenty, commenced the study of my present profession. This did not occur until after I had been married some three years. I lived in the country then, or rather, summered there, in a beautiful little village in the interior of the State, in a pleasant, old-fashioned house, which my father built, and which, as I was his only heir, I supposed of course I owned. Some half a dozen miles from the village was a fine trout stream, to which my wife and myself used occasionally to go on a fishing excursion. On such occasions we went on horseback, as the road was somewhat rough, and my wife was as much at home in the saddle as I was. This, I repeat, was a good while ago, and we were both a score of years younger than we are now. Well, I started out alone one day to visit this trout stream, anticipating a good time with its speckled, and usually greedy inhabitants. I say I was alone, and yet there was with me, all the way, and all the time, one who can talk, reason, philosophise, understand things as well as you or I; and one, to all appearance, as much and distinctly human as you or I."

"Impossible!" exclaimed Smith, "we can't go that, Doctor. I can't stand my quarter of that."

"Foolish man!" continued the Doctor; "I say I was alone; let me demonstrate my proposition. Blackstone says, and what he says every lawyer will concede is the end of the law, and the beginning too, for that matter, that when a woman becomes a wife, she loses her identity, becomes nobody; that her husband absorbs her existence, as it were, as he does her goods and chattels, in his own. Now, sir, do you comprehend? My wife was with me, and she, being according to law nobody, of course I was alone. You, sir, being a law abiding man, must admit that my proposition is Q.E.D.

"The doctrine of absorption, as I call it, is convenient. It promotes harmony of action, by subjecting it to the control of a single will, thus avoiding all embarrassment from a conflict of opinion between man and wife. So, on my way to the trout stream (I say *my* way, for though my wife was on horseback by my side, yet she being, according to the best legal authorities, nobody, you see I was alone), I thought I would enlighten the good lady in regard to the true position, or rather the no position at all, which she occupied. Our way lay for a couple of miles along an old road, towards a clearing which had been abandoned, and through which the stream flowed. The tall old trees spread their long arms over us, clothed in the rich verdure of spring, and the breeze, so fresh and fragrant, moaned, and sighed, and whispered among the leaves.

"'My dear,' said I, blandly, as we rode along, the birds singing merrily among the branches above us, 'do you know that you are NOBODY?'

"'Nobody, Mr. W----,' (I was simply Mr. W----then; I had not become, nor even dreamed that I should become a Doctor), 'Nobody, Mr. W----? Did you say nobody?'

"'Absolutely nobody,' said I. 'A perfect nonentity. You are less even than a legal fiction.'

"'Look you,' said she, as she applied the whip to her pony, in a way that brought him, with a bound, across the road directly in front of me (she rode like a belted knight), obstructing my progress, 'Look you, Mr. W----,' and there was a red spot on her cheek, and her eye sparkled like the sheen of a diamond, 'let us settle this matter now. I can bear being of small consideration, occupying very little space in the world, but to be stricken out of existence entirely, to possess no legal identity, to be regarded as absolutely nobody, is a thing I don't intend to stand--mark that, Mr. W----.'

"'Keep cool, my dear,' said I; 'let us argue this matter.' I was calm, for I knew the law was on my side; I had the books, and the courts, and the statutes all in my favor. I was fortified, you see.

"'Argue the matter!' she exclaimed; 'not till it is admitted that I'm somebody. If I'm nobody, I can't be argued with, I can't reason, nor talk. Now, Mr. W----, I've a tongue.'

"'Gospel truth,' said I, 'whatever the authorities may say. But we will admit, for the sake of the argument, that you are somebody; Blackstone says'----

"'Out on Blackstone,' she exclaimed; 'what do I care for Blackstone, whose bones have been mouldering in the grave for more than a hundred years, for what I know. Don't talk to me about Blackstone.'

"'But, my dear, you are *my* wife, and Blackstone says'--

"'I don't care a fig what Blackstone says. If I *am* your wife, I am my mother's daughter, and my brother's sister, and Tommy's mother, and there are four distinct individualities all centered in myself.'

"'But,' said I again, 'Blackstone says'--

"'Confound that Blackstone,' she exclaimed; 'I do believe he has driven the wits out of the man's head. Now, look you, Mr. W----, you invited me to ride with you; you now say I am nobody. Very well. If nobody leaves you, I suppose you won't be without company, for somebody certainly left home with you this morning, and has rode with you thus far. So, good-bye, Mr. W----; success to your fishing, Mr. W----,' and she struck into a gallop towards home.

"'Hallo!' said I, 'I give up the point. I take back all I said. *Culpa mea*, my good wife. If Blackstone does say'--

"'Not a word more about Blackstone,' said she, shaking her whip, half serious half playfully, at me; 'if I go with you, I go as somebody--a legal entity.'

"'Very well,' said I, 'we'll drop the argument.'

"'Not the argument, but the fact, Mr. W----; and admit that Blackstone was a goose, and that his law, like his logic, is all nonsense when measured by the standard of common sense and practical fact. Admit that a woman, when she becomes a wife does not become a mere nonentity, or I leave you to journey alone.'

"'Very well, my dear, let us see if we cannot compromise this matter. Suppose we allow his philosophy to stand as a general truth, making you an exception. We'll say that wives in general are nobody, but that you shall be exempt from the general rule, and be considered always hereafter, and as between ourselves, as somebody.'

"You see the shrewdness of my proposition. Firstly, it saved Blackstone; secondly, it saved *me*, let me down easy; and thirdly, it appealed to the womanly vanity of my wife, and it took.

"'Oh, well,' she said, as she brought her pony alongside of me, and we jogged along cosily together, 'I see no objection to that. Other wives can take care of themselves. But this compromise, as between *us*, Mr. W----, must be a *finality*. No Nebraska traps, Mr. W----. No Kansas bills hereafter. It must be a finality, mind.'

"'Very well,' said I; and a robin that was building its nest on a limb that hung over the road, paused in its labors, and burst into song, and the burden of its lay seemed to be a compromise, which, in truth, should be a FINALITY.

"We were successful in our fishing, and we followed the old-fashioned custom as to bait. We discarded the fly, using only the angle-worm. At the foot of the ripples; under the old logs; where the water went whirling under the cavernous banks; in the eddies; among the driftwood; everywhere, we found trout--not large, none weighing over six ounces, and few less than three. We caught my basket full in less then two hours, and then rode home. It was a day of enjoyment to us, you may be sure.

"And now I appeal to you, in all seriousness, my friend," the Doctor continued, addressing himself to Spalding, "if there is not something due to the wives and mothers of the present generation? Is there not some relaxation of the law necessary in vindication of the civilization of the age, against the legal barbarisms still remaining on the statute books, and adhered to by the common law, in regard to wives and mothers? Is the current of progress to flow by them for ever, bearing no reforms which shall affect them? Do not misunderstand me. I am no advocate of the practices of the 'strong-minded women,' who hold their conventions and public meetings, who unsex themselves by mounting the forum, and, throwing off the retiring modesty of the true woman, seek to secure notoriety at the price of popular contempt. But there are evils which bear heavily, too heavily, upon the women even of this country, and which, for the credit of the civilization of the age, should be corrected. As calm-minded, philanthropic men, we, the American people, should look into this subject, and, regardless of jeer and scoff, do what justice, humanity, and the right demand of us, in regard to some of the social and legal inequalities between the sexes, pertaining to the married state."

"It is one of the mysteries of our system of jurisprudence," replied Spalding, "that while everything else is on the move, while progress is written in letters of living light upon all other things, that remains stationary--at least in a comparative sense. The world moves on, civilization advances, science and the arts stride forward, but the law stands still. A principle which may have been somewhat changed, modified, bent, if you please, into an adaptation to the exigencies of the present, and a fitness for the changed circumstances of the times in which we live, is suddenly thrown back into its old position by the exhumation of some 'decision' from the dust of ages, made by some judge away back in the olden times, resurrected by the research of some antiquarian lawyer, who loves to delve among the rubbish of past generations. The learning, the wisdom, the philosophy of the present is discarded, and the spirits of a lower civilization are conjured from the darkness of vanished centuries, to settle rules for the government of commerce, personal conduct, and the social relations of the times in which we live. There seems to be something paradoxical in the idea that the older the decision the better the law--the more ancient the commentator, the profounder the wisdom of his axioms. This might be well, were it true that civilization is 'progressing backwards,' the science of government retrograding. In that case, it would of course be true, that the nearer you approach the fountain, the purer the stream would be. But such is not the fact. In all these attributes the world is on the advance, the science of government progressive; and to make the wisdom of centuries ago override the wisdom, or overshadow the light of the present, is a paradox peculiar to our system of jurisprudence. There are lawyers and judges, who enjoy a high reputation, whose fame rests upon their profound research among the worm-eaten tomes of black-letter law, and whose glory consists in their familiarity with the opinions and axioms of men who lived and died so long ago that their very tombs are forgotten. This class of lawyers and jurists hold in contempt all the learning, the philosophy, the practical wisdom of the present --rejecting everything that is not bearded and hoary with age. Seated in their libraries, in the midst of their ponderous octavos, their Roman and black-letter volumes, they reject with disdain the commentators, the opinions of the jurists of the present century; and brushing away the cobwebs and dust from the covers of their treasured relics of bygone ages, they clasp them in a loving embrace close to their hearts, exclaiming, 'These are my jewels.' Whatever has not the sanction of ancient authority, is folly to them--worse than folly, for it is innovation, and that is rank impiety.

"I remember an anecdote of the celebrated William Wirt, related to show how ready his mind was, how instant in activity, and how suddenly it would flash with an eloquence, superior to that exhibited by the most elaborate preparation. He was arguing a cause before the Supreme Court of the United States, and laid down, as the basis of his argument, a principle to which he desired to call the particular attention of the judges. The opposing counsel interrupted him, calling for the authority sustaining his principle,--'The book--the book!' demanded his adversary. 'Sir, and your honors,' said Wirt, straightening himself up to his full height, 'I am not bound to grope my way among the ruins of antiquity, to stumble over obsolete statutes, or delve in black letter law, in search of a principle written in living letters upon the heart of every man.' If the idea contained in this answer of Wirt, were more fully appreciated by our modern jurists, it would be all the better for the country.

"The common law is said to be the perfection of reason. This is doubtless true, but it is the perfection of the reason of the present, as well as of the past. Its principles are elastic, suiting themselves to the civilization of all ages. They are progressive, keeping pace with the progress of all times. They are not immutable, save in the element of right, and they therefore shape themselves to all circumstances, moving along with the onward march of trade, the commerce, the social relations, and business of the people. The learning of to-day, the wisdom, the philosophy of to-day is profounder than that of any preceding century, and it is folly to overthrow it by, or compel it to give place to, the learning, the wisdom, the philosophy of departed and ruder ages.

"In regard to your question, whether there is not some relaxation of the law necessary, in vindication of the civilization of the age, against the legal barbarisms remaining upon the statute book, and in the common law in regard to our wives, I answer frankly that I do not know about that. The law, as you read it in Blackstone, and as you expounded it to your wife, on your fishing excursion, has been somewhat modified. Wives have been given a ***status*** by modern legislation; and a woman, by becoming a wife, does not now cease to be a legal entity. The law permits her to retain and control her property irrespective of her husband, and she has, therefore, thus far, ceased to be 'nobody.' But my private opinion is, that, as a general thing, the women of this country get along very well, even under the pressure of the 'barbarisms' of which you speak. They manage, one way and another, to get the upper hand of their legal lords, law or no law. If their existence, in the light of authority, is 'less than a legal fiction,' they come to be regarded, or make themselves felt in the world as practical facts. They are quite as apt to be at the top, as at the bottom of the ladder, notwithstanding what 'Blackstone says' about their legal position. There is, doubtless, a good deal of abuse of authority on the part of husbands, but the women get their share of the good that is going in the world, as a general thing. If the law is against them, they manage to usurp full an even amount of privilege and authority, and keep along about in line with the other sex. I never knew an out and out controversy between a man and his wife, in which the former did not get the worst of it in the end; and as to the impositions, which as a melancholy truth are too frequent, they are about as much on one side as the other. It is not to legal enactments that we must look for the cure of unhappiness incident to the married state, but to a reform in temper and habits of life. Besides, I do not believe the wives of this country would accept of a strict legal equality at all, if it were tendered them as a FINALITY. I believe they would prefer remaining as they are; for by being so, they are left to the resources of their own genius, to win by their tact, what is not guaranteed by law. I know that there are a good many crazy-headed people in pantaloons as well as petticoats, who go about laboring for the 'emancipation of women,' as if the heavens and earth were coming together. But those of them who wear skirts, generally have delicate white hands, flowing curls, flashing black eyes, and the gift of oratory--and a desire to exhibit them all; while those in pantaloons have their hair combed smoothly back, as if preparing to be swallowed by a boa-constrictor, wear white cravats, talk softly, and show a good deal of the whites of their eyes, from a chronic habit of looking up towards the moon and stars. As a general thing, these latter are of no practical use in the world, and make as good a tail to the kite of the 'strong-minded women' as anything else. But these people represent a very small portion of the American women, and until the masses demand 'emancipation,' I rather think that matters had better be permitted to remain as they are. The women will take care of themselves--no fear of that."

CHAPTER XXII.
A BEAUTIFUL FLOWER--A NEW LAKE--A MOOSE--HIS CAPTURE--A SUMPTUOUS DINNER.

We started the next morning on an exploring voyage up the right-hand stream, which enters this beautiful lake some half a mile west of the one we had looked into the day before. On either hand, as we passed along the narrow channel, was a natural meadow, covered with a luxuriant growth of rank grass and weeds, conspicuous among which was a beautiful flower, the like of which I have never seen anywhere else. I am no botanist, and therefore cannot describe it in the language of the florist, so that the learned in that beautiful science might classify it. It resembles somewhat the wild lily in shape, growing upon a tall, strong stem, almost like the stem of the flag. The flower itself is double, and its deep crimson--the deepest almost of any flower I have ever seen--shone conspicuously, as it waved gracefully in the breeze above the surrounding vegetation. It has one defect, however; it is without fragrance, I infer from the fact that its roots spread far out every way, and reach down into the water beneath, that it can hardly be transferred to the garden, or become civilized. It would be a great acquisition to the collection of the florist if it could, for I know of no flower that excels it in richness of color, gracefulness of appearance, or in gorgeousness of beauty.

We saw abundance of deer feeding quietly upon the narrow meadows, and upon the lily pads on our way. We had no inclination to injure them, and we let them feed on. Some of them were hugely astonished, however, at our presence, and dashed away, whistling and snorting, into the forest. Two miles from the lake, we came to a rocky barrier, down which the stream, came rushing and roaring, for fifty or sixty rods, in a descent of perhaps sixty feet in all. Around these rapids the boats were carried, and we found, above them, the water deep and sluggish, flowing through a dense forest, the tall trees on the banks stretching their leafy arms across the narrow channel, forming above it an arch delightfully cool, through which the sunlight could scarcely penetrate. We followed this channel a long way, when we came to a little lake or pond, four or five miles in circumference. It was a perfect gem, laying there all alone, so calm, so lovely in its solitude, with no sign of civilization around it, no sound of civilization startling its echoes from their sleep of ages, no human voice having perhaps ever been heard upon its shore since the red man departed from the hunting-ground of his fathers. The shores all around it were bold and rocky, save on the western side, where a broad sandy beach, of a quarter of a mile in extent, lay between the water and the shadow of the deep forest beyond. A solitary island of half a dozen acres, covered with majestic pines and tall, straight spruce trees, rises near the centre of the lake, adding a new charm to its quiet beauty. The waters of this little lake are clearer and more transparent than those of any other we had seen; we could see the white shells on its sandy bottom, fifteen feet below the surface. This peculiarity induced us to believe that we were above the stratum of iron ore which seems to underlay most of this wild region, coloring, while it does not render impure, the waters of most of these lakes and rivers. I have frequently, in my wanderings in these northern wilds, stumbled upon outcropping orebeds, which, were they nearer market, or more accessible to the energy and enterprise of the American people, would be capable of building up gigantic fortunes, but they are all valueless here, and probably will continue so for generations to come.

We saw the fresh tracks of a moose on the sandy beach, tracks that had been made that morning, and we concluded to spend the day here, in the hope of securing one of these gigantic deer. We rowed to the island, intending to encamp there. We entered a little bay, of half an acre, the points forming it coming within a few yards of each other, and the branches of the trees intertwining their long arms lovingly above. As we landed, our dogs began nosing and dashing about, as if suddenly roused into excitement by the hot scent of some animal that had been disturbed by our coming. They broke into a simultaneous cry, and plunged like mad into the thicket. We pushed our boat back towards the open water, when we heard the plunge of some animal into the lake, on the other side of the island. Martin, who was in the leading boat with me, by a few vigorous pulls at the oar, rounded the point between us and the spot where we had heard the plunge, and there, not ten rods from the shore, making for the mainland, was the game which, of all others, we most desired to see.

"A moose! by Moses!" exclaimed Martin, in huge excitement. "Hurrah! hurrah! A moose! he's ours! he can't escape!" and away he dashed in pursuit. The other boats now hove in sight, and a loud hurrah! went up from each, when they saw the nature of the game that had been started. There was no difficulty in overtaking the animal, desperate as were his efforts to escape. We shot past him, and turned him back in a direction towards the island again, and I picked up my rifle to settle the matter.

"Don't shoot him," said Martin; "don't shoot him yet; he can't get away, and if you kill him, he'll sink; and if he don't, we can't get him into the boat. Let us drive him back to the island." The other boats were, by this time, up with us, every man in a wild state of excitement, eager to be first in at the death. We had headed the animal towards the island, with our three boats so arranged, as that he could swim in no other direction, without running one of them down. The dogs had started a deer that had taken to the water, on the other side of the island.

"Look here!" said I; "gentlemen, this game is mine. I claim him by right of discovery, and my right must not be interfered with."

"Very well," the Doctor answered, "we'll only take a hand in his capture if he's likely to escape. So, go ahead."

As we came within a few yards of the shore, and we could see that the animal's hoofs touched the bottom, I aimed carefully at his head, and fired. He made one desperate lunge forward, and turned over on his side, dying with scarcely a straggle, the ball having passed directly through his brain.

This was the first and only live moose I have ever seen. He was not a large one, being, probably, a three-year-old, but well-grown. We should have called him a monster, had we not, before that time, seen in various museums the stuffed skins of those a quarter or a third larger. He would have weighed, as shot, probably between five and six hundred pounds. He had made this solitary island his home, as we ascertained by his spoor and other signs that we found upon subsequent explorations. We saw his bed but a few rods from where we landed, and from which our dogs had aroused him, though they, in their excitement, had overrun his scent, and dashed off after a deer.

We had now accomplished one of the objects of our journey in this direction, and as the law we had imposed upon ourselves had reached its limits, prohibiting our shooting another moose that day, even should an opportunity occur, we concluded to return to our shanty, on the lake below. We, therefore, dressed our moose, and taking with us the skin and hind quarters, started down stream to a late dinner on Little Tupper's Lake. Indeed, there was a sort of necessity for our doing so. We had left our provisions there, calculating to return in the afternoon, not having taken with us even pepper or salt, wherewith to season the food which, upon constraint, we might cook during our absence. A few crackers, in the pockets of each, was all, in the provision line, that we had provided ourselves with, and though, when we saw the moose-tracks in the sand, we had concluded to rough it, for a single night, for the chance of securing such rare game, yet having secured it, that part of our mission was accomplished, and we turned towards home.

On our return to the lake, Spalding and myself rowed across to the mouth of a cold brook, to procure a supply of fresh trout, upon which, with our moose and bear-meat, to dine. This we soon accomplished, and on our arrival home, we found huge pieces of moose and bear roasting before a blazing fire. The meat was supported upon long sticks, one end of which was sharpened, and the meat spitted upon it, and the other thrust into the ground, in a slanting direction, so as to bring the roasting pieces into a proper position before the fire. The meat was removed occasionally, and turned, until the roasting process was completed, and then served up on clean birch bark, just peeled from the trees, in the place of platters. We had tin plates, knives, and forks, with us, also a tea-kettle, tin cups, and tea of the choicest quality, sugar, pepper, salt, and pork. The man who cannot make a meal where the viands present are moose-meat, bear, jerked venison, fresh trout, and pork, and for drink the best of tea and the purest and coldest spring water, had better keep out of the Rackett woods.

The people, whoever they were, who prepared the camp in which we were domiciled, had an eye to convenience and comfort. The shanty was built of logs, on three sides, the crevices between which were filled with moss, and the sloping roof neatly covered with bark, in layers, like an old-fashioned roof, covered with split shingles. The front was open, and directly before it was a rough fire-place, with jams, made of small boulders, laid up with clay, regularly-fashioned, as if intended for a kitchen. This fire-place was three or four feet high, and served an excellent purpose, with reference to our cookery, and the lighting of our shanty at night. It served, also, to conduct the smoke upward, and prevented it from being blown into our faces, as we sat in front, at once, of our sleeping-place and our camp-fire. The only things that reminded us of civilization, aside from what we carried with us, were the innumerable crickets that, through all the night, kept up their chirruping in the crevices of this rude fireplace. There was something old-fashioned and sociable in their song. These, with the shrill notes of the little peepers along the shore, were old sounds to us, familiar voices, and they fell pleasantly on the ear. We had finished our meal, and taken to our pipes in the evening, as the sun went down among the old forests, away off in the west. The greyness of twilight came stealing over the water, and grew into darkness in the beautiful valley where that lake lay sleeping. The stars stole out silently, and set their watch in the sky, and calmness and repose rested upon everything around us.

"I remember," said Smith, "the first year that I was in college, of hearing two learned professors disputing about what sort of animal it was that made the piping noise we hear in the marshy places, and stagnant pools, in the spring time, usually known as peepers. One insisted that it was a newt, or small lizard; and I remember that he went to his library, and brought a volume which proved his theory to be correct. The other denied the authority of the author, and insisted that the peeper was a frog. The discussion excited my curiosity, and I made up my mind to satisfy myself on the subject, if possible, by occular demonstration. There was a small marshy place, half a mile, or so, from the college grounds, from which I had heard, in my walks, the music of the peepers coming up every evening, in a loud and joyous chorus. I watched by it a number of evenings, and though there were a plenty of peepers, piping merrily enough, yet I could not get sight of one to save me. I began to think it was a myth, the viewless spirit of the bog, that made all the noises about which the learned professors had been disputing. At last, however, I got sight of a peeper, caught him in the act, and saw that it was, in fact, a little frog, nothing more, nothing less. He was not more than three feet from me, and though, when I moved, he hid himself in the muddy water, yet I managed to capture and take him home alive. He was a little animal, certainly, not larger than a half-dollar piece, and it was marvellous how a thing so small could make such a loud and piercing noise. I took him to my room, and placed him in a water-tight box, in which I fashioned an artificial bog, in the hope that he would confirm my testimony by his piping. The second evening, as I sat in my room, poring over the recitations of the morrow, he lifted up his voice, loud, shrill, and clear, as when singing in his native marsh. I hurried, in triumph, to the learned disputants about his identity, and in their presence, he furnished unanswerable evidence that the peeper was a frog, and not a newt. I was complimented by both the learned pundits, as though I had added a great item to the aggregate of human knowledge."

"You *did* do a great thing, my friend," said Spalding, "you solved a mystery about which men, wise in the learning of the books, had perhaps been disputing for centuries. What are the peepers? asked the naturalist, who listened to their piping notes from the marshy places in the spring time. It was a matter of small practical importance, what they were. Still it was a question which MIND wanted to have solved. Its solution would do no great amount of good to the world. But then it was a mystery which it was the business of mind to lay bare; and what more has science done in tracing the history and progress of this earth of ours, as written upon the rocks, among which geology has been so long delving? 'What are the peepers?' asked the naturalist. 'They are newts, little lizards,' answers a learned pandit. 'They are spirits of the bog, myths, that hold their carnival in the early grass of the marshy pools,' says the theorist and poet, who **believes** in the idealities of a poetic fancy. 'They are frogs,' says a third, who is ready to chop any amount of logic in favor of his system of frogology, and hereupon columns of argument, and pages of learned discussion, have been held over the identity of the jolly peepers of the spring-time.

"But you discarded logic, threw away argument, and came down to the sure demonstrations of sober fact. You watched by the marshy pool, and caught the 'peeper' in the act, took him '*in flagrante, delicto*,' as the lawyers say, and thus ended the theoretical discussion about the 'peepers.' You placed another fixed fact upon the page of natural history.

"And how often has the wisdom of the schools, the philosophy of the profoundest theorists, been overthrown by the simple demonstrations of practical facts? For a thousand years the world was in pursuit of the giant power that lay hidden in heated vapor, the steam that came floating up from boiling water. That power eluded the grasp and baffled the research of human genius, which was looking so earnestly after it, until ingenuity gave it up, and philosophy pronounced it a delusion. Not far from the beginning of the present century, practical experiment began to develop the mysterious power of steam. Rudely and imperfectly harnessed, at first, it still made the great wheel revolve, and men talked about making it a great motor for mechanical purposes. Philosophy volunteered its demonstrations of the absolute impossibility of such a thing. Still human ingenuity felt its way carefully onward, until the great fact was developed, that steam was in truth capable of moving machinery, was endowed almost with vitality, and could be made to throw the shuttle and spin. Ingenious men hinted that it might be made to propel water-craft in the place of wind and sails, and thus be harnessed into the service of commerce, as it had already been into that of manufactures. Here again philosophy interposed its axioms, and declared the scheme among the wild vagaries of a distempered fancy. But years rolled on, and the tall ship that swung out upon the broad ocean, and moved forward when the air was still and calmness was on the face of the deep, forward in the eye of the wind--forward in the teeth of the storm, that stopped not for billow or blast, gave the lie to philosophy, and scattered the theory of the wise like chaff.

"The lightning, that fierce spirit of the storm, that darted down on its mission of destruction from the black cloud floating in the sky, became a thing of interest to the mechanical world, and the question was asked, 'Why cannot the lightning be harnessed into the service of man, and be made utilitarian?' Philosophy sneered at the wild delusion, but see how that same subtle and mysterious agency has been conquered? Note how truthfully it carries every word intrusted to its charge, along thousands of miles of the telegraph wire, with a speed, in comparison with which, sound is a laggard, a speed that annihilates alike space and time. Men looked into a mirror, and seeing their own counterpart, a *fac-simile* of themselves reflected there, began to ask, 'Why may not that shadow be fixed; fastened in some way, to remain upon the polished surface that gives it back, even after the original may be mouldering in the grave?' Here again philosophy laid its finger upon its nose, and winked facetiously, as if it had found a new subject for ridicule, in the stupendous folly of such an inquiry. But from that simple question, rose up the Daguerreian art; an art which fixes upon metallic plates, upon paper, the shadow of a man, of palace and cottage, of mountain and field, giving thus a picture ten thousand times truer to nature than the pencil of the cunningest artist. These and a thousand other mighty triumphs of human ingenuity have fought their way onward to their present position, against the fogyism of philosophy, the inertia of the schoolmen. They have been the sequence of cold, resistless demonstrations of experiment and fact. The world would stand still but for the spirit of research for the practical; for experimental, and not theoretical knowledge, that is abroad. It is this spirit that moves the world in all its present matchless career of progress, and distinguishes our era above all others of the world's existence. You may be thankful, my friend, that you have been able to add another fixed fact to the stock of human knowledge, even though it be only that the 'peeper' is a frog, and not a 'newt' or a 'myth.'

"But who would suppose that such a tiny little frogling could make such a loud, shrill, and ear-piercing sound? Who would think that a million of such puny things, could make the air of a summer evening so full of the music of their songs? I remember how, in my boyhood, I listened to their voices, which came up loudest, shrillest, merriest, when twilight was spreading its grey mantle over the earth;

while the song of the birds was hushing into silence, and the coming darkness was lulling the things of the day into repose; Oh! how merrily they sang along the little brooklet that took its rise in a spring in the meadow, and wended its way among the young grass, just springing into verdure, to the beautiful lake beyond. Their song is in my ear now, and that meadow, that beautiful lake, the tall hills on the summits of which the departing sunlight lingered, the tall maples that clustered in their cone-like beauty around that gushing fountain, the clustered plum trees, the giant oak, spared by the woodman's axe when the old forest was swept away, the fields, the 'Gulf' in the hill-side, and the beautiful creek, that came cascading down the shelving rocks, and leaping over precipices in which the speckled trout sported: all these are before me now--a vision of loveliness, all the more dear because stamped upon the memory when life was young. Oh! Time! Time! the wrecks that lie scattered in thy pathway! That little brooklet, and the peepers, the fountain, the maples, and the meadow, are all gone. The brave old oak was riven by the lightning. The fields have crept up to the very summit of the hills, and even the stream that came down from the mountain has vanished away, save when the rains, or the melting snows send it in a freshet over the rocks where, when I was a boy, it was cascading always. That beautiful meadow, too, is gone, and the streets of a modern village, with blocks of houses, and stores, and shops, occupy the place where I swung my first scythe. The old log-house vanished years and years ago. A steamboat ploughs its way through that beautiful lake, and the things of my boyhood are but visions of memory, called up from the long, long past. Not one landmark of the olden time remains. Oh! Time! Time!"

CHAPTER XXIII.
THE CRICKET IN THE WALL--THE MINISTER'S ILLUSTRATION--OLD MEMORIES.

We spent the following day in drifting quietly around the lake, floating lazily in the little bays, under the shadow of the tall trees, and lounging upon small islands, gathering the low-bush whortleberries which grew in abundance upon them. We filled our tin pails with this delicious fruit for a dessert for our evening meal. On one of these islands we found indications of its being inhabited by wood rabbits, and we sent Cullen to the shanty for the dogs to course them, not however with any intention of capturing them, but to enjoy the music of the chase, and hear the voices of the hounds echoing over the water. We landed them upon the island, and began beating for the game. The hounds understanding that their business was the pursuit of deer, and having hunted the island over thoroughly, came back to us, and sat quietly down upon their haunches, as much as to say there was nothing there worth looking after. But we had seen one of the little animals that had been roused from its bed by the dogs, and we called their special attention to the fact by leading them to the spot, and bidding them to "hunt him up." They understood our meaning, and started on the trail, with a loud and cheerful cry. For half an hour, they coursed him round and round the island, making the lake vocal with their merry music. We might have shot the game they were pursuing fifty times, but we had no design against its life. The little fellow did not seem to be greatly alarmed, for we noted him often, when by doubling he had temporarily thrown off the dogs, squat himself down, and throw his long ears back in the direction of the sound that had been pursuing him; and when the dogs straightened upon his trail, and approached where he sat, he would bound nimbly away among the thick bushes to double on them again.

We called off the dogs and passed on to float along under the shadow of the forest trees and the hills, and take an occasional trout by way of experiment among the broken rocks along the shore. We had dispatched Cullen to the shanty to prepare dinner for us by six o'clock, at which hour we were to be at home. Cullen had promised, to use his own expression, "to spread himself" in the preparation of this meal, and he kept his promise. On our return, we found a sirloin of moose roasted to a turn, a stake of bear-meat broiled on the coals, a stew of jerked venison, and as pleasant a dish of fried trout and pork as an epicure could desire. Our appetites were keen, and we did ample justice to his cookery. This was one of the most delightful evenings that I have ever spent in the northern woods. There was such a calm resting upon all things, such an impress of repose upon forest and lake, such a cheerful quiet and serenity all around us, that one could scarcely refrain from rejoicing aloud in the beauty and the glory of the hour. As the sun sank to his rest behind the western hills, and the twilight began to gather in the forest and over the lake, the moon rose over the eastern high lands, walking with a queenly step up into the sky, casting a long line of brilliant light across the waters, showing the shadows of the mountains in bold outline in the depths below, and paling the stars by her brightness above. We all felt that we were recruiting in strength so rapidly in these mountain regions, where the air was so bracing and pure, under the influence of exercise, simple diet, natural sleep, and the absence of the labors and cares of business, that we were contented, notwithstanding the monotony that began to mark our everyday proceedings.

"I have been listening," said Spalding, as we sat upon the rude benches in front of our camp-fire, indulging in our usual season of smoking after our meals, "to the song of the crickets in those rude jams, and they call up sad, yet pleasant memories from the long past; of the old log house, the quiet fire-place, the crane in the jam, the great logs blazing upon the hearth of a cold winter evening, the house dog sleeping quietly in the corner, and the cat nestled confidingly between his feet. Oh! the days of old! the days of old! These crickets call back with these memories the circle that gathered around the hearth of my home, when I was young. Father, mother, brothers, sisters, playmates, and friends. How quietly some of them grew old and ripe, and then dropped into the grave. How quietly others stole away in their youth to the home of the dead, and how the rest have drifted away on the currents of life and are lost to me in the mists and shadows of time. Even the home and the hearth are gone; they

'Battled with time and slow decay,'

until at last they were wiped out from the things that are. The song of the peepers is a pleasant memory, and comes welling up with a thousand cherished recollections of our vanished youth; but the song of the cricket that made its home in the jams of the great stone fire-place is pleasanter, and the memories that come floating back with his remembered lay are pleasanter still. He was always there. He was not silent, like the out-door insect, through the spring month and the cold of winter, piping only in sadness when the still autumnal evenings close in their brightness and beauty over the earth; but he sang always, and his chirrup was heard at all seasons. In the winter the fire on the hearth warmed him; in the summer he had a cool resting place, and he was cheerful and merry through all the long year. And this reminds me of an anecdote of a venerable minister, who passed years ago to his rest. He was a Scotchman, and when preaching to his own congregation at Salem, in Washington comity, he indulged in broad Scotch, which to those who were accustomed to it was exceedingly pleasant. I was a boy then, and was returning with my father from a visit to Vermont. We stopped over the Sabbath at Salem, and attended worship in the neat little church of that pleasant village. There were no railroads in those days. The iron horse had not yet made his advent, and the scream of the steam whistle had never startled the echoes that dwell among the gorges of the Green Mountain State. Oh! Progress! Progress! I have travelled that same route often since, more than once within the year, and I flew over in an hour what was the work of all that cold winter day that brought us at night to that neat little village of Salem. I thought, as I dashed with a rush over the road I once travelled so leisurely, how change was written upon everything; how time and progress had obliterated all the old landmarks, leaving scarcely anything around which memory could cling. Well! well! it is so everywhere. All over the world, change, improvement, progress are the words. The venerable minister, for his locks were grey, and time had ploughed deep furrows down his cheeks, and draws palpable lines across his brow, was, as my memory paints him, the personification of earnestness, sincerity and truth. The text and the drift of the sermon I have forgotten, save the little fragment that fixed itself in my memory by the singularity of the figure by which he illustrated his meaning. He was speaking of the operation of the Holy Spirit upon the human heart, and how gently it won men from their sinful ways. He said, 'It was not boisterous, like the rush of the tempest; it was not fierce, like the lightning; it was not loud, like the thunder; but it was a still sma' voice, like a wee cricket in the wa's.' I regard the cricket that chirruped in the wall as an institution. One of the past to be sure, swept away by the current of progress, whose course is onward always; over everything, obliterating everything, hurling the things of today into history, or burying them in eternal oblivion. In this country there is nothing fixed, nothing stationary, and never has been since the first white man swung his axe against the outside forest tree; since the first green field was opened up to the sunlight from the deep shadows of the old forests that had stood there, grand, solemn, and boundless since this world was first thrown from the hand of God. There will be nothing fixed for centuries to come. The tide of progress will sweep onward in the future as it has done in the past. Onward is the great watchword of America, and American institutions; onward and onward, over the ancient forests; onward, over the log-houses that stood in the van of civilization; over the great fire-places; over the cricket in the wall; over the old house dog that slept in the corner; over the loved faces that clustered around the blazing hearth in the days of our childhood; over everything primitive, everything, my friends, that you and I loved, when we were little children, and that comes drifting along down on the current of memory--bright visions of the returnless past. Ah, well! it is best that it should be so. It is best that the world should move on; that there should be no pause, no halting in the onward march. What are we that the earth should stand still at our bidding, or pause to contemplate our tears? Dust to dust is the great law, but so long as a phoenix rises from the ashes of decay, what right have we to murmur? Time may desolate and destroy, but man can build up and beautify. True, his works perish as he perishes, but new works and new men are rising forever to fill, and more than fill, the vacancies and desolations of the past. Go ahead then, world! Sweep along, Progress! Mow away, Time! Tear down temple and stronghold; sweep away the marble palace and log-house! sweep away infancy and youth, manhood and old age; wipe out old memories, and pass the sponge over cherished recollections. The energy and the ingenuity of man are an over-match even for time. From the ruins of the past, from the desolations of decay, new structures will rise, and a new harvest, more abundant than the old, will spring up from the stubble over which Time's sickle has passed. Recuperation is a law stronger than decay, and it is written all over the face of the earth."

CHAPTER XXIV.

THE ACCIDENTS OF LIFE--"SOME MEN ACHIEVE GREATNESS, AND SOME HAVE GREATNESS THRUST UPON THEM"--A SLIDE--RATTLESNAKES AT THE TOP AND AN ICY POOL AT THE BOTTOM--A FANCIFUL THEORY.

While we sat thus conversing, our boatmen went down along the beach, and around a little point that ran out into the lake, to bathe. They were jolly, but uncultivated men, given to rudeness and profanity of speech when out of our immediate presence, and by themselves, and we heard from them, while they were splashing and struggling in the water, expressions somewhat inelegant as well as profane.

"I have often thought," said Spalding, as we listened to the rude and sometimes profane speech of our men, "how vast the influence which circumstances or accident, over which men have no control, have upon their conduct and destiny in this world, if not in the next. The poet has well said,

'Full many a gem of purest ray serene
The dark unfathomed caves of Ocean bear;
And many a flower is born to blush unseen,
And waste its sweetness on the desert air.'

"These rude men are but testifying to the great truth, that man is the creature, in a greater or less degree, of circumstances; that he is great or small, polished or rude, wise or simple, according to the accident of his birth, or the surroundings in the midst of which his journey of life lays. True, there *are* intellects that will work themselves into position, men who will hew their way upward in spite of the difficulties which beset them, as there are others who will plunge down to degradation and dishonor, in defiance of tender rearing, of education, of association, and all the allurements to an upward career that can be presented to the human understanding. But these are so rare, that they may be properly regarded as exceptions to the general rule; so rare, indeed, as to prove its truth. You and I can look around us, and from among our acquaintances select many men and women, whose genius and solid understanding, and whose virtues too, have remained undeveloped, and probably will do so till they die, from lack of opportunity for their exercise. Accident seems to have stricken them from their legitimate sphere. Circumstances, for which they were not responsible, and over which they could exercise no control, have barred them out from their seeming true position in the world, and the genius which was intended for the daylight and the eagle's flight towards the sun, is left to skim in darkness along the ground, like the course of the mousing owl. We have all seen another thing, which baffles our philosophy, while it proves the truth of the theory of which I am speaking. We have seen men, and see them every day, who, from no quality of heart or mind seem fitted to rise in the world, occupying commanding positions to which accident has lifted them; whose genius commands no admiration, whose virtues are of a doubtful character, and who possess no one quality which entitles them to our respect or the respect of the world. As the former are the victims of circumstance, these latter are its creatures. Both are the sport of fortune; the one class its victims, and the other its favorites. How is all this to be accounted for? And where rests the responsibility of failure, and where the credit of success? Are there accidents floating about among the paths marked out on the chart of life by the Deity, which jostle his creatures from the destiny intended for them? Or were men thrown loose upon the currents of life, to take their chances of good and evil, to be virtuous or vile, according to the influences among which they were floating, to be fortunate or otherwise, as the means of advancing themselves drifted within their reach? If so, where rests the responsibility, I ask again, of failure, and where the credit of success? Children are born into the world under strangely different influences. One first sees the light in the haunts of vice and crime, amidst the corruptions which fester away down in the depths of a great city. The influences which surround it are only and always evil. They are such in infancy, in childhood, in youth, and in manhood. Another is cradled under the influence of intelligences, piety, virtue; having around it always the safeguards of refined and Christian civilization. What is the difference in the degree of responsibility attached to the future of these antipode beginnings? Can you tell me where, and how these wide, terribly wide distinctions are to be reconciled? When and where the career of these germs of being, starting from points so wide asunder, are to meet, and how the balances of good and evil, of suffering and enjoyment of sinning and retribution, are to be adjusted at last? I have been asking myself, too, while listening to the speech of these men, so thoughtlessly uttered, where these profane epithets, these impious expressions, are to rest at last? Who can tell whether they do not go jarring through the universe, marring the music of the spheres, throwing discord into the anthems of the morning stars when they sing together, a wail among the glad voices of the sons of God, when they shout for joy? In this world, and to the dulness of human perception, when the sound of the impious words has died away, or a smile comes back to the face clouded by the angry thought, the effect seems to have ceased; but it may not be so. The word or the thought may be wandering for ages, vibrating still, away off among the outer creations of God. The angel that bore them at the beginning from the lips or the heart, may be flying still, and generations and centuries may have passed, before his journeying with them shall have ceased.

"It is a fanciful idea, that whatever we say or think, is immortal; that every word we utter goes ringing through the universe forever; that every thought of the heart becomes a creation, a thing of vitality in some shape, starting forward among the things of some sort of life, never to die! I have sometimes, in my dreamy hours, speculated upon the truth of such a theory, and reasoned with myself in favor of its reality. All I can say in its favor, however, is that I cannot disprove it. It may be true, or it may not. There are other mysteries quite as incomprehensible, the results of which we can see, without being able to penetrate the darkness in which they dwell. But assuming its truth, and appreciating the consequences which would follow, we should rule the tongue with a sterner sway, and guard the heart with a more watchful care than is our wont. Think of the obscene word becoming a living entity, the profane oath a thing of life; the filthy or impure thought, assuming form and vitality, all starting forward to exist forever among the creations of infinite purity. Who would own one of these ogres in comparison with the beautiful things of God? Who would say of the obscene word, the profane oath, or the filthy or impious thought, 'this is mine. I made it. I am the author of its being--its creator!' And yet it may be so. If it is, there are few of us who have not thrown into life much, very much to mar the harmonies of nature, to throw discord among the spheres."

"Your statement," remarked Smith, "that accident has much to do with making or marring the fortunes of men, is doubtless true. Men are destroyed by accident, and their lives are sometimes saved by it. And if you'll put away metaphysics, come out of the cloud in which you have hid yourself in your dreamy speculations, I will furnish you with a case in point, showing that a man may get into a very unpleasant predicament, where he runs a great risk and gets some hard knocks, and yet be able to thank God for it, in perfect earnestness of spirit. A case of the kind came under my own observation, and while there was not much philosophy, or abstract speculation about it, there was a great deal of hard practical fact. It happened when I was a boy, at the old homestead, in the valley that stretches to the southwest from the head of Crooked Lake. That valley is hemmed in by high and steep hills, and at the tune of which I speak, was much more beautiful in my view than it is now. There was no village there then, and the farms which stretched from hill to hill were greatly less valuable than they are now; but the woods and pastures, and meadows, lay exactly in the right places, and had among them partridges, and squirrels, and pigeons, and cattle, and sheep enough to make things pleasant; besides, there were plenty of trout in those days, in the stream that flows along through the valley mid-way between the hills. On the north side, coming down through a gorge, or 'the gulf,' as we used to call it, was a stream which, in the dry season of the year, was a little brook, trickling over the rocks, but which, in the spring freshets, or when the clouds emptied themselves on the mountain, was a wild, foaming, roaring, and resistless torrent. In following this stream into 'the gulf,' you walked on a level plain between walls of rock, rising two or three hundred feet on either hand, and a dozen or more rods apart, until you came to 'the falls,' down which the stream rushed with a plunge and a roar, when its back was up, or over which, in the dry season, it quietly rippled. These 'falls' were not perpendicular, but steep as the roof of a Dutch barn, and it was a great feat to climb them when the stream was low. Ascending about fifty feet, you came to a broad flat rock, large and smooth as a parlor floor, and which in the summer season was dry. Well, one day, in company with a boy who was visiting me, I went up to the 'falls,' and we concluded to climb the shelving rocks to the 'table;' and taking off our shoes and stockings, entered upon the perilous ascent--for such to some extent it was. Hands and feet, fingers and toes, were all put in requisition. My friend began the ascent before I did, and was half way up when I started. I ought to have said, that at the foot of the 'falls,' was a basin, worn away by the torrent, and in which the water, clear and cold, then stood to the depth of three or four feet. We were toiling painfully up, when I heard a rush above, and in an instant my friend came like an arrow past me, sliding down the shelving rocks on his back, or rather in a half-sitting posture, his rear to the rocks. I won't undertake to say that the fire flew as he went by me, for the rocks were slate, and therefore such a phenomenon was not likely to occur, but the entire absence of the seat of my friend's pantaloons, and the blood that trickled down to his toes, showed that the friction was considerable. As he passed me, I heard him exclaim, 'thank God,' and the next instant he plunged into the cold water at the base of the falls. What there was to be thankful for in such a descent over the rocks, I could not at the time comprehend, as the chances were in favor of a broken back, or neck, or some other consummation equally out of the range of gratitude, in an ordinary way. He came up out of the water blowing and snorting like a porpoise with a cold in his head, and waded to the shore. 'Come down,' he shouted, which I did, not quite so far or fast as he did, but fast enough to make an involuntary plunge, head foremost, into the pool at the bottom. The occasion of his catastrophe was this: he had ascended so near the table rock, that his hands were upon it, and was lifting himself up, when, as his eyes came above the surface, the edge upon which his hands with most of his weight rested, gave way, and he started for the basin below. But he had a view of what satisfied him that to this accident he owed his life, and it was a sense of gratitude for his escape, that prompted the exclamation I heard as he went bumping past me. Coiled on the rock above, and within reach of his face, were several large rattlesnakes, and he always insisted that one made a spring at him, as his hands gave way, and he put out for the basin into which he plunged. He was a good deal bruised, but his escape from the poisonous reptiles reconciled him to that."

CHAPTER XXV.
HEADED TOWARDS HOME--THE MARTIN AND SABLE HUNTER--HIS
CABIN--AUTUMNAL SCENERY.

We concluded that we would break up our camp in the morning, and drift leisurely back towards civilization. We had tarried upon this beautiful lake until we had explored its romantic nooks, and we started on our return to our old camping ground at the foot of Round Pond. We had refrained for two days from disturbing the deer, and our supply of fresh venison was entirely exhausted. Just at the outlet of the lake we were leaving, is a little bay, towards the head of which are a great number of boulders, laying around loose, scattered about like haycocks in a meadow, only a great many more to the acre. The water about these boulders is shallow, and the lily-pads and grasses make a luxuriant pasture for the deer. Among these boulders, and concealed by one of them, save when his head was up, was a deer. While he fed we could see nothing of him, but when he raised his head to look around him, that alone was visible above the rock. Smith and myself were in the leading boat, he in the bow with his rifle. As the current swept near the rocks where the deer was feeding, we let our little craft drift quietly in that direction. As we came within shooting distance, say from fifteen to twenty rods, Smith adjusted his rifle, and as the animal raised its head above the rock, he sighted him carefully, and fired. It was a beautiful shot. There was nothing of the animal but the head visible, and the bullet, true to its aim, struck it square between the eyes, and it fell dead. This shot, together with the glory of killing the bear, elated Smith wonderfully, and upon the strength of them, he assumed the championship of the expedition.

We drew the deer into the baggage-boat, and sent forward our pioneer to erect our tents, and prepare a late dinner, at our old camping ground, while we landed with the dogs on the island near the head of Round Pond, or Lake, to course whatever game they might find upon it. They soon burst into full chorus, and dashed away. The island is small, containing only a few acres, and the game could not, therefore, take a wide range After a single turn, a deer broke, like a maddened warhorse, from the thicket, and plunging into the lake, struck boldly for the mainland, five hundred yards distant. We were near by with our two boats when he took to the water, and we thought we would accompany him as an escort to the shore; so we rowed up, and with a boat on each side, and within ten feet of him, as he swam, escorted him towards the forest. We treated him with great respect, offering him no indignity, interfering with him in nothing; and yet the old fellow seemed very far from appreciating our politeness, or relishing our company. The truth is, he was horribly frightened, and he struggled desperately to rid himself of our association; but we stuck by him like his destiny, talking kindly to him, endeavoring to impress upon his mind that we meant him no harm--indeed, that we were his friends. But, I repeat, he did not appreciate our politeness. By-and-by his feet touched the sand, and he bounded forward, as much as to say, "Good-bye, gentlemen," when a simultaneous yell from all six of us, and the discharge of four rifles in quick succession over him, added wonderfully to the energy of his flight. He will be likely to recognise us if he ever meets us again, and if the past furnishes any admonitions to his kind, he will give us a wide berth.

We rowed leisurely along the eastern shore, and in a deep bay found excellent fishing, at the mouth of a cold mountain brook. On the banks of this bay we found the winter hut of a martin and sable trapper. It had an outer and inner apartment, the latter almost subterranean. The hut was composed of small logs, which a single man could lay up, the crevices between which were closely packed with moss, and the roof covered with two or three layers of bark. The doorway was sawed through these logs, and a door, constructed of bark, was made to fit it; a rude hearth of sandstone was built in one corner, and a hole was open above it to let out the smoke.

Against the outside of this pen, only about ten feet square, logs were leaned up, the ends of which rested upon the ground, the interstices between them carefully stopped with moss, and the whole covered with bark; the ends consisted of stakes, driven into the ground and chinked with moss. Into this sleeping apartment a door was cut from the parlor, large enough for a man to pass by getting down on all-fours; while within was a plentiful supply of boughs from the spruce and fir tree. In this hut, now so dark, and in which the air was so dead and fetid, a solitary trapper had wintered, pursuing his occupation of martin and sable hunting--the which, if tolerably successful, would yield him some two or three hundred dollars the season. He carried into the woods a bag of flour or meal, a few pounds of pork, pepper, salt, and tea; and this, with the game he killed, made up his supply of food. With no companion but his dog, he had probably spent two or three months, and very possibly more, in this lonely cabin.

We arrived at our camp towards evening, and dined sumptuously on fresh venison and trout. Our pioneer had provided a luxurious bed of boughs within, and had fashioned rude seats in front of our tents. He had rolled the butt of a huge tree, which he had felled, to the proper place, against which to kindle our camp-fire, and we had a pleasant place to sit, with our pipes, in the evening, looking out over the water, listening to the pile-drivers, half a dozen of which were driving their stakes along the reedy shore, with commendable diligence. The sunlight lay so beautifully on the hillsides, and contrasted so admirably with the deep shadows of the valley beneath, the lake was so calm and still, the old woods stood around so moveless and solemn, that one could scarcely persuade himself that he was not looking upon some gigantic picture, the fanciful grouping and transcendent coloring of some ingenious and winning artist.

"The hillsides about these lakes," remarked the Doctor, "must be superlatively beautiful in the fall, when the forest puts on its autumnal foliage. They present such a variety of trees, of so many different kinds, and the hills and mountains are so admirably arranged, that they must be gorgeous beyond description. However we may prefer the green and *living* beauty of spring, when everything is so full of vitality, so buoyant and free, yet the autumn scenery is the most magnificent of any in the year."

"Every season has its charms," said Spalding, "Even the winter, with its cold, its dead and cheerless desolation, has its robe of chaste and peerless white, which, as well as that of the spring-time, the summer, and the autumn, has been the theme of song. I agree with you, that in gorgeousness of beauty, there is no season so rich as the autumn. Spring-time has its pleasant scenery, its genial days, its deep green, its flowers, and its singing birds; and these are all the more lovely because they follow so closely upon the cold storms, and bleak winds, the chilling and blank desolation of winter. We love the spring because of its freshness, its pervading vitality, its re-cuperating influences. Everybody loves the spring-time; everybody talks about the spring-time; poets sing of it; orators praise it; 'fair women and brave men' laud it; so that were spring-time human, and possessing human instincts, and subject to hu-man frailties, it would have plenty of excuse, for becoming a very vain personage.

"Somebody has called the autumnal days the 'saddest of the year.' I have forgot-ten who he was, if I ever knew; but in my judgment, he was all wrong. Dark days there are--damp, chilly, misty, wet, and unpleasant days in autumn; days that make one relish a corner by an old-fashioned fire. There are gusty, windy, capricious days in autumn, which nobody cares to praise, when the northwest wind goes sweep-ing over the forest, roaring among the trees, and whirling the sere leaves along the ground, and which, to tell the truth about them, are anything but pleasant. But 'some days *must* be dark and dreary,' and they serve to give the sunlight of a bright to-morrow a keener relish, and a lovelier comparative beauty. To call the fall days the 'saddest of the year' is an absurdity, poetical I admit, but still an absurdity. There is nothing sad in a cold, or a wet, a drizzly, a gusty, or a stormy day; much there may be that is unpleasant, much that one may be disposed to quarrel with, but they are anything but sad.

"A calm autumnal day in the country is a great thing, a beautiful thing, a thing to thank God for; a thing to make one happy, buoyant of spirit, full of gratitude to the great Creator; a thing to make one merry, too, not with a loud and boister-ous mirth, but with a heart full to overflowing with cheerfulness, and a calm joy. To see the bright sun standing in his glory up in the sky, shedding his placid light over the earth, when the air is clear, the winds hushed, and the leaves are still and moveless on the trees; and then to look along the hillsides, and mark the bright sunlight, and the deep shadows, the green of the fir, the hemlock, and the spruce, the yellow of the birch, the crimson of the maple, the dark brown of the beech, the grey of the oak, the silver glow of the popple, and the varying shades of all these, mingling and blending in all the harmony of brilliant coloring. Why, these hillsides are decked like a maiden in her beauty, like a bride robed for the altar! Talk about springtime, or summer! Green on the hillside! green in the meadows and pastures! green everywhere--all around is changeless and everlasting green! as if hillside and valley, forest and field, had but a single dress for morning, noon, and night, and that only and always green! True, there is the music of the birds, joyous notes and variant, happy and hilarious, in the spring-time, but there is no cricket under the flat stone in the pasture, his song is not heard in the stone wall, or in the corner of the fences; no music of the katydid; no tapping of the woodpecker on the hollow tree, or the dead limb; no chattering of the squirrel, as he gathers his winter store; no pattering of the faded leaves, as they come so quietly down from their places; no falling of the ripened nuts, loosened from their burs or shucks by the recent frosts. All these sounds belong to the calm autumnal days, and while they differ the whole heavens from the merry songs of spring, there is nothing sad about them. No! No! nothing sad. I remember (and who that was reared in the country does not) when I was a boy, how I went out in the sunny days of autumn, after the frosts had painted the hillsides, to gather chestnuts; and when the breeze rustled among the branches, how the nuts came rattling down; and how if the winds were still, I climbed into the trees and shook their tops, and how the chestnuts pattered to the ground like a shower of hail. I remember the squirrels how they chattered, and chased each other up and down the trees, or leaped from branch to branch, gathering here and there a nut, and scudding away to their store houses in the hollow trees, providing in this season of plenty for the barrenness of the winter months. I remember, too, how we gathered, in those same old autumnal days, hickory-nuts and butter-nuts by the bushel; and how pleasant it was in the long cold winter evenings, to sit around the great old kitchen fire-place, cracking the nuts we had gathered when the green, the yellow, the crimson, the brown, the grey, and the pale leaves were on the trees. Pleasant evenings those seem to me now, as they come floating down on the current of memory from the long past, and dear are the faces of those that made up the tableaux as they were grouped around those winter fires. Logs were blazing on the great hearth, and the pineknots, thrown at intervals on the fire, gave a bold and cheerful light throughout that capacious kitchen. I remember how the winter wind went glancing over the house-top, whirling, and eddying, and moaning around the corners, hissing under the door and sending its cold breath in at every crevice; and how the windows rattled when the blast came fiercest, and how the smoke would sometimes whirl down the great chimney, I remember well where my father's chair was always placed; and where my mother sat of those winter evenings, when her household cares were over for the day, plying her needle, or knitting, or darning stockings, or mending garments, for such employment was no dishonor to the matrons of those days. With these for the leading figures, I remember how seven brothers and sisters were grouped around, and how the old house dog had a place in the corner, and how lovingly the cat nestled between his feet. Cherished memories are these pleasant visions and they come to me often, vivid as realities. But the dream vanishes, the vision fades away, and I think of the six pale, still faces as I saw them last, and of the names that are chiseled upon the cold marble that stands through the sunny spring-time, the heat of summer, the autumnal days, and the storms and tempests of winter, over the graves of the dead."

CHAPTER XXVI.
A SURPRISE--A SERENADE--A VISIT FROM STRANGERS--AN INVITATION TO BREAKFAST--A FASHIONABLE HOUR AND A BOUNTIFUL BILL OF FARE.

The evening was calm, and the lake slept in stirless beauty before us. The shadows of the mountains reached far out from the shore, lieing like a dark mantle upon the surface of the waters, above and beneath which the stars twinkled and glowed like the bright eyes of seraphs looking down from the arches above, and up from the depths below. The moon in her brightness sailed majestically up into the sky, throwing her silver light across the bosom of the lake; millions of fireflies flashed their tiny torches along the reedy shore; the solemn voices of the night birds came from out the forest; the call of the raccoon and the answer, the hooting of the owl, and the low murmur of the leaves, stirred by the light breeze that moved lazily among the tree-tops, old familiar music to us, were heard. This latter sound is always heard, even in the stillest and calmest nights. There may be no ripple upon the water; it may be moveless and smooth as a mirror, no breath of air may sweep across its surface, and yet in the old forest among the tree-tops, there is always that low ceaseless murmur, a soft whispering as if the spirits of the woods were holding, in hushed voices, communion together. We had retired for the night under the cover of our tents. My companion had sunk into slumber, and I was just in that dreamy state, half sleeping and half awake, which constitutes the very paradise of repose, when there came drifting across the lake the faint and far off strains of music, which, to my seeming, exceeded in sweetness anything I had ever heard. They came so soft and melodious, floating so gently over the water, and dying away so quietly in the old woods, that I could scarce persuade myself of their reality. For a while I lay luxuriating as in the delusion of a pleasant dream, as though the melody that was abroad on the air was the voices of angels chanting their lullaby into the charmed ear of the sleeper. Presently, Smith raised his head, supporting his cheek upon his hand, his elbow resting upon the ground, and after listening for a moment, opened his eyes in bewilderment exclaiming, as he looked in utter astonishment about him, "What, in the name of all that is mysterious, is that?"

Spalding and the Doctor followed, and their amazement was equalled only by their admiration when

"Oft in the stilly night"
came stealing in matchless harmony over the water, "A serenade from the Naiads, by Jupiter!" exclaimed Smith.

"A concert, by the Genii of the waters!" cried the Doctor.

"Hush!" said Spalding, "we are trespassing upon fairy domain; the spirits of these old woods, these mountains and rock-bound lakes, are abroad, and well may they carol in their joyousness in a night like this."

In a little while the music changed, and

"Come o'er the moonlight sea"
came swelling over the lake. And again it changed and

"Come mariner down in the deep with me"
went gently and swiftly abroad on the air. The music ceased for a moment, and then two manly voices, of great depth and power, came floating to our ears to the

words:

> "'Farewell! Farewell! To thee, Araby's daughter,'
> Thus warbled a Perl, beneath the deep sea,
> 'No pearl ever lay under Onan's dark water,
> More pure in its shell than thy spirit in thee.'"

"That's flesh and blood, at least," exclaimed the Doctor, "and I propose to ascertain who are treating as to this charming serenade in the stillness of midnight."

We went down to the margin of the lake, and a few rods from the shore lay a little craft like our own, in which were seated two gentlemen, the one with a flute and the other with a violin. They had seen our campfire from their shanty on the other side of the lake, and had crossed over to surprise us with the melody of human music. And pleasantly indeed it sounded in the stillness and repose of that summer night in that wild region. The echoes that dwell among those old forests, those hills and beautiful lakes, had never been startled from their slumbers by such sounds before, and right merrily they carried them from hill to hill, and through the old woods, and over the calm surface of that sleeping lake, and with a joyousness, too, that told how welcome they were among those wild and primeval things.

After listening to their music for half an hour, we invited our new friends ashore. We found them to be two young gentlemen from Philadelphia, who had just graduated at one of the Eastern colleges, and who had concluded to spend a month among these mountains and lakes, before entering upon the study of the profession to which they were to devote themselves. They had been close friends from their childhood, and room-mates during their collegiate course. They had cultivated their taste for music, until few mere amateurs could equal their skill upon their respective instruments, or in harmony of voice. They were highly intelligent and courteous gentlemen, and if their future shall equal the promise of the present, they will make their mark in the world. We accepted, at parting, their invitation to breakfast with them on the morrow, and at one o'clock they left us to return to their shanty over the lake. We sent one of our boatmen to row them home; and as they started across the water, they treated us to a concert to which it was pleasant to listen. There is something surpassingly sweet in the music of the flute and violin in the hands of skillful performers; and yet, to my thinking, it falls far short of the melody of the human voice. I have listened to some of the most celebrated singers, and of the most distinguished performers, but it appears to me now, that I never, on any other occasion, heard the melody of the human voice, or instrumental music half so enchanting, as that which came floating over the lake on that calm summer night. There was a volume and compass about it which can never be reached in a concert room. It was not loud, but it seemed to fill all the air with its sweetness. It came over the senses like a pleasant dream, as it went swelling up to the hills that skirted the lake, floating away over the water, and dying away in lengthened cadence in the old forests. Every other sound was hushed; the voices of the night-birds were stilled; even the frogs along the shore suspended their bellowing, and all nature seemed listening to the new harmony that thus fell like enchantment upon the repose of midnight. The music grew fainter and fainter as it receded, until only an occasional strain, wavy and dream-like, came creeping like the voice of a spirit over the water, and then it was lost in the distance. The frogs resumed their roaring, the night-birds lifted up their voices; the raccoon called to his fellow, and was answered away off in the forest; the pile-driver hammered away at his stake, the old owl hooted solemnly from his perch, and we retired to our tents to talk over the romance of our serenade, and to dream of Ole Bull and the Swedish Nightingale.

The morning broke bright and balmy. A pleasant breeze swept lazily over the lake, lifting the thin mist that hung like a veil of gauze above the water. We left our tents standing, and crossed over to the shanty of our friends of the previous evening to breakfast. We found them living like princes. Their two boatmen had built them a log shanty; open in front, and covered with bark so as to be impervious to the rain, while within was a luxurious bed of boughs. Around the campfire were benches of hewn slabs, and a table of the same material. A few rods from the door a beautiful spring came bubbling up into a little basin of pure white sand, the water of which was limpid and cold almost as ice-water. They had been here for a week, hunting and fishing. They had employed their leisure in jerking the venison they had taken, of which they had some four or five bushels, and which they intended to take home with them, to serve, together with the skins of the deer they had slain, as trophies of their success.

They received us cordially, and we sat down to a breakfast, which, for variety, at least, rivalled the elaborate preparations of the Astor or the St. Nicholas; albeit, the cookery, as an abstract fact, might have been of the simplest. We had venison-steak, pork, ham, jerked venison stew, fresh trout, broiled partridge, cold roast duck, a fricassee of wood rabbits, and broiled pigeon upon our table, coming in courses, or piled up helter-skelter on great platters of birch bark, some on tin plates, and now and then a choice bit on a chip! We had coffee, and tea, and the purest of spring water, by way of beverage, and truth compels me to admit, that under the advice of the Doctor, a drop or two of Old Cognac may have been added by way of relish, or to temper the effect of a hearty meal upon the delicate stomachs of some of the guests. We were exceedingly fashionable in our time for breakfasting this morning, and it was eleven o'clock before we rose from table. The sun was travelling through a cloudless sky, and his brightness lay like a mantle of glory upon the water, while his heat gave to the deep shadows of the old trees, whose long arms with their clustering foliage were interlocked above us, a peculiar charm. The description which we gave of the beautiful lake we had left the day before, the story of the moose and the bear we had killed, together with our quit-claim of the shanty we had, inhabited, brought our friends to the conclusion to drift that way for a week or so.

It was amusing to hear Smith relate the manner of capturing the bear, the glory of which achievement he had won by the tossing up of a dollar; how he had started out alone in one of the boats with his rifle to look into a little bay half a mile below the shanty, where be left the rest of us sleeping after dinner; and how, as he was floating along under the shadow of the hills, at the base of a wall of rocks some forty feet high, rising straight up from the water, he heard something walking just over the precipice; and how he picked up his rifle that lay in the bottom of the boat, to be ready for any emergency; and then how astonished he was to see a great black bear walk out into view along the edge of the rocks above, and how carefully he sighted him; and how, at the crack of his rifle, the animal came tumbling down the cliff, and how quick he reloaded and gave trim a settler in the shape of a second bullet; and how he tugged, and strained, and lifted to get him into the boat, and how astonished we all were when he returned with his prize to camp. While relating this wonderful achievement, he winked at the Doctor, as much as to say, "fair play; remember our compact; stand by me now." And the Doctor did stand by him, boldly endorsing, with a gravity that was refreshing, every invention of Smith's prolific imagination, on the subject of his slaughtering the bear.

We left our new friends in the afternoon; they to start in the morning for our old camping-ground on the lake above, and we down the stream on our retreat from the wilderness. We came back to our tents, after securing a string of trout from the mouth of the little stream across the bay. Our evening meal was over, and we sat around our campfire just as the sun was hiding himself behind the western highlands, when, from a little hollow in the forest behind us, and but a short way off, we heard the call of a raccoon. Martin started over the ridge with the dogs, and in five minutes he hallooed to us to come with our rifles for he had the animal "treed," and ready to be brought down at "a moment's warning." We went over to where he was, and sure enough, away up in the top of a tall birch, sat his coonship, looking quietly down upon the dogs that were baying at the foot of the tree.

"Gentlemen," said Spalding, "we will not all fire at this animal as we did at Smith's bear. One bullet is enough for him, and if he gets down among us, I think six men will be a match for one 'coon,' so we need not be inhuman through a sense of danger. Whose shot shall he be?"

"I move that Spalding have the first shot," said Smith; and the motion was carried.

"Do I understand you, gentlemen," Spalding inquired, adjusting himself, as if preparing to bring down the game, "that I am to have this first shot, and that no one is to fire until I have taken a fair shot at him?"

We all answered, "Yes."

"Are you perfectly agreed in this, and do you all pledge yourselves to abide the compact?" Spalding inquired again, bringing his rifle to a present, and looking up at the game.

"All agreed," we answered, with one voice.

"Very well, gentlemen," said Spalding, shouldering his rifle, "there's one life saved anyhow. That animal up there has been in great peril, but he's safe now. I don't intend to fire at him sooner than ten o'clock to-morrow, and if I understand our arrangements, we leave here in the morning at six."

"Sold, by Moses!" exclaimed Martin, as he broke out into a roar that you might have heard a mile; "I thought the Judge meant something, by the time he wasted in talkin' and gettin' ready to shoot."

"Spalding," inquired Smith, "do you expect us to keep this compact?"

"Of course I do," he replied; "did any of us peach when you opened so rich in the matter of your bear? Did any one break his compact with you on that subject? Absolve us from our agreement about the bear, and you may take my shot at that animal up in the tree."

"I wasn't born yesterday," Smith replied, "and I can't afford to exchange the glory of killing the bear in my own way, and baring three responsible endorsers, for the honor of shooting a coon. Gentlemen," he continued, "I move that that coon be permitted to take his own time to descend from his perch up in the tree-top there;" and the motion was carried unanimously.

CHAPTER XXVII.
WOULD I WERE A BOY AGAIN.

"We have played the boy again, yesterday and to-day, pretty well," remarked Smith, as we sat in front of oar tents in the evening, smoking our pipes. "And I am half inclined to think we have started for home too soon, after all. Spalding's moralizing for the last two or three days deceived me. I thought, as he was becoming so serious, he must be getting tired of the woods; but his proposition yesterday to escort that deer to the shore, and frighten him almost to death, his jolly humor with our young friends over the way, and the trick he played on as in regard to the raccoon this evening, satisfies me that he's got a good deal of the boy in him yet. We shall have to retreat from the woods slower than I thought, to exhaust it."

"If the cares of business or the duties of life did not call us back to civilization" said the Doctor, "I could almost spend the summer among these lakes, only for the luxury of feeling like a boy again. When I listen to the glad voices of the wild things around as, I can almost wish myself one of them."

"That coon, for instance," interrupted Smith, "that came so near getting shot by his chattering."

"I call the gentleman to order," said I; "the Doctor has the floor."

"I sometimes think that it is no great thing after all to be human;" the Doctor continued, bowing his acknowledgments for my protecting his right to the floor. "Mind is a great thing, but there is more of sorrow, anxiety, and care clustering about it, than these wild things we hear and see around us suffer through their instincts. Reason, knowledge, wisdom, are great things. To stand at the head of created matter, to be the noblest of all the works of God, the only created thing wearing the image, and stamped with the patent of Diety, are proud things to boast of. But great and glorious and proud as they are, they have their balances of evil. They bring with them no contentment, no repose, while they heap upon us boundless necessities and limitless wants. We are hurried through life too rapidly for the enjoyment of the present, and the good we see in prospect is never attained. When we were boys we longed to be men, with the strength and intellect of men; and now that we are men, with matured powers of body and mind, true to our organic restlessness and discontent, we look back with longing for the feelings and emotions of our boyhood. What a glorious thing it would be if we could always be young--not boys exactly, but at that stage of life when the physical powers are most active, and the heart most buoyant. That, to my thinking, would be a better arrangement than to grow old, even if we live on until we stumble at last from mere infirmity into the grave, looking forward in discontent one half of our lives, and backward in equal discontent the other."

"You remind me," said Spalding, "of a little incident, simple in itself, but which, at the time, made a deep impression upon my mind, and which occurred but a few weeks ago. Returning from my usual walk, one morning, my way lay through the Capitol Park. The trees, covered with their young and fresh foliage, intertwined their arms lovingly above the gravelled walks, forming a beautiful arch above, through which the sun could scarcely look even in the splendor of his noon. The birds sang merrily among the branches, and the odor of the leaves and grass as the dews exhaled, gave a freshness almost of the forest to the morning air. On the walk before me were two beautiful children, a boy of six and a little girl of four. They were merry and happy as the birds were, and with an arm of each around the waist of the other, they went hopping and skipping up and down the walks, stopping now and then to waltz, to swing round and round, and then darting away again with their hop and skip, too full of hilarity, too instinct with vitality, to be for a moment still. The flush of health was on their cheeks, and the warm light of affection in their eyes. They were confiding, affectionate, loving little children, and my heart warmed towards them, as I saw them waltzing and dancing and skipping about under the green foliage of the trees. "'Willy,' said the little girl, as they sat down on the low railing of the grass plats, to breathe for a moment, and listen to the chirrup and songs of the birds in the boughs above them, 'Willy, wouldn't you like to be a little bird?'

"'A little bird, Lizzie,' replied her brother. 'Why should I like to be a little bird?'

"'Oh, to fly around among the branches and the leaves upon the trees,' said Lizzie, 'and among the blossoms when the morning is warm, and the sun comes out bright and clear in the sky. Oh! they are so happy,'

"'But the mornings aint always warm, and the sun don't always come up bright and clear in the sky, Lizzy,' said her brother, 'and the leaves and blossoms aint always on the trees. The cold storms and the winter come and kill the blossoms and scatter the leaves, and what would you do then? I shouldn't like to be a bird, but I *should* like to be a big strong man like father.'

"'Please tell me what tune it is?' said the little boy, addressing me.

"I told him, and he turned to his little sister, saving, 'Come, Lizzie, we must go; mother said we must be home by half-after seven, and it's most that now;' and he put his arm lovingly around her neck, and she put hers around his waist, and they walked away towards home, talking about the leaves and the blossoms on the trees, the merry little birds, the bright sunshine, and the pleasant time they had had in the park that morning.

"It was a pleasant thing to see those two little children, so confiding, so earnest and true in their young affections, clinging to each other so closely, as if no shadow could ever come between them, or tarn their hearts from each other. How natural was that simple question put by that little girl to her brother, 'Wouldn't you like to be a little bird?' It was the thought of a pure young mind, that sees only the bright sunshine of to-day, whose life is in the present, and to which there is no forebodings of darkness in the future. There was philosophy, too, in the answer of her brother, a simple but suggestive sermon, 'But the sun' said he, 'don't always come up bright and clear; the mornings aint always warm; the leaves and blossoms aint always on the trees. The cold storms, and the winter come and kill the blossoms and scatter the leaves, and what would you do then?' To finite minds like ours, it would seem to have been a more beautiful arrangement of nature, could it have been, that we could always have the spring time in its glory with us; if the leaves and the blossoms were always young and fresh and fragrant; if the cold storms of winter could never come to 'kill the blossoms and scatter the leaves;' if the sun would always come up bright and clear; if the birds were always merry, and their glad voices always on the air. This world would be a paradise then, and one older and wiser in the learning of the schools, but not wiser or better in the heart's affections, than that little girl, might well wish to be a little bird, to fly around among the branches, the green leaves, and the blossoms on the trees. And yet what presumption in finite man to sit in judgment upon, or criticise the wisdom of the Omnipotent God! How know we but that a single change, the slightest alteration of a simple law, would go jarring through all the universe, throwing everything into confusion, and bringing utter chaos, where now all is order. The mother sees her little child die, she lays it in its coffin, and surrenders it to the grave, and her heart rebels against the Providence that snatched away her treasure. In her agony, she appeals reproachfully to Heaven, and asks, 'Why am I thus bereaved?' Foolish mother! impeach not the wisdom of your bereavement. Mysterious as it may be, know this, that in the councils of eternity your sorrows were considered, and the decree which took from you your darling, was ordered in mercy. Pestilence sweeps over the land; a wail is on the air. Peace, mourners, be still! The pestilence has a mission of mercy, mysterious as it may be to us. The storm lashes the ocean into fury; tall ships, freighted with human souls, go down into its relentless depths; a shriek of agony comes gurgling up from the devouring waters; a cry of woe is heard from a thousand homes over the wrecked and the lost. Peace, again, mourners! The storm has a mission of mercy. It may never be comprehended by us here, but when the veil shall be lifted, as in God's good time it doubtless will be, we shall see how the pestilence and the storm, that cost so many tears, were essential to the harmony of a glorious system, a perfect plan, and that seeming sorrow was at last the occasion of unspeakable joy. Let no man say that this or that law, or operation of nature, were better changed, until he can fathom the designs of God; till he can create a planet, and send it on its everlasting round; till he can place a star in the firmament; till he can breathe upon a statue, the workmanship of his own hands, and be obeyed when he commands it to walk forth a thing of life; till he can dip his hand into chaos and throw off worlds. The 'cold storms of winter' are essential to the enjoyment of the brightness and glory, the genial sunshine, the pleasant foliage, the blossoms and the odors of spring. They have their uses, and chill and dreary and desolate as they may be, they are parts of an arrangement ordered by infinite goodness and omnipotent wisdom.

"'I should like to be a big strong man like father is!' How like a boy was this? Thirsting for the strength, the might and power of manhood! And this is the aspiration of the young heart always; to be mature, strong to grapple with the cares, and wrestle with the stern actualities of life. How little of these does childhood know! How little does it calculate the chances, that when, in the long future, it shall have attained the full strength and maturity of life, when manhood shall be in the glory and strength of its prime, and it looks forward into the dark cloud beyond, and backward into the bright sunshine of the past, the aspiration, the hope will change into regret, and the yearning of the heart, speaking from its silent depths, will be, 'would I were a boy again!'"

CHAPTER XXVIII.
HEADED DOWN STREAM--RETURN TO TUPPER'S LAKE--THE CAMP ON THE ISLAND.

We started down stream again at six o'clock in the morning, intending, if possible, to reach Tupper's Lake before encamping for the night. It would make for us a busy day to accomplish so much; but going down stream and down hill are very different things from going up, as any gentleman may satisfy himself by rowing against a current of two miles the hour, or toiling up an ascent of three or four hundred feet to the mile, and then retracing his steps. We accomplished more than half the distance, and that over the worst of the journey, by twelve o'clock, and we halted for dinner and a *siesta*. If there is one thing in life which can lay any claim to being considered a positive luxury, it is a nap on a mossy bank, in the deep shadows of the forest trees, after a hearty meal, of a warm summer day. There should be, in order to its full appreciation, a mixture of weariness with a due proportion of laziness. Too much of either detracts from the enjoyment of its beatitudes. To *feel* the sensation of resting, that weariness is leaving you, and that the process of recuperation is an active, living agency, going on all through the system, while the natural love of repose is being gratified as an independent emotion, constitute the very perfection of mere animal enjoyment. The musquitoes at midday have gone to their rest, or if a straggler comes buzzing and singing about your ears, you are lulled rather than disturbed by his song. If he takes his drop of blood from your veins, the tickling of his tiny lance is but a pleasant titilation, and you let him feed on, almost grateful for his kindness in keeping you from sleeping too soundly, or losing in utter oblivion the full extent of the luxury of perfect repose.

After an hour's rest, we launched our little fleet upon the river again, and while the sun was yet above the western highlands, we stood upon the broad flat rock at the mouth of Bog River, looking out over Tupper's Lake, one of the most beautiful sheets of water that the sun or the stars ever looked upon. Our sea-biscuit was getting low, and our egress from the wilderness was therefore becoming, in some sort, a necessity. There was no lack of venison, or fish, but these are rather luxuries than actual necessaries, and they were becoming somewhat stale to as. The staff of life is bread, and of this we had but two days' supply. It is entirely true that our jerked venison, now dry and hard as chips, could, if necessary, be made to furnish, to some extent, a substitute; still, while "it is written that man shall not live by bread alone," it is equally the law that he cannot very well get along without it.

We launched our boats upon the lake and rowed to the head of Long Island, where we put up our tents for the night. I have spoken so often of the loveliness of the evenings on these beautiful lakes, that to attempt a description of the one we enjoyed on this romantic island, would be only a tiresome repetition. But there was a splendor about the heavens above, and their counterpart in the depths below, which I have scarcely ever seen equalled. There was no moon in the early evening, and so pure and clear was the atmosphere, so moveless and still the waters, that the stars seemed to come out in vaster numbers, and with an intenser glow, and to be reflected back from away down in the lake with a brighter refulgence; the hills along the shore seemed to stand up in bolder outline; the bays to lay in deeper shadow; while the tall peaks stood in grim solemnity, like pillars supporting the mighty arches of the sky.

"I was asking myself," said Smith, as we sat looking out over the water, in the evening, or gazing down into the glowing depths, and listening to the night voices, faint and far off in the old forests, as they came floating over the lake, "I was asking myself, as we journeyed around the falls to-day, and as we stood on the rock where the river comes leaping down and plunging into the lake, whether the march of improvement would ever spread a Lowell around those falls, or subject those wild waters to the uses of civilization. Whether progress would ever invade those mountain regions; or the ingenuity of man ever discover uses for these rocks and boulders, or coin wealth from the sterile and sandy soil of this old wilderness? Hitherto a country like this has been regarded of no value, save for the timber which it grows; and when that is exhausted, as fit only to be abandoned to sterility and desolation. But who can tell whether there may not be in these boulders, these rocks, this sandy and unproductive soil, unknown wealth, held in reserve to reward the researches of science in its utilitarian explorations. I am not now speaking of gold, or silver, or any other dross, which men have hitherto wasted their toil to accumulate; but of new discoveries, and new purposes to which these now useless things may be applied; discoveries which may send the tide of emigration surging up from the valleys to mountain regions like these. May it not be that science, while delving among the wrecks of vanished ages, may stumble upon some new principle, or combination of the elements of which these old rocks are composed, that shall give them a value beyond that of the richest lowlands, and make them the centre of a dense and cultivated population?"

"Your question," answered Spalding, "is suggestive. Did you ever think what gigantic strides the world has made within the memory of men now living, and who are yet unwilling to be counted as old? Look back for only fifty years, and note what a stupendous leap it has taken! Where then were the iron roads over which the locomotive goes thundering on its mission of civilization? where the telegraph, that mocks at time and annihilates space? Hark! there is a new sound breaking the stillness of midnight, and startling the mountain echoes from their sleep of ages! It is the scream of the steam-whistle, the snort of the iron horse, the thunder of his hoofs of steel, rushing forward with the speed of the wind, shaking the ground like an earthquake as he moves. A new motor has been harnessed into the service of man, and made to fly with his messages swifter than sound? It is the winged lightning; and as it flashes along the wires stretched from city to city, and across continents, carries with unerring certainty every word committed to its charge. Ocean steamers have made but a ferriage of seas. The photographic art has made even the light of the sun a substitute for the pencil of the artist. Everywhere, in all the departments of science, in every branch of the arts, improvement, progress, has been going on with a sublimity of achievement unknown in any age of the past. These things are mighty motors which push along civilization, throwing a wonderful energy into the forward impulse of the world. But remember, that though these results are brought about by the advance in the mechanic arts, yet that advance is based upon a deeper philosophy, a profounder wisdom, than mere perfectability in those arts. Take the steam-engine--it is a great contrivance, a wonderful invention; but the greatest of all was the discovery of the principle and operation, the practical phenomena of steam itself. The telegraphic machine was a great invention; but the great thing was the development of the science of electricity, the discovery of the secret agency which sent forward the thought entrusted to it swifter than light. The daguerrian instruments, the metallic plates, the prepared paper, were great inventions; but vastly greater was the discovery and development of the phenomena and affinities of light, the mystery of solar influences.

"There is hope for the world in all this mighty progress, for with it will one day come the development of the true nature and theory of government, the true solution of the great theory of the social compact, the proper adjustment of the relations of man to man, a right appreciation of the nature and value of human rights. It is bringing forward the masses, elevating the millions who work. It will rouse into activity their innate energies, and bring forth their inward might. It creates THOUGHT to guide the hands that set all this vast machinery in motion. It diffuses and strengthens intellectuality, and the pride of intellectuality, making of the men who work something more than mere machines themselves. It is developing and perfecting a mightier engine than any of man's invention; one that tyrants cannot always control, that kings cannot always manage. That engine is the human mind. Like the steam-engine, it is gathering power, and capability for the exercise of power, and the time will come when it will go crashing, with resistless energy, among thrones, overturning despotisms, upheaving dynasties, sweeping away those false theories of governmental institutions, which guarantee to one class of people a life of luxurious idleness, coupled with a prerogative to rule; and which dooms another class to an hereditary servitude, changeless as fate, and relentless as the grave. It will vindicate the rights, and ennoble the destiny of the masses of the people who work.

"But where is this career of progress to end? Is there a limit to this onward movement? We know that the world has made greater advancement in the present century, than it did in the five thousand years preceding it, and that new discoveries in the sciences and the arts are being made every day. Nature has been compelled, and is still being compelled, to yield up secrets which have been for centuries regarded as beyond the power of human capacity to penetrate. How is this? Is the world to go on thus, always? Is this rush of progress to remain unchecked, always? If so, what mystery, even of Omnipotent wisdom, will remain unsolved at last? What results will not human energy be able to accomplish? Is the time to come when man shall be able to shape out of clay, fashion from wood, or stone, an image of himself, and, breathing upon it, command it to walk forth a thing of life, and be obeyed? Will he be able to search out a universal antidote to disease? Will he discover the means of supplying the human frame with such recuperative power as will nullify the law that prescribes to all flesh the dilapidation and decay of age, of weakness and of death? Will he search out some secret agency which will hold his body in perpetual youth, defying alike the attritions of age, and the ravages of disease? Will he discover how it is that time saps the strength, and steals away the vigor of the human system, and a remedy for exhausted and wasted energies? It is not my purpose to advance a theory based upon an affirmative answer to these inquiries, but when we contemplate the stupendous pace at which the world is moving forward, who will venture to assert where the limit to this progress is to be found? You tell me that man cannot **create**; that he can only combine into new shapes elements which God has furnished to his hands. I do not know this. That he *has* not created I admit; but that he has not capabilities, as yet undeveloped, as a creator, I do not KNOW. I will not venture the assertion that the time will ever come when he will have discovered wherein lies the mystery of life; that he will ever find an antidote to disease; that he will search out some recuperative agency stronger than the law of decay, and that will hold the human system in the perpetual vigor, and bloom, and beauty of maturity. I will not assert that science will, at last, be carried to such perfection, that there shall be no more infirmities of age; that the pestilence will be stayed from walking in the darkness, and destruction from wasting at noonday; that men will cease to grow old, save in years, or that death will be compelled to seek its victims only through the channel of accidents, against which forecast will not, and science has no opportunity to guard. What I mean to say is, that I do not KNOW that just such results are beyond the capabilities of human progress. Measuring the future by the past, I cannot demonstrate that such results may not one day be attained."

"The good time of which you speak," said the Doctor, "when there shall be no more infirmity of age, no growing old, save in years; when there shall be no wasting by disease, through the perfectability of the curative science, or the discovery of some recuperative agency, stronger than the law of decay, will never come. When it is granted, as an abstract proposition, that the capabilities of science are sufficient to counteract the mere wasting influence of time upon the human system, you are met by a great practical fact which will overturn your theory. The excesses of the world are a much more fruitful source of disease and death than the attritions of age. There is a constant struggle on the part of nature to build up and beautify, to strengthen and recuperate, against the results of human excesses. Not one in a million of those who pass away every year, die from the effects of age, as a primary cause. Hence, you must not only perfect science, but you must perfect the morals and the habits of the human family, before you can exempt them from decay and death. The instincts of men, the appetencies which they possess in common with the whole animal creation, are each made the source of disease, and premature decay. Some men eat too much; some drink too much; some sleep too much; some waste their vital energies in sensual indulgence, while all have some vicious habit (I mean with reference to the preservation of life), known or unknown to the world, which, sooner or later, undermines the constitution, and helps on the work of dilapidation. These excesses will always exist; they are inherent in the human constitution, resulting from the very nature of man; they are an inevitable sequence of his physical structure, and his intellectual life. To avoid them implies absolute perfectability in every attribute, and that makes him a god. Until man shall have become infinite in wisdom, as well as immaculate in purity, he will continue to indulge, to a greater or less extent, in excesses of some sort, and those excesses will always be an overmatch, when superadded to the natural law of decay, for the recuperative efforts of science. You must create a radical reform in every department of life; in business, in social habits, in the fashions, in the mode of living, in everything, before you can hope to reach the

Utopia of which you speak. The outrages perpetrated upon nature by the conventionalities of the world alone, would be an insurmountable barrier to the realization of your idea. The necessity for excessive labor to satisfy artificial wants hews away at one end of society, and the indulgence of idleness and ease, at the other. Exposure to the elements, to heat and cold, buries its millions; and too great seclusion, in pursuit of comfort in heated rooms, and a confined and corrupted atmosphere, buries its millions also. Lack of wholesome food fills thousands of graves, and the results of abundance fill other thousands. Lack of appropriate clothing, fitted for the constitution and the seasons, engenders disease and death; and an excess of the same article, fashioned as stupendous folly only can fashion it, engenders vastly more disease and death. There are elements of decay and death furnished to men and women, tempting their weakness, and forced upon their adoption by the conventionalities of life, every day, every hour, and everywhere. It is a part of our civilization, an offshoot of the very progress of which you speak, a sort of necessity in practical results, at least, that men **shall** so live as to wage war against nature, and against themselves; that they shall hurry themselves, or be hurried by inevitable circumstances, into the grave at the earliest possible moment. You may, therefore, dismiss from your mind, my friend, the fanciful idea, that science will ever enable the world to dispense with the cemeteries, or that the cities of the dead will, through its agency, cease to flourish. You will find that as science closes up one avenue to the grave, men will force a way to it through another. We shall have to live as our fathers lived, be subject to disease as they were, grow old as they grew old, and die as they died. We must submit to the law which has written the doom of decay upon all things, which has made us mortal, and when our time comes we must be content to pass away as the countless millions who preceded us have done."

"Well," said Spalding, as he knocked the ashes from his pipe, and rose to retire, under the cover of the tent, for the night, "be it as you say, what matters it? 'I would not live always.' Give to us the hope of an hereafter, a faith that looks through the valley of the shadow of death, and sees immortality, a world of glory beyond, and what matters it how soon the hour of our departure shall come?"

CHAPTER XXIX.

A MYSTERIOUS SOUND--TREED BY A MOOSE--ANGLING FOR A POWDER HORN-

-AN UNHEEDED WARNING AND THE CONSEQUENCES.

As Spalding ceased speaking, there came from away off, over the forest in the direction of the tall mountain peaks, a faint sound like the boom of a cannon, so distant that it could scarcely be heard, and yet it was distinct and palpable to the senses. I say that it came from the direction of the mountains, seen dim and shadowy in the distance, and yet none of us were quite sure of this. We all heard it, but not one of us could assert that the direction from which it came was a fixed fact in his mind.

"There, Judge" said Cullen, "I've hearn that sound often among the mountains, and when I've been driftin' about on these lakes, it never seems much louder or nearer. It always seems to come from the mountains, and yet you'll hear it while shantyin' at their base, and it sounds just as faint and far off as it did just now. What it is, or where it comes from, I won't undertake to say. The old Ingins who, five and twenty year ago, fished and hunted over these regions, told of it as a thing to wonder at, and that it was handed along down from generation to generation, as one of the mysteries of this wilderness. I mind once I was out among the Adirondacks, trappin' martin and sable. I shantied for a week with Crop, under the shadow of Mount Marcy. It was twenty odd year ago, and that old mountain stood a good deal further from a clearin' than it does now. Crop and I had a good many hard days' work that trip; but we got a full pack of martin and sable skins, and two or three wolf scalps, besides a bear and a painter, and we didn't complain. Wal, one afternoon, we put up a shanty in an open spot two miles from our regular campin' ground, and built our fire for the night. There was no moon, and though the stars shone out bright and clear, yet in the deep shadow of the forest it was dark and gloomy enough. We had eaten our supper, and I was smokin' my last pipe before layin' myself away, when all at once the forest was lighted up like the day. It was all the more light from the sudden glare which broke upon the darkness, and there, for an instant, stood the old woods, lighted up like noon, every tree distinct, every mountain, every rock, and valley, as perfect and plain to be seen as if the sun was standin' right above us in the sky. Crop was as much astonished as I was, and he crept to my feet and trembled like a coward, as he crouched beside them. I looked up, and flyin' across the heavens was a great ball of fire, lookin' for all the world as if the sun had broke loose, and was runnin' away in a fright. A long trail of light flashed and streamed along the sky where it passed. It was out of sight in a moment, and the fiery tail it left behind faded into darkness. A little while after, maybe ten minutes after it disappeared, that boomin' sound came driftin' down the wind, and I somehow tho't it was mixed up in some way with that great ball of fire that flew across the sky. Maybe I was wrong, but I've always tho't it was the bustin' into pieces of that fiery thing that lighted up the old woods that night, that broke the forest stillness, like a far off cannon. I never heard it so loud at any other time, and when I hear it now, I always say to myself, there goes another of Nater's fireballs into shivers. I've hearn it in the daytime, when the air was still, and the forest voices were hushed, but I never at any other time, day or night, saw what I suspicioned occasioned it. The Ingins used to say it came from the mountains, but it don't. I've hearn some folks pretend that it comes from the bowels of the airth, but it don't; its a thing of the air, and I've a notion it travels a mighty long way from its startin' place afore it reaches us.

"Talkin' about that trip among the Adirondacks, puts me in mind of an adventer I had with a bull moose, on one occasion among them. There are times when sich an animal is dangerous. I've hearn tell of elephants gittin' crazy and breakin' loose from their keepers, or killin' them, and makin' a general smash of whatever comes in their way. I believe its so sometimes with a bull moose; and when the fit is on the animal forgets its timid nater, and is bold and fierce as a tiger. I've seen two sich in my day; one of 'em sent me into a tree, and the other put me around a great hemlock a dozen or twenty times, a good deal faster than I like to travel in a general way, and if I hadn't hamstrung him with my huntin' knife, maybe he'd have been chasin' me round that tree yet. Wal, as I was sayin' I was out among the Adirondacks one fall, airly in November; I'd wounded a deer, and sent Crop forward on his trail to overtake and secure him. It was a big buck, with long horns, and Crop had a pretty good general idea of what sich things meant. He was cautious about cultivatin' too close an acquaintance with such an animal, unless something oncommon obligated him to do so. I heard him bayin' a little way over a ridge layin' gist beyond where I shot the buck. I warn't in any great hurry, for I knew Crop would attend to his case, and I tho't I'd wipe out my rifle afore I loaded it again. I was standin' by the upturned roots of a tall fir tree that had been blown down, and in fallin' had lodged in a crotch of a great birch, maybe twenty feet from the ground, and broke off. I stepped onto the butt of the fallen spruce, and was takin' my time to clean my gun, when I heard a crashin' among the brush on the other side of the ridge, as if some mighty big animal was comin' my way. I walked pretty quick along up the slopin' log till I was, maybe fifteen feet from the ground, and I saw Crop comin' over the ridge, in what the Doctor would call a high state of narvous excitement, with his tail between his legs, lookin' back over his shoulder, and expressin' his astonishment in a low, quick bark, at every jump, at something he seemed to regard as mighty onpleasant on his trail. I didn't have to wait long to find out what it was, for about the biggest bull moose I ever happened to see, came crashin' like a steam-engine after him. He wasn't more than two rods behind the dog, and if I ever saw an ugly looking beast, that moose was the one. Every hair seemed to stand towards his head, and if he wasn't in earnest I never saw an animal that was. He was puttin' in his best jumps, and the way he hurried up Crop's cakes was a thing to be astonished at. The dog didn't see me, and seemed to be principled agin stoppin' to inquire my whereabouts. He dashed under the log where I stood, and the moose after him like mad. He seemed to be expectin' aid and comfort from me, as the papers say, and was wonderin', no doubt, where me and my rifle was all this time. I called after him, but he was in a hurry and couldn't stop, for there was a thing he didn't care about shakin' hands with, not three rods from his tail. He heard me, though, and took a circle round a great boulder, and the moose after him, and as he got straightened my way, I called him again, and he saw me. He leaped onto the log and came runnin' up to where I stood, and was mighty glad to be out of the way of them big hoofs and horns that were after him. He was safe now, and he opened his mouth and let off a good deal of tall barkin' at his enemy. The moose saw us, and his fury was the greater because he couldn't get at us. He kept chargin' back and forth under the log we were perched on, and if there wasn't malice in his eye, I wouldn't say so.

"When I first saw him, I was standin' with the butt of my rifle on the log, my hand graspin' the barrel, and as I caught it up suddenly to load, the string of my powder-horn caught between the muzzle and the ramrod, broke, and the horn fell to the ground. Here was a fix for a hunter to be in. My rifle was empty, and every grain of powder I had in the world was in the horn, fifteen feet below me, on the ground. To go down after it was a thing I was principled agin undertaking considerin' the circumstance of that bull moose with his great horns and the onpleasant temper he seemed to be in. What to do I didn't know. I hollered and shouted at the kritter, thinkin', maybe, that the voice of a human might scare him; but it only made him madder, and every time I hollered he charged under the log more furiously than before. I threw my huntin' cap at him, but he pitched into it, and if he didn't trample it into the ground, as if it was a human, you may shoot me. After a while, he got tired of dashin' back and forth, under the log, and took a stand two or three rods off, and as he eyed us, shook his great horns and stamped with his big hoofs, as much as to say, 'very well, gentlemen, I can wait, don't hurry yourselves, take your time; but I shall stay here as long as you stay up there. And when you do come down, we'll take a turn that won't be pleasant to some of us.' Crop and I took the hint and sat still, thinkin' maybe he'd get over his pet and move off; but he did'nt lean that way at all. He seemed to've made up his mind to stay there as long as we stayed on the log, be the same more or less. We'd sat there maybe an hour, when I happened to think of a trollin' line and some fishhooks I had in my pocket, and it came across me that possibly I might fish up my powder horn. So tyin' half a dozen hooks to the end of my line, I laid down on the log to angle for my powder-horn. When I laid down, the old bull made a pass under the log, as if he expected me down there, and charged back again, as if he was disappointed in not runnin' agin me. But he saw 'twan't no use, and took his old stand agin. I dropped down the grapnel, and after a great many failures, I hooked into the string of the powder horn, and hoisted away. I hauled it up mighty quick, for the old bull seemed to be suspicions that something was goin' on that might have something to do with his futer happiness, and when he got sight of it, the pass he made was a thing to stand out of the way of. But he was too late; the powder-horn was safe, and I notified him, as Squire Smith did the cats, to leave them parts in just one minute by the clock. He did'nt pay any attention to the warnin'. I loaded my rifle carefully, and while I was puttin' on the cap, asked the gentleman if he calculated to move on, and let peaceable people alone. He didn't condescend to answer a word, looking for all the world like a tiger in savageness. 'Very well,' said I, as I sighted him between the eyes, 'on your head be it,' and pulled. The ball went crashin' through his skull into his brain, and he went down. Crop knew what that meant. He didn't wait to run down the log, but leaped to the ground, and had his teeth in the animal's throat before the echoes of my rifle were done dancin' around among the mountains. I loaded my gun before I came down, thinkin' maybe there might be another bad tempered moose about, but there wasn't. Crop and I learned what we ought to've know before, and that was that it's a safe thing for a hunter to have an extra horn of powder in his pocket, and a loaded rifle in his hand when a mad bull moose is on his trail, and that a slantin' tree is a good thing to get onto at sich a time."

CHAPTER XXX.
GOOD-BYE--FLOATING DOWN THE RACKETT--A BLACK FOX--A TRICK UPON THE MARTIN TRAPPERS AND ITS CONSEQUENCES.

We rose with the dawn the next morning, and before the sun was above the hills we were on our way down the lake, to separate as we struck the Rackett; the Doctor and Smith to return by the way of Keeseville and the Champlain, and Spalding and myself to drift down that pleasant stream to Pottsdam, and thence to the majestic St. Lawrence, to spend a fortnight among the "Thousand Islands" of that noble river. Near the outlet of the lake is a bold rocky bluff, rising right up out of the deep water twenty feet, against which the waves dash, and around which a romantic bay steals away to hide itself in the old woods. This beautiful bay is always calm, for even the narrow strait which connects it with the open water is divided by a rocky, but wooded island, shutting out alike the winds and the waves from disturbing its repose. It is surrounded by gigantic forest trees, whose shadows make it a cool retreat in the heat of noon, and whose dense foliage fills the air with freshness and fragrance when the sun is hot in the sky. Towards its head, a cold stream comes creeping around the boulders, and dancing and singing down the rocks from a copious spring, a short way back in the forest. Near where this brook enters we landed at seven o'clock to breakfast. We supplied ourselves with fish by casting across the mouth of the little stream, while our boatmen were preparing a fire. Our sail of eight miles down the lake furnished us with appetites which gave to the beautiful speckled trout we caught there a peculiar relish. We arranged matters so that the Doctor and Smith were to return in one boat to the Saranacs, while Spalding and myself were to move on down the Rackett with the other two. Cullen and Wood were to go with us to Pottsdam, from whence our route lay by railroad to Ogdensburgh. We had, on entering the woods, dispatched our baggage to the former place to await our arrival there. At nine o'clock we launched out upon the lake again. There are two outlets which enter the Rackett, half a mile apart, down the right hand one of which the Doctor and Smith's course lay, and ours down the left. We shook hands with our friends, and lay upon our oars while they passed on towards home, wishing them a pleasant voyage, and a safe return.

"I say," shouted Smith, as they were about rounding a point that would hide them from our view, "remember our compact about killing the bear. The glory of that achievement belongs to me, you know. Don't say a word about it when you get home till you see me. I haven't fully made up my mind as to the manner of capturing him, and there must be no contradictions on the subject."

"Go ahead," replied Spalding, "we'll be careful of your honor. Drop us a line at Cape Vincent, when you've digested the matter, and we'll stand by you. Good-bye!"

"Good-bye!" And our friends disappeared from our sight on their voyage home.

"And so," said Spalding, "we are to leave this beautiful lake, and these old forests so soon. I could linger here a month still, enjoying these shady and primitive solitudes. To you and I, the quiet which one finds here is vastly more inviting than it is to the friends who have just left us. The Doctor, of necessity, leads a life of activity, feeling physical weariness as the result of his labors, but little of that strong yearning for intellectual repose which those in your profession or mine so often feel. Smith's life demands excitement. The absence of the cares and toil of business occasions a restlessness and desire of change, which makes him discontented here. With them the great charm of this wild region is its novelty. They enjoy its beauties for a season with peculiar relish, but as these become familiar, the spell is broken, and they turn towards home without a regret To you and I, there is something beyond this. We, too, feel and appreciate the beauty of these lakes and mountains The hill-sides and placid waters, the forest songs, and wild scenery are pleasant to us; but we enjoy them the more from the intellectual relaxation, the mental quiet and repose, which we find among them. We feel that we are resting, that the process of recuperation, intellectual as well as physical, is going on within us. We can almost trace its progress, and we feel that the time spent by us here is full of profit as well as pleasure. At all events, it is so with me, and if duty to others, whose interests it is my business to serve, did not demand my return, I could enjoy another month here with unabated pleasure."

"You have left me little," I replied, "to add to what you have already said, in expressing the sources of my enjoyment among these beautiful lakes. Fishing and hunting, considered in the abstract, are things I care but little about. They are pleasant enough in their way, but what brings me here is the strong desire as well as necessity for the repose of which you speak. There is a luxury in intellectual rest, when the brain is wearied with protracted toil, which far surpasses the mere animal enjoyment which follows relaxation from physical labor. That rest I cannot find in society. I must seek it among wild and primeval solitudes, where I can be alone with nature in her unadorned simplicity, away from the barbarisms, so to speak, of civilization, where I can act and talk and think as a natural, and not an artificial man, where I can be off my guard, and free from the weight of that armor which the conventionalities of life, the captions espionage of the world compels us to wear, un-tempted by the thousand enticements which society everywhere presents to lure us into unrest."

We drifted leisurely down the left hand channel, and entered the Rackett, bidding good-bye to the beautiful lake as a bend in the river hid it from our view. A mile below the junction, the river runs square against a precipice some sixty feet in height, wheeling off at a right angle, and stretching away though a natural meadow on either hand, of hundreds of acres in extent. At the base of this precipice, formed by the rocky point of a hill, the water is of unknown depth. Above, and fifty feet from the surface of the river, there are ledges of a foot or two in width, like shelves, along which the fox, the fisher, and possibly the panther, creep, instead of travelling over the high ridge extending back into the forest. As we rounded a point which brought us in view of this precipice, Spalding, who was in the forward boat, discovered a black object making its way along the face of the rocks. A signal for silence was given, and the boats were permitted to float with the current in the direction of the precipice. We were forty rods distant, and the animal, whatever it was, had no suspicion of danger. It paused midway across the rocks, looked about, nosing out over the water, and sat down upon its haunches, as if enjoying the beauty of the scenery around it. In the meantime, the boats had drifted within twenty rods, and Spalding, taking deliberate aim, fired. At the crack of the rifle, the animal leapt dear of the ledge, struck once against the face of the rock some twenty feet below, and then went, end over end, thirty feet into the river. As he struck the water he commenced swimming round and round in a circle, evidently bewildered by Spalding's bullet, or the effect of his involuntary plunge down the rocks. Our men bent to their oars, and had got within five or six rods of it, when it straightened up in alarm for the shore.

"Hold on, Cullen," said I, "lay steady for a moment." I drew upon the animal, and just as it reached the shore, fired, and it turned over dead. We found it to be a black fox, that had walked out upon the ledge, and thus been added another victim to the indulgence of an idle curiosity. Spalding's bullet had grazed its belly, raking off the hair and graining the skin; mine had gone through its head.

"There, Judge," said Cullen, as he lifted the animal into the boat, "is a kritter that isn't often met with in these parts, and the wonder is, that he didn't discover us as we floated down the stream. He's about the cunningest animal that travels the woods. He's got an eye that's always open, a delicate ear, and a sharp nose, and he keeps 'em busy, as a general thing. He never neglects their warnin', but puts out about the quickest, whenever they notify him that there's an enemy about. I've had a good deal of trouble with them in my day, when I've been out trappin' martin. They'll manage to spring the trap and carry off the bait. When one of them chaps gets on a line of traps, there's no use in talkin'. The game's up, and the trapper may make up his mind to get rid of the varmint in some way, or locate in another range of country. He'll find his traps sprung and his bait gone. Or if a martin has been in ahead of the fox, he'll find only the skull, the end of the tail, the feet, and a few of the larger bones, and they'll be picked mighty clean at that. You've seen a martin trap, or if you haven't, I'll try and describe one so that you'll understand it. It's a very simple contrivance, and if a martin was not a good deal more stupid than a goose, he'd never be caught in one of them. We drive down a couple of rows of little stakes, plantin' the stakes close together, and leaving between the rows a space of six or eight inches. The rows are may be a foot and a half long. We then cut and trim a long saplin', say five or six inches across at the butt, and leaving one end on the ground, set the other, may be two feet high, with a kind of figure four, so that when it falls, it will come down between the rows of stakes. We fix the bait so that a martin in getting at it, will have to go in between the rows of stakes, and displace the trap sticks, when down comes the pole upon him and crushes him to death. We talk about a *line* of traps, because we blaze a line of trees, sometimes for miles, and set a trap every twenty or thirty rods. I've had a line of a dozen miles or more, in my day, in a circle around my campin' ground. In minding our traps, we follow the line of marked trees from one to the other, and so never miss a trap, nor get lost in the woods.

"I mind once, a good many years ago, Crop and I was over towards the St. Regis, on a cruise after martin and sable, and anything else in the way of game we could pick up. I'd laid out my trappin' arrangements on a pretty large scale, and was doin' a little better than midlin', when I found that my traps were sprung by some animal that helped himself to the bait, without leavin' his hide as a consideration for set- tin' of 'em. After a few days, I found that whatever it was, understood the line as well as I did, for he took the range regular, and not only stole the bait, but ate up half a dozen martin, that had given me a claim on their hides by springin' my traps. This was a kind of medlin' with my private concerns that I didn't like, and I was bound to find out who the interloper was, and if possible, to make his acquaintance. There was no snow on the ground, and I couldn't get at his track. So I made up my mind to watch for him. Well, one day I spoke to Crop to stay by the shanty and take care of the things, while I went to find out who it was that was medlin' with our property, and started off on my line of traps. I got up into the crotch of a great birch near one of 'em, and sat there with my rifle, waitin' for something to turn up. It was a little after noon when I got located. The sun travelled slowly along down towards the western hills, his bright light, in that calm November day, makin' the rocky ranges and the bare heads of the tall peaks shine out in a blaze of glory. The livin' things of the old woods were busy and jolly enough. An old owl came flying lazily out of the thick branches of a hemlock, and lightin' within a dozen feet of me, opened his great round eyes in astonishment, and as the bright sunlight dazzled him, he squinted and turned his cat-like face from side to side, as if makin' up his mind that he'd know me the next time we met. By-and-by he opened his hooked beak, and great red mouth, and roared out, 'Hoo! hohoo! hoo!' as much as to say, 'who the devil are you?' I didn't answer a word, and after a little, he flew back to his shadowy perch among the dense foliage of the hemlock. A black squirrel came hopping along with his mouth full of beech nuts, and running nimbly up the tree on which I was perched, and out upon one of the great limbs, deposited his store in a hollow he found there. He caught sight of me as he came back, and seating himself upon a branch, not six feet from my head, began chatterin' and barkin' as if givin' me a regular lecter for invadin' his premises, and takin' possession of his tree. He didn't seem to understand the matter at all, and I didn't undertake to explain the reason of my being there. After a little, he went off about his business, and left me to attend to mine. A raccoon came nosing along, stoppin' every little way to turn over the leaves, or pull away the dirt from a root with his long hands, tastin' of one thing and smellin' of another in a mighty dainty way. When he came to my tree, he seemed to think that there might be something among its branches worth looking at. So he came clambering up its rough bark towards where I sat. He came up on the other side of the tree from me, till he got about even with my huntin'-cap, and then came round to my side, and there we were, face to face, not two feet apart. I reckon that coon was astonished when our eyes met, for with a sort of scream he let right loose, and dropped twenty feet to the ground like a clod, and the way he waddled away into the brash, mutterin' and talkin' to himself, was a thing to laugh at.

"The sun was, may be, an hour high, when lookin' along the line of marked trees, I saw a black animal come trotting mighty softly towards the trap I was watchin'. I knew him at once. He was a black fox, and I knew that he was the gentleman that had been makin' free with my property for the last few days. He trotted up to the trap, and walked carefully around it, nosin' out towards the bait, but keepin' out from under the pole. He seemed to understand what that pole meant, and that if it fell on him, he'd be very likely to be hurt. After a little, he trotted out to the other end of the pole, and gettin' on to it, walked carefully along to within ten or twelve feet of the bait; if he didn't begin jumpin' up and down till he sprung the trap, you may shoot me. When he'd done that job, he went back, and gettin' hold of the bait with his teeth, drew it out and began very cooly to eat it. By this time I'd brought my rifle to bear upon the gentleman, but I gave him a little law, to see what his next move would be. After he'd finished the bait, and found there warn't any more to be come at, he stretched himself on his belly along the ground, and began lickin' his paws, and passing them over his cheeks, as you've seen a cat do. After he'd washed his face awhile, he sat himself down on his haunches, curled his long bushy tail around his feet, and looked about as if considerin' what he should do next. Just then I paid my respects to him, and as my rifle broke the stillness of the forest, he turned a double summerset, and after kickin' around a little, laid still. I came down from my perch, and took the gentleman to the shanty and added his hide to those of the martins I'd taken. My traps warn't disturbed after that, and I carried home a pack of furs that bro't me near two hundred dollars."

CHAPTER XXXI.

OUT OF THE WOODS--THE THOUSAND ISLANDS--CAPE VINCENT--BASS FISHING HOME--A SEARCHER AFTER TRUTH--AN INTERRUPTION--
FINIS.

We floated quietly down the Rackett, carrying our boats around the falls, shooting like an arrow down the rapids, or gliding along under the shadows of the gigantic forest trees that line the long, calm reaches of that beautiful river. We shook hands and parted with our boatmen at the pleasant village of Pottsdam, where we arrived the second evening after leaving Tupper's Lake. We found our baggage, and it was a pleasant thing to change our long beards for shaved faces, and our forest costume for the garniture of the outer man after the fashion of civilization. We took the cars for Ogdensburgh, and the next morning found us steaming up the majestic St. Lawrence, towards that paradise of fishermen, the Thousand Islands. We stopped a couple of days at Alexandria Bay, and passed on to Cape Vincent, a beautiful village situated a mile or two below where the river takes its departure from the broad lake beyond. This pleasant little town is built upon a wide sweep of tableland, overlooking the river in front, and the open lake on the west. It is accessible both by the lake and river, having two or three arrivals' and departures of steamboats each way daily, and being the terminus of the Rome and Watertown Railroad, the great thoroughfare between Kingston and the central portion of the Tipper Provinces and the States. It is a delightful place in the hot summer months, with a climate unequalled for healthfulness, a cool breeze always fanning it from the water, and in the vicinity the best bass fishing to be found on this continent.

Opposite, and just below the town, is Carlton Island, on which stand the ruins of an old French fortification, the walls and trenches and the solitary chimneys, from which the wooden barracks have rotted or been burned away, remain as melancholy testimonials of the bloody strifes between the red men of the forest, and the pioneers of civilization who were driving them from the hunting grounds of their fathers.

The black bass of the St. Lawrence and Ontario, are the "gamest" fish that swim, and they are nowhere found in such abundance as in the neighborhood of Cape Vincent. On the outer edge of the bar, near the head of Carlton Island, we caught between seventy and eighty in one afternoon, weighing from three to five pounds each, every one of which fought like a hero, diving with a plunge for the bottom, skiving with a rush down, across, or up the river; leaping clear from the water and shaking his head furiously, to throw the hook loose from his jaw, before surrendering to his fate. In Wilson's Bay, a sweet place, three miles from the village by water, or one and a half by land, we caught as many more on another afternoon. We took a sail-boat and glided round Lighthouse Point (a pleasant drive of two miles from the village), out into the lake, and steered for Grenadier Island, five miles distant, on which we tented for the night, and the bass we brought home the next day were something worth looking at. Near the upper end of Long Island are other prolific bass shoals, where the fisherman may enjoy himself. Indeed, he can scarcely go amiss in the surrounding waters.

The black bass of the St. Lawrence are not only game fish, but are, in excellence of flavor, scarcely excelled by any fish of this country. Baked or boiled, they have few superiors, and as a pan fish, are excelled only by the brook-trout of the streams. The season for taking them commences in July; and continues through September. August is the best month in the year for the bass fishermen. If, during that month, he will supply himself with a strong bass-pole, a strong treble-action reel, stout silk lines, and proper hooks, and visit Gape Vincent, he will find boatmen with a supply of minnows, ready to serve him; and if he fails to enjoy himself for a fortnight among the black bass of the St Lawrence and Ontario, he may count himself as a man who is very hard to please.

We spent a pleasant week at Cape Vincent, and then turned our faces home-ward, invigorated in strength and buoyant in spirits, to begin again a round of toil, from which we, at least, could claim no further exemption.

"H----," said a friend of mine, as he stalked into my sanctum, a few days after my return, and seated himself at my elbow, as if for a private and confidential talk, "did Smith really shoot the bear, the skin of which he brought home, and which he exhibits with such triumph. Tell me, honestly, as between you and me, did he in fact shoot him?"

"Smith certainly did shoot that bear," I replied.

"But is the marvellous story he tells about the manner of killing him really true?"

"That, of course, I cannot tell," I replied, "as I have never heard the story."

"Why," said my friend, "he tells about a beautiful lake, lying away back in the northern wilderness, above which Mount Marcy, and Mount Seward, and other nameless peaks of the Adirondacks, rear their tall heads to the clouds, throwing back the sunlight in a blaze of glory; on which the moonbeams lie like a mantle of silver, while away down in its fathomless depths the stars glow and sparkle, like the sheen of a million of diamonds. Of the old forests and trees of fabulous growth, stretching away and away on every hand, throwing their sombre shadows far out over the water, in whose tangled recesses countless deer and moose, and panthers, and bears range, and among whose branches birds of unknown melody carol. That one side of this beautiful lake is palisadoed by a wall of rocks, stand straight up sixty feet high, near the top of which is a shelf or narrow pathway, along which two men can scarcely walk abreast. That he was passing along this pathway one afternoon, examining the rocks, and looking for geological specimens. Below him was a preci-pice of fifty feet, against the base of which the waves, when the winds swept over the lake, dashed. Around him the birds that build their nests in the crevices of the rock were whirling and screaming, while before him lay the beautiful lake, motion-less and calm, as if it had fallen asleep and was slumbering sweetly in its forest bed. That he was passing leisurely along with his rifle at a trail, admiring the transcen-dent loveliness of the scenery around him, where the rugged and the sublime, the placid and the beautiful, were so magnificently mingled, when, in turning a sharp angle, a huge bear"

"Copy!" shouted the printer's devil, as he came plunging down three steps at a bound from the compositors' room above. "Copy!" he screamed, as he dove into the outer office where that article was usually kept, but found none.

"Mr. H.," said he, as he opened my door so gently, with a voice so quiet, and a look so innocent, that one might well be excused for believing that he had never spoken a loud word in his life, "Mr. H----, the foreman desired me to ask you for some copy."

"You see, my friend," said I to the anxious inquirer after truth, "that I am exceedingly busy just now. You will excuse me, therefore, for referring you to the Doctor and Spalding, who know all about the matter. Good day." And my friend departed without finishing the story Smith told him about his killing the bear. I have never heard the balance of that story yet.

And now, Reader, a word to you, and I have done. When the sun comes up over the city, day after day, pouring his burning rays along the glimmering streets, shining on and on in a changeless glare, till he hides himself in the darkness again; when your strength wilts under the enervating influences of the summer heats, and you pant for the forest breezes and the "cooling streams," remember that the same wild region I have been describing, the same pleasant rivers, beautiful lakes, tall mountains, and primeval forests are there still, all inviting you to test their recuperative agencies. The same singing birds, the fishes and the game are there waiting your pleasure. Visit them when the summer heat makes the cities a desolation. Give a month to the enjoyment of a wilderness-life, and you will return to your labors invigorated in strength, buoyant in spirit--a wiser, healthier, and a better man.

FINIS.

www.bookjungle.com *email: sales@bookjungle.com fax: 630-214-0564 mail: Book Jungle PO Box 2226 Champaign, IL 61825*

The Codes Of Hammurabi And Moses
W. W. Davies

QTY

The discovery of the Hammurabi Code is one of the greatest achievements of archaeology, and is of paramount interest, not only to the student of the Bible, but also to all those interested in ancient history...

Religion ISBN: *1-59462-338-4* **Pages:132**
MSRP $12.95

The Theory of Moral Sentiments
Adam Smith

QTY

This work from 1749. contains original theories of conscience amd moral judgment and it is the foundation for systemof morals.

Philosophy ISBN: *1-59462-777-0* **Pages:536**
MSRP $19.95

Jessica's First Prayer
Hesba Stretton

QTY

In a screened and secluded corner of one of the many railway-bridges which span the streets of London there could be seen a few years ago, from five o'clock every morning until half past eight, a tidily set-out coffee-stall, consisting of a trestle and board, upon which stood two large tin cans, with a small fire of charcoal burning under each so as to keep the coffee boiling during the early hours of the morning when the work-people were thronging into the city on their way to their daily toil...

Pages:84

Childrens ISBN: *1-59462-373-2* *MSRP $9.95*

My Life and Work
Henry Ford

QTY

Henry Ford revolutionized the world with his implementation of mass production for the Model T automobile. Gain valuable business insight into his life and work with his own auto-biography... "We have only started on our development of our country we have not as yet, with all our talk of wonderful progress, done more than scratch the surface. The progress has been wonderful enough but..."

Pages:300

Biographies/ ISBN: *1-59462-198-5* *MSRP $21.95*

The Art of Cross-Examination
Francis Wellman

QTY

I presume it is the experience of every author, after his first book is published upon an important subject, to be almost overwhelmed with a wealth of ideas and illustrations which could readily have been included in his book, and which to his own mind, at least, seem to make a second edition inevitable. Such certainly was the case with me; and when the first edition had reached its sixth impression in five months, I rejoiced to learn that it seemed to my publishers that the book had met with a sufficiently favorable reception to justify a second and considerably enlarged edition. ..

Pages:412

Reference   **ISBN:** *1-59462-647-2*   *MSRP $19.95*

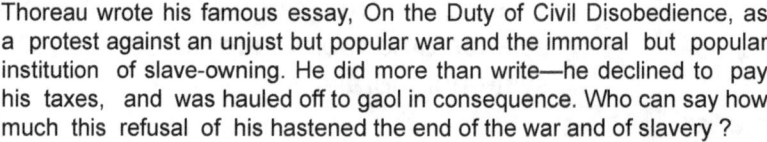

On the Duty of Civil Disobedience
Henry David Thoreau

QTY

Thoreau wrote his famous essay, On the Duty of Civil Disobedience, as a protest against an unjust but popular war and the immoral but popular institution of slave-owning. He did more than write—he declined to pay his taxes, and was hauled off to gaol in consequence. Who can say how much this refusal of his hastened the end of the war and of slavery ?

Law   **ISBN:** *1-59462-747-9*   **Pages:48**

MSRP $7.45

Dream Psychology Psychoanalysis for Beginners
Sigmund Freud

QTY

Sigmund Freud, born Sigismund Schlomo Freud (May 6, 1856 - September 23, 1939), was a Jewish-Austrian neurologist and psychiatrist who co-founded the psychoanalytic school of psychology. Freud is best known for his theories of the unconscious mind, especially involving the mechanism of repression; his redefinition of sexual desire as mobile and directed towards a wide variety of objects; and his therapeutic techniques, especially his understanding of transference in the therapeutic relationship and the presumed value of dreams as sources of insight into unconscious desires.

Dream Psychology
Psychoanalysis for Beginners

Sigmund Freud

Pages:196

Psychology   **ISBN:** *1-59462-905-6*   *MSRP $15.45*

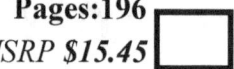

The Miracle of Right Thought
Orison Swett Marden

QTY

Believe with all of your heart that you will do what you were made to do. When the mind has once formed the habit of holding cheerful, happy, prosperous pictures, it will not be easy to form the opposite habit. It does not matter how improbable or how far away this realization may see, or how dark the prospects may be, if we visualize them as best we can, as vividly as possible, hold tenaciously to them and vigorously struggle to attain them, they will gradually become actualized, realized in the life. But a desire, a longing without endeavor, a yearning abandoned or held indifferently will vanish without realization.

Pages:360

Self Help   **ISBN:** *1-59462-644-8*   *MSRP $25.45*

QTY

The Rosicrucian Cosmo-Conception Mystic Christianity *by Max Heindel* ISBN: *1-59462-188-8* **$38.95**
The Rosicrucian Cosmo-conception is not dogmatic, neither does it appeal to any other authority than the reason of the student. It is: not controversial, but is: sent forth in the, hope that it may help to clear... New Age/Religion Pages 646

Abandonment To Divine Providence *by Jean-Pierre de Caussade* ISBN: *1-59462-228-0* **$25.95**
"The Rev. Jean Pierre de Caussade was one of the most remarkable spiritual writers of the Society of Jesus in France in the 18th Century. His death took place at Toulouse in 1751. His works have gone through many editions and have been republished... Inspirational/Religion Pages 400

Mental Chemistry *by Charles Haanel* ISBN: *1-59462-192-6* **$23.95**
Mental Chemistry allows the change of material conditions by combining and appropriately utilizing the power of the mind. Much like applied chemistry creates something new and unique out of careful combinations of chemicals the mastery of mental chemistry... New Age Pages 354

The Letters of Robert Browning and Elizabeth Barret Barrett 1845-1846 vol II ISBN: *1-59462-193-4* **$35.95**
by Robert Browning and Elizabeth Barrett Biographies Pages 596

Gleanings In Genesis (volume I) *by Arthur W. Pink* ISBN: *1-59462-130-6* **$27.45**
Appropriately has Genesis been termed "the seed plot of the Bible" for in it we have, in germ form, almost all of the great doctrines which are afterwards fully developed in the books of Scripture which follow... Religion/Inspirational Pages 420

The Master Key *by L. W. de Laurence* ISBN: *1-59462-001-6* **$30.95**
In no branch of human knowledge has there been a more lively increase of the spirit of research during the past few years than in the study of Psychology, Concentration and Mental Discipline. The requests for authentic lessons in Thought Control, Mental Discipline and... New Age/Business Pages 422

The Lesser Key Of Solomon Goetia *by L. W. de Laurence* ISBN: *1-59462-092-X* **$9.95**
This translation of the first book of the "Lemegton" which is now for the first time made accessible to students of Talismanic Magic was done, after careful collation and edition, from numerous Ancient Manuscripts in Hebrew, Latin, and French... New Age/Occult Pages 92

Rubaiyat Of Omar Khayyam *by Edward Fitzgerald* ISBN:*1-59462-332-5* **$13.95**
Edward Fitzgerald, whom the world has already learned, in spite of his own efforts to remain within the shadow of anonymity, to look upon as one of the rarest poets of the century, was born at Bredfield, in Suffolk, on the 31st of March, 1809. He was the third son of John Purcell... Music Pages 172

Ancient Law *by Henry Maine* ISBN: *1-59462-128-4* **$29.95**
The chief object of the following pages is to indicate some of the earliest ideas of mankind, as they are reflected in Ancient Law, and to point out the relation of those ideas to modern thought. Religion/History Pages 452

Far-Away Stories *by William J. Locke* ISBN: *1-59462-129-2* **$19.45**
"Good wine needs no bush," but a collection of mixed vintages does. And this book is just such a collection. Some of the stories I do not want to remain buried for ever in the museum files of dead magazine-numbers an author's not unpardonable vanity..." Fiction Pages 272

Life of David Crockett *by David Crockett* ISBN: *1-59462-250-7* **$27.45**
"Colonel David Crockett was one of the most remarkable men of the times in which he lived. Born in humble life, but gifted with a strong will, an indomitable courage, and unremitting perseverance... Biographies/New Age Pages 424

Lip-Reading *by Edward Nitchie* ISBN: *1-59462-206-X* **$25.95**
Edward B. Nitchie, founder of the New York School for the Hard of Hearing, now the Nitchie School of Lip-Reading, Inc, wrote "LIP-READING Principles and Practice". The development and perfecting of this meritorious work on lip-reading was an undertaking... How-to Pages 400

A Handbook of Suggestive Therapeutics, Applied Hypnotism, Psychic Science ISBN: *1-59462-214-0* **$24.95**
by Henry Munro Health/New Age/Health/Self-help Pages 376

A Doll's House: and Two Other Plays *by Henrik Ibsen* ISBN: *1-59462-112-8* **$19.95**
Henrik Ibsen created this classic when in revolutionary 1848 Rome. Introducing some striking concepts in playwriting for the realist genre, this play has been studied the world over. Fiction/Classics/Plays 308

The Light of Asia *by sir Edwin Arnold* ISBN: *1-59462-204-3* **$13.95**
In this poetic masterpiece, Edwin Arnold describes the life and teachings of Buddha. The man who was to become known as Buddha to the world was born as Prince Gautama of India but he rejected the worldly riches and abandoned the reigns of power when... Religion/History/Biographies Pages 170

The Complete Works of Guy de Maupassant *by Guy de Maupassant* ISBN: *1-59462-157-8* **$16.95**
"For days and days, nights and nights, I had dreamed of that first kiss which was to consecrate our engagement, and I knew not on what spot I should put my lips..." Fiction/Classics Pages 240

The Art of Cross-Examination *by Francis L. Wellman* ISBN: *1-59462-309-0* **$26.95**
Written by a renowned trial lawyer, Wellman imparts his experience and uses case studies to explain how to use psychology to extract desired information through questioning. How-to/Science/Reference Pages 408

Answered or Unanswered? *by Louisa Vaughan* ISBN: *1-59462-248-5* **$10.95**
Miracles of Faith in China Religion Pages 112

The Edinburgh Lectures on Mental Science (1909) *by Thomas* ISBN: *1-59462-008-3* **$11.95**
This book contains the substance of a course of lectures recently given by the writer in the Queen Street Hall, Edinburgh. Its purpose is to indicate the Natural Principles governing the relation between Mental Action and Material Conditions... New Age/Psychology Pages 148

Ayesha *by H. Rider Haggard* ISBN: *1-59462-301-5* **$24.95**
Verily and indeed it is the unexpected that happens! Probably if there was one person upon the earth from whom the Editor of this, and of a certain previous history, did not expect to hear again... Classics Pages 380

Ayala's Angel *by Anthony Trollope* ISBN: *1-59462-352-X* **$29.95**
The two girls were both pretty, but Lucy who was twenty-one who supposed to be simple and comparatively unattractive, whereas Ayala was credited, as her Bombwhat romantic name might show, with poetic charm and a taste for romance. Ayala when her father died was nineteen... Fiction Pages 484

The American Commonwealth *by James Bryce* ISBN: *1-59462-286-8* **$34.45**
An interpretation of American democratic political theory. It examines political mechanics and society from the perspective of Scotsman James Bryce Politics Pages 572

Stories of the Pilgrims *by Margaret P. Pumphrey* ISBN: *1-59462-116-0* **$17.95**
This book explores pilgrims religious oppression in England as well as their escape to Holland and eventual crossing to America on the Mayflower, and their early days in New England... History Pages 268

QTY

The Fasting Cure *by Sinclair Upton*   ISBN: *1-59462-222-1*   **$13.95**

In the Cosmopolitan Magazine for May, 1910, and in the Contemporary Review (London) for April, 1910, I published an article dealing with my experiences in fasting. I have written a great many magazine articles, but never one which attracted so much attention... New Age/Self Help/Health Pages 164

Hebrew Astrology *by Sepharial*   ISBN: *1-59462-308-2*   **$13.45**

In these days of advanced thinking it is a matter of common observation that we have left many of the old landmarks behind and that we are now pressing forward to greater heights and to a wider horizon than that which represented the mind-content of our progenitors... Astrology Pages 144

Thought Vibration or The Law of Attraction in the Thought World   ISBN: *1-59462-127-6*   **$12.95**

by William Walker Atkinson   *Psychology/Religion Pages 144*

Optimism *by Helen Keller*   ISBN: *1-59462-108-X*   **$15.95**

Helen Keller was blind, deaf, and mute since 19 months old, yet famously learned how to overcome these handicaps, communicate with the world, and spread her lectures promoting optimism. An inspiring read for everyone... Biographies/Inspirational Pages 84

Sara Crewe *by Frances Burnett*   ISBN: *1-59462-360-0*   **$9.45**

In the first place, Miss Minchin lived in London. Her home was a large, dull, tall one, in a large, dull square, where all the houses were alike, and all the sparrows were alike, and where all the door-knockers made the same heavy sound... Childrens/Classic Pages 88

The Autobiography of Benjamin Franklin *by Benjamin Franklin*   ISBN: *1-59462-135-7*   **$24.95**

The Autobiography of Benjamin Franklin has probably been more extensively read than any other American historical work, and no other book of its kind has had such ups and downs of fortune. Franklin lived for many years in England, where he was agent... Biographies/History Pages 332

Name	
Email	
Telephone	
Address	
City, State ZIP	

☐ **Credit Card**   ☐ **Check / Money Order**

Credit Card Number	
Expiration Date	
Signature	

Please Mail to: Book Jungle
PO Box 2226
Champaign, IL 61825
or Fax to: 630-214-0564

ORDERING INFORMATION

web*: www.bookjungle.com*
email*: sales@bookjungle.com*
fax*: 630-214-0564*
mail*: Book Jungle PO Box 2226 Champaign, IL 61825*
or PayPal *to sales@bookjungle.com*

Please contact us for bulk discounts

DIRECT-ORDER TERMS

**20% Discount if You Order
Two or More Books**
Free Domestic Shipping!
Accepted: Master Card, Visa,
Discover, American Express